Acceptance

The
Realm Series

Acceptance

C.R. Rice

Acceptance
Copyright © 2024 C.R. Rice. All rights reserved.

Published By: 4 Horsemen Publications, Inc.

4 Horsemen Publications, Inc.
PO Box 417
Sylva, NC 28779
4horsemenpublications.com
info@4horsemenpublications.com

Cover by Autumn Skye
Typesetting by Valerie Willis

All rights to the work within are reserved to the author and publisher. No part of this publication may be reproduced, stored in a retrieval system, or transmitted in any form or by any means, electronic, mechanical, photocopying, recording, scanning, or otherwise, except as permitted under Section 107 or 108 of the 1976 International Copyright Act, without prior written permission except in brief quotations embodied in critical articles and reviews. Please contact either the Publisher or Author to gain permission.

All characters, organizations, and events portrayed in this novel are either products of the author's imagination or are used fictitiously.

All brands, quotes, and cited work respectfully belongs to the original rights holders and bear no affiliation to the authors or publisher.

Library of Congress Control Number: 2024940246

Paperback ISBN-13: 979-8-8232-0595-5
Hardcover ISBN-13: 979-8-8232-0596-2
Audiobook ISBN-13: 979-8-8232-0598-6
Ebook ISBN-13: 979-8-8232-0597-9

DEDICATION

For Zayn, I'll meet you where the fallen stars lie.

For Cory, for all your love and support,
no matter what happens, you are always there.

For my Wonder Twin, Dani, for being the friend
and supporter I never knew I needed.

For Nana and Pappy, for reading every word
I've ever written, no matter how
dark, twisted, or painful.

I love you all.

Table of Contents

Dedication	v
Prologue	ix
Chapter One	1
Chapter Two	4
Chapter Three	9
Chapter Four	14
Chapter Five	21
Chapter Six	28
Chapter Seven	33
Chapter Eight	39
Chapter Nine	43
Chapter Ten	48
Chapter Eleven	52
Chapter Twelve	56
Chapter Thirteen	61
Chapter Fourteen	65
Chapter Fifteen	69
Chapter Sixteen	74
Chapter Seventeen	80
Chapter Eighteen	84
Chapter Nineteen	88
Chapter Twenty	93
Chapter Twenty-One	98
Chapter Twenty-Two	101
Chapter Twenty-Three	104
Chapter Twenty-Four	107

DEDICATION

Chapter Twenty-Five 111
Chapter Twenty-Six 114
Chapter Twenty-Seven 118
Chapter Twenty-Eight 121
Chapter Twenty-Nine 124
Chapter Thirty 127
Chapter Thirty-One 131
Chapter Thirty-Two 135
Chapter Thirty-Three 139
Chapter Thirty-Four 143
Chapter Thirty-Five 147
Chapter Thirty-Six 152
Chapter Thirty-Seven 157
Chapter Thirty-Eight 161
Chapter Thirty-Nine 164
Chapter Forty 167
Chapter Forty-One 170
Chapter Forty-Two 174
Chapter Forty-Three 178
Epilogue 183
The Realm Series 186
C.R. Rice 187
Book Club Question 189

Prologue

Nothing good would be done on this night, for this was a night specifically designed for misdeeds to be done. Thick, menacing clouds patrolled the skies, obscuring the pearlescent full moons that hung above. A storm was building, and as thunder rolled with deafening intent, lightning crashed with devastating intensity. The smell of an impending heavy rain weighed in the air.

People hid in their homes, silent prayers for safety tumbling from their lips, while animals burrowed deeper into their burrows, clinging to one another in fear. Only their fear was not caused by the storm, but by the menacing secrets it promised to hide.

A familiar figure, draped entirely in red, tore from the shadows and stormed out into the foreboding night. Everything in its posture pointed to complete displeasure with its current knowledge. Wind tore and rain slashed; thunder exploded through the air, and lightning crashed into a nearby tree, setting it ablaze. None of this stopped the figure, nor was a step halted or hesitated as it plunged forward.

A large building loomed in the not so far distance. Its shattered windows and littered yard gained no attention as the figure slipped through the rotten, broken door. If the figure possessed the ability to smell, its stomach would certainly have turned at the noxious odors that filled the decrepit space. Thankfully, it did not.

The house became nondescript as the figure focused on its single goal, the back room. Lightning sliced the sky outside, momentarily filling the room with light as the figure stepped inside. A large table sat at its center, covered with scraps of paper, broken swords, and dirty artifacts. But those weren't what would capture a passerby's eye. No, if any had glanced inside at the moment of that lightning strike, they would have caught sight of the rainbow of robed figures that surrounded that table. At the head of one end stood one draped in white, while the colors that flanked darkened until they were met with black at the other.

ACCEPTANCE

The one in red let the door fall back on its hinges as it made its way between the ones in orange and yellow.

"You are late," said the great one in white.

"Things have gotten messy," said Red.

The one in black dropped its hooded head to the side. "Have they? We haven't noticed."

If Red had a spine, it would have shivered beneath the bitter words.

White chose this moment to speak and spare Red from another blizzard. "We have set everything in motion. The last moments are approaching. Has everyone completed their *approved* missions?"

A rough gravel noise rumbled, fluttering the robes of one side. "Of course," spoke Grey.

Red's sleeves bunches and shook in palpable anger. "You toy with things."

The shoulders of Grey's robe lifted and fell once more. "Some things are meant to be toyed with."

"Enough," said Black. "Tonight is the last night before everything changes. Freedom is near. The games are in motion, and we mustn't make any errors."

The earth shook beneath their hovering robes, tipping the artifacts to their sides and tumbling to the ground. Doors screeched on corroded hinges as the last of the glass clattered from shattered windows.

The robed figures pulled themselves up. "So, it has begun."

One by one, the colored figures faded away. Their robes rustling in the heavy winds as they rushed to complete the next step in their plan. Each was eager to forge their path before the rest.

Red lingered. Its hooded form shook, and a deep growl rumbled from within as it faced off with Grey. "You won't win."

Slowly, Grey brought its head back, feeling the fabric falling from its face, the silver of its eyes glinting in the darkness as lightning slashed. "If you are clinging to the belief that this will end in any victory, then you have already lost."

Chapter One

Unknown location – Thane

Thane clenched his jaw as a surge of helplessness flooded his body. Averie was disappearing, fading into nothing just inches away, and there was nothing he could do but force what he hoped was a reassuring smile as he said, "Never give in."

His body jerked as Averie launched herself at him before disappearing completely. "Damn it!" he roared into the stagnant world surrounding him. "Karen, we—" Panic squeezed his heart when he turned and found himself utterly and completely alone.

The world he found himself in bore a striking resemblance to the purgatory he had been confined to, yet had a distinct, *wrong* quality to it. Gone were the other lost souls and the soft warmth of the blazing sun. In their place was silence and a haunting chill.

"Hello?! Is anywhere there?!" Thane turned in a slow circle, his eyes tracking every inch in search of movement. "HELLO!"

Silence.

Thane's chest rose and fell with more force than a storm's crashing of waves as panic leeched itself into his bones. He had never been fearful of being alone until now. When being alone for an eternity threatened his sanity.

"Hello! DAMNIT SOMEONE ANSWER ME!!"

Again and again, he cried out for someone, anyone, to answer him. To tell him he wasn't alone. His feet pounded against the ground, and his arms pumped furiously at his sides as he crossed the park and raced up the hill. The familiar parking lot remained as empty as the park. A single moment was wasted before Thane took off once more.

ACCEPTANCE

His brain struggled to comprehend what had happened. *Averie will be okay. She has to be.* The thought played on a reassuring loop in his mind as his body moved of its own accord. Effortlessly, he dodged low branches, leapt over large boulders, and sidestepped lifted roots as he raced down the familiar, worn path that joined the park and small town they had grown up in.

Relief fluttered like trapped butterflies as the edge of the path opened then withered with the revelation of the pastel, *empty* town. "No," he whispered. His chest rose with forced breath, and his body threatened to collapse as the last dredges of hope swept away in the silent wind.

You can't stop, Thane. You can never *stop. No matter how hard things get, you have to do everything you can to protect the ones you love.*

Thane's knees stiffened, his fall averted, as his old mentor's words echoed in his mind. Spine straight, Thane forced himself to take slow, measured steps toward the seemingly desolate town until he stood at its edge. Cupping his hands to his mouth, he tried again.

"Hello? Is anyone there?"

His heart pounded with panic once again as the deafening silence suffocated any hope of an answer. "Relax," he forced out. "Everyone just went to their houses. At the exact same time. No big deal. Check the buildings."

So he did. Building by building, Thane methodically combed through each one, determined to leave no stone unturned. His desperation grew more palpable with each empty dwelling until all that remained were the homes of the lost souls.

Unable to contain himself, his slamming of doors reverberated through the deserted town, vying with his desperate plea for an answer as he relentlessly uncovered the harsh reality. He was alone. Resolution settled its burden upon his shoulders as he left the last house. Their *house*. It, too, was empty. Sagging to the porch stairs, Thane hung his hands over his legs and let his head drop to his chest.

"This can't be happening," he whispered, his voice cracking with despair.

Time stretched on endlessly, each second feeling like an eternity. As the false sun began to disappear below the horizon, a shadow enveloped Thane's hunched body, shielding him from the comforting warmth.

Like the sudden crack of lightning, the realization jolted through him and sent a shiver down his spine. Thane's head snapped up, his eyes widening in astonishment as his jaw dropped.

A man, clothed half in a black so deep it rivaled all darkness and half in a white so pure it nearly blinded him, stood a scant foot away. On the blackened side, the man wore form-fitted armor, which included fingerless gauntlets that extended into long, black-tipped fingers with razor-sharp nails. On the opposite side, he wore armor of pure white that reminded Thane of the definition of fantasy gear.

Cascading down to his waist, the man's hair mirrored the pristine essence of his other half, dancing in an otherworldly breeze that he couldn't even feel. His eyes, mirroring the depth of his blackened attire, lacked any white sclera, intensifying their enigmatic allure.

CHAPTER ONE

"What would you do to see her again?" beckoned a rasp.

"Who are you?"

A subtle tilt of the newcomer's head preceded, "Is that really your biggest concern right now?"

Thane narrowed his eyes and straightened to his full height. "I've been calling out. I searched everywhere. You were nowhere, and you didn't answer. So yes, that is my concern."

A moment of obvious contemplation passed before the man nodded. "You may call me Dar."

"Where were you?"

Dar's head shifted to the other side. "Here."

Thane's cheek twitched in irritation. "Is that so?"

"Yes."

"Why didn't you answer?"

"I didn't know you."

"I haven't seen you here before."

"Have you been here long?"

Thane pondered the question and shrugged. "Couple months. I think. Is time the same here as back there?"

Dar's cheek twitched as he fought a smile and shook his head. "I am afraid that is not possible."

Frustration flared in Thane's blue eyes. "Trust me, I know how long I have been dead."

Dar rocked back on his heels and slid his hands into his pockets. "I have no doubt about that. But that does not mean you have been *here* for that long. This is a very special place. One that does not get new … additions. People or places."

"Stars, I hate this Realm," Thane cursed. "Do any of you speak in anything but riddles?" he asked as he descended the stairs.

For every step Thane took down, Dar took a casual one back. "How about a game?"

Thane popped his neck from side to side and looked up at the darkened sky. "What kind of game?"

"Question for question, answer for answer. I will be honest as long as you promise to do the same. Do we have a deal?"

"Fine," Thane sighed.

Dar nodded and smiled wide. "I have always loved a deal. Go on then, ask away."

"You said this is a special place." Thane paused until Dar nodded in agreement before mindfully phrasing his question. "What is it called?"

"We call it the Membrane," Dar answered immediately. "Who are you?"

Thane blinked several times at the swift response and cleared his throat. "Thane. What is the Membrane?"

Dar's eyes flared with light. "A place worse than hell, purgatory, and eternity put together. A prison for those that cannot be controlled."

3

Chapter Two

HEART REALM

REBELLION'S ENCAMPMENT – DARK MOUNTAIN

Outside the mountain, only chaos and death existed. The clash of swords and dying cries of Shadowed, beast, and human rose to a crescendo in a horrifying ballad of war. Sera and Lucas tore a path through the Rebellion forces with merciless precision. Their bodies shifting and melding alongside one another as their blades slayed, consumed souls, and conquered with terrible power. Countless lives ended beneath their assault, each one bringing them closer to their destination.

"What's the plan?" Lucas asked as he drove his sword through another. The soul blade in his hand hissing as it sucked at the remnants of the warrior's soul and left nothing but its husk behind. Lucas grit his teeth as the blade plunged its talons deeper into his arm, and fresh power coursed through his veins.

Sera swiped her blade across a grizzled man's exposed throat and wrinkled her nose in disgust as blood splattered along her white top. "Find Averie. Kill any that get in your way."

Lucas smiled at the prospect. The more lives he claimed, the stronger he became. To wield a soul blade came at a cost to one's life, shortening it while granting your remaining days the taste of power. But when one's life was already gone, the price wasn't that high.

Lucas shifted his weight to the left, dodging a blow before their blades clashed together. The man shoved forward, attempting to throw Lucas off balance. Lucas parried and pulled a hidden dagger from his waist and plunged it through the abdomen of his opponent. The man's eyes widened in disbelief. A smile curved Lucas's lips

CHAPTER TWO

as he lifted a foot and kicked him from his blade. Sparing the man a second glance, Lucas's lips pursed at the thought of the dying man's soul, one that his blade wouldn't get to taste as another enemy crept up from the side.

"We aren't moving fast enough," Sera snapped. Though they had made it halfway to where she sought, the Rebellion warriors continued to pour out, blocking her path and slowing her progress. "Cover me."

Lucas rolled his eyes. "As if I weren't already."

Sera sheathed the swords at her hips, closed her eyes, and called forth her shadows. The familiar burn of their presence traced her spine. One by one they reached out, stretching from the depths of trees, beasts, Shadowed creatures, and humans alike. A soft sigh left her parted lips as the tentacle-like strands reached out, their chilling essence welcome in the heat of battle. When she opened her eyes, they bathed the world in their presence. Terrified screams wailed as her shadows pulled men and women, foe and ally, to the ground, indiscriminate as they were in their hunt.

Lucas growled and deflected another blow. "You are taking ours down with you!"

Sera shrugged and thrust her arms out, sending those that lingered from her side out in a sea of reaching hands. "Sacrifices must be made." *Mine included.*

Silas brought his swords down in a signature "X," dicing the goat-legged creature in front of him. Wiping the sweat from his eyes, he released a growl of frustration.

"There's too many of them!"

"Thanks! Didn't notice." Ryan panted and swung his scythe once more.

"Where did she even get these things?" Silas winced and wiped at the green, sticky liquid on his hands.

"Watch out!" Ryan called.

Silas turned a moment too late. A large horned bear rammed his side and sent him flying from the room.

"Silas!" Ryan called, his feet already carrying him after the other man.

"Stop! He'll be fine," Hex called, kicking a spiked beast through a portal. "We need you here!"

The echo of terrified screams claimed their attention. They were used to the cries of pain and deathly gasps of those slain, but fear was not something openly heard in the throes of battle. Hex, Snip, and Ryan turned horrified eyes to the battlefield.

"What's going on?" Ryan asked.

Hex and Snip exchanged a worried glance and took a step toward the broken edge.

Snip cursed beneath his breath as another group of grotesque creatures limped and prodded into the cavern. A twitch in his cheek showed his growing impatience before he swiped his foot along the slick ground, opening the earth beneath the gathering of enemies. A cruel smirk lifted his cheeks as his irises consumed his eyes,

ACCEPTANCE

and his leg jerked back. The earth slammed together, trapping the enemy between the earth below and life above, leaving only their twitching hands on its surface.

Snip leapt over the severed appendages and landed atop a large boulder. His eyes widened and jaw dropped as he watched shadows cascade from Sera's body. Distorted limbs ripped and tore indiscriminately through the battlefield. Disembodied hands with talon claws pierced, bisected, and severed all they passed through.

"What is it?" Hex called as he slammed his hand down on the dented head of a three-eyed, nine-fanged, spider-like creature. A flash of light burst through its eyes as its essence was purged, turning the thing to ash. Hex dropped to one knee at the sudden explosion.

"Shit," Snip cursed, earning a raised brow from his brother and a chuckle from Ryan.

"Teaching him the foul language of your world, I see." Hex panted as he glared at Ryan.

Ryan brought his mighty scythe down in a soul-severing arch. "Not my fault. He has the mind of a child, soaks up everything he hears and says it at the most inappropriate times. Besides, do you think I don't know what Crixus and Fornax translate to?"

Hex glowered, the moment distracting him just long enough for a Shadowed to pierce his flesh with a soul blade. Hex roared at the searing pain. His body quaked as the devilish sword attempted to rip his soul free. A soul that wasn't his to take. Hex's head dropped to his chest as his body leaned forward, his teeth elongating and eyes glowing furiously. His fingers lengthened and nails sharpened to rival the deadliest blade. Fury and pain fed his frenzy as his hands tore through the Shadowed's flesh like a warm knife through butter.

The Shadowed fell in lifeless pieces to the floor. Its tainted blood sizzled against the ground as the clatter of soul blade meeting stone echoed. Instead of being satisfied with his victory, the scent of the fallen enticed the demon inside. Hex's metamorphosis continued until he was something far from human. His hair grew until it tumbled down his back, and with every inch it grew, the darkness of his hair was washed away, transformed into a blinding white. Ryan watched in unveiled fascination as Hex's transformed appearance halted their attackers in place.

Snip vaulted from the boulder and seized his brother's shoulders. "Stop," he ordered. "Stop it now."

The command fell upon deaf ears as Hex's demonic side continued to unveil. Ryan took a daring step forward, the blade of his scythe scratching the stone as he moved. Hex stiffened at the sound and fixed his unholy, swirling black-and-red eyes on Ryan.

Snip's head whipped to his friend. "Don't move!" he warned.

Ryan, though his curiosity officially peaked, adhered to Snip's warning. Snip had been the thorn in his side for decades, but never once in that time had he ever seen the fear that now blazed in the darkness of his eyes.

CHAPTER TWO

Snip took advantage of his brother's fixation on Ryan to slap Hex across his cheek. A furious roar tore from Hex's throat as his eyes snapped back to Snip. "That's enough, Hex! Get control of yourself!"

Hex jerked from Snip's hold and leapt back, landing in an attack-ready crouch. His hands clutched his head. The Shadowed, their eyes gleaming with hunger, converged on the brother who seemed unaware of their presence.

Snip cursed and disappeared into nothingness. Ryan frowned, then nearly drove his scythe through Snip when the man reappeared from behind and pulled him through a portal. The world swirled before his eyes in a swirling distortion of reality. Ryan's stomach rolled at the unexpected travel. Acid burned a path up his throat as he landed on unsteady feet and dropped to his knees. His chest heaved in deep breaths, a dire mistake, as his body retched from the battle-tainted air filling his lungs. It wasn't until the world had stopped spinning that he noticed they were now sheltered behind the large boulder.

One battle waged at their backs while death rained down before them.

"What are you doing?! We can't leave him!" Ryan snapped. Rising on unsteady feet, Ryan shoved from Snip's side and rounded the boulder.

Snip rolled his eyes and reached out to fist the back of Ryan's shirt and used it to jerk him back down. "I wouldn't look if I were you."

With narrowed eyes, Ryan ignored the man's suggestion and, instead, lifted his scythe, prepared to join Hex in battle, and froze. Ice ran through his veins when he looked over the top of the boulder and watched Hex rip and tear his way through the Shadowed, Abarimon, and hooved creatures with his bare hands and, much to Ryan's disgust, *teeth*.

Hex used his claws to slice through flesh, body, and bone. The liquid sounds of vanquished beings echoed in the mountain. A creature too hungry for a victory stepped a mite too close and found its neck locked within Hex's jaw. Guttural roars shook the crumbling mountain as he fought like the crazed beast he appeared to be.

What felt like hours but was mere seconds passed, and all lay slain at Hex's feet. Snip glanced over the top of the rock and nodded in satisfaction. Clapping a hand on Ryan's shoulder, he said, "You stay here. I'll be right back."

Ryan stood in shocked silence. Not because he didn't have anything to say, but because he wasn't sure how to put the gruesome scene into words. He had been in battles before, survived wars, and committed unnatural acts, but the things he had just witnessed were bound to haunt his nights for years to come.

Snip circled the rock and, with his hands in his pockets, strolled up to the monstrous version of his brother, a cheery, whistled tune on his lips. The beastly form of Hex held its fixed, swirling gaze upon his brother's approaching body. Hex stiffened as the mind of the beast melded with that of the man. Snip smiled and continued to whistle his merry tune before rapidly knocking his brother once, twice, three times upside his silver-skinned skull.

ACCEPTANCE

Hex fell to one knee, his body collapsing in on itself at the blow. When next he stood, his hand rubbed frantically at the spot he had been struck and appeared to be completely normal once more.

"Crixus, Snip!" Hex cursed. "What in Fornax did you do that for?!"

Snip rolled his eyes. "Seriously? Do you see what you have done?"

Hex glanced around the broken room and sucked a harsh breath through his teeth and ran a blood-soaked hand through his hair. "I seemed to have gone a bit overboard."

"Oh, did you? Is that what you think? You went a bit overboard? Crixus, Hex, I think you tried to eat that one!" Snip chided as he kicked the nearly headless thing from beside his foot.

Hex frowned and opened his mouth to retort, when untamed, inhuman cries sounded from behind.

Ryan whirled as the hair at the back of his neck rose. His scythe lifted on instinct and blocked the impending blow. "Incoming!" Ryan called, cutting the first monster down as another wave broke through the opening. An angry growl rumbled his chest as Ryan lifted his blade and swiped it through the air, clearing his path and bringing him back to Hex and Snip's side.

"Do you think you can control yourself this time?" Snip asked as he released the pulsing black vines from his hands.

Hex rolled his eyes in answer and did the same. In the next moment, the trio was once more thrown into a fight for their lives. The air was filled with a fine mist of red, black, and green liquid as wounds were inflicted and taken.

Concern grew as the enemy forces continued to advance without pause, while energy levels dwindled. Snip stumbled back into the side of the mountain, his chest heaving as he fought to catch his breath. Unbeknownst to him, a slithering, snake-like Shadowed slipped through the darkness and leapt, its mouth open and fanged teeth jutting out as it launched itself at Snip.

A curse broke free as, faster than light, Hex lunged forward, his hands wrapping around the long-necked creature, crushing it in his grip. "Pay attention!" he snapped.

Movement from inside the mountain caught Snip's eye as he dropped another lifeless corpse to the ground. "About damn time," he panted. Hex turned pulsing red eyes to where his brother stared and hissed a breath. Ryan followed and found his relief short-lived when a chill racked his spine.

Reinforcements had arrived.

Silas stepped from the mouth of the mountain, his body alive with power. Callen loomed just behind, his eyes molten and body poised for action. But it was Averie, arriving unbothered and bored, that had the feeling of unease filling the air.

Chapter Three

Inside the Mountain – Callen and Averie

They were going to lose. *He* was going to lose. Breath rattled in his chest. Sweat poured down the sides of his face. He was running low on energy, and that thought alone had him down on one knee. Callen's eyes clicked to Averie's prone body. He was tired. Ichor splattered the walls and pooled on the floors. Endless creatures were strewn about the room, and still they came. Callen's eyes shuttered.

You made a promise! his soul screamed. Only it wasn't his voice that spoke. It was Thane's. Energy pulsed through his tired body and renewed his drive. Callen opened his eyes and felt the burn of unleashing his power. His vision broadened as he let it flow free, stretching to a near 360-degree view of his surroundings bathed in silver. The grotesque creatures lumbered and slithered toward him, closer and closer, until they froze altogether. The agonized gargles of their companions echoed in the room. Empty sockets of the ones in front of him, once fixed on him, shifted to something over his shoulder.

He was half turned to the source when the room filled with a blinding, warm, and golden light. Callen lifted an arm to shield himself as it crept up his body and washed away the sickening darkness of the Shadowed. As quickly as it had arrived, the light faded away, and in its place, an icy chill settled in the air. Confusion wrinkled his brow as he lowered his arm and blinked to clear his spotted vision as he gaped at the sight laid out before him. The Shadowed creatures no longer stood before him. There were only piles of ash. Shock swamped his mind as he turned, his breath caught in his chest.

"Averie," he gasped.

ACCEPTANCE

She stood strong, her head tilted slightly down as she admired her work. When her fervid gaze met Callen's, he was nearly blinded by its light. A slow, menacing smile spread across her face, making her teeth gleam and eyes shine.

"Way to be a slacker, Frosting," she said.

Callen missed the way her smile dimmed at the words as his shoulders sagged in relief. "He is alright." Callen shook his head at the memory of Thane. "I should have known he would find his way."

Averie's smile tightened as she looked over at Callen's haggard state. *Well, this won't do.* Every inch of him screamed of wear and exhaustion. Blood dripped from his face and hands. Black, green, and red liquid splattered his clothes, while the tension of more encroaching Shadowed had his shoulders bunching. "Need a little jumpstart?" she asked with a playful quirk of her brow.

Callen frowned. "A jumpstart?"

Averie's smile widened, this time in genuine excitement as she rolled her shoulders and glanced at the first wave of Shadowed filtering through the door. "I would run while you still have the chance," she cautioned. They met her warning with the growls and snarls reminiscent of the animals they had become. "Suit yourself," she mumbled.

The glow consumed her body once more, the heat rising in her chest and expanding to the top of her head and down to the tips of her toes. When the force of power buzzed along her skin and began to raise the hair on her arms, she lifted her hand, aiming in Callen's direction. Static popped and cracked the air as light shot from her hand and plunged into Callen's chest.

Callen gnashed his teeth as unfamiliar power ripped through his veins with a searing intensity. His mind screamed at the force while his body began to rise. The well of power inside him overflowed, chasing away his fatigue and filling him with boundless foreign energy.

Averie lowered her hand and eyed the wave of Shadowed clawing their way through each other to get into the room. A sigh puffed her cheeks. "Shall we begin?"

Callen stood with his head bowed and chest rising with heavy breaths. Steam rolled from his exposed skin, bathing him in a demonic aura that was accented when his head snapped up. His eyes were encased in living, molten silver that leeched into the bulbous, pulsing veins around his eyes.

Without answering, he spun away from Averie and focused on the reinforcements ripping their way through the doorway. Two thundering steps forward brought him a foot away from the closest defiled enemy. Thin, boney arms ended in dagger-like claws that windmilled wildly in his direction. Callen stepped to the side, easily dodging the mindless creature, and pushed his hand smoothly through the air. An arsenal of thin spikes rose from the black mountain floor and plunged into all that stood in his path. Callen pulled his arm back, and the spikes melted into the floor as though they had never been.

The satisfying thump of bodies colliding with the unforgiving stone echoed in the still chamber. Without sparing a glance back, Callen stepped over the fallen

CHAPTER THREE

corpses and led the way into the hall. White scorch marks peppered a path down the chamber in stark contrast to the midnight stone.

"They went this way," Callen growled as he led the way down the hall and into what had been their main gathering area.

"Did they?" Averie asked, her words heavy with sarcasm as she slid over a large boulder. "I figured they went the other way, you know, opposite of the clear incinerated path."

Callen shook his head as he stepped into the large open room, his mouth opening to retort, when a body came soaring past them and collided with the wall with a resounding thud. A painful groan morphed into an angry growl as the victim rose on unsteady legs.

Averie leaned forward, curious who had survived such a blow, and gasped. Silas stepped from the cloud of debris, his grip tightening on the jagged, deadly swords in his hands. The remains of his tattered shirt were being devoured by a sage-colored flame, making him look every bit like a being of the underworld. Another growl rumbled in his chest as he ripped the burning fabric clear of his body, revealing angry pink skin. Sweat, blood, and other unpleasant liquids splattered his face and chest and spiked his hair erratically around his head. But none of these things compared to the haunting, murderous glow in the depths of his teal eyes.

A swarm of mangled Shadowed and monstrous, snarling animals crept into sight. Silas bared his teeth and took deliberate steps forward, all the while twirling his battle-stained blades over his wrists. Over and over, they spun through the air, each arch bringing a louder pop to the air until steady streams of blue electricity danced up and down the blades.

A foreboding smile curved his lips as in one moment, he was slowly progressing forward, and the next, he was in the center of the confused, unearthly creatures. Silas moved like a man possessed. He drove one sword through a scaled and slithering snakelike Shadowed and swung the other across a fur-covered, eyeless creature with a spear.

Agony infused roars, gargles, and howls pierced the air, seeming to feed Silas's frenzy. Only after he had decapitated two more and severed another's arm did the disorganized horde realize what was happening, but it was already too late. Silas lifted his electrified swords high into the air, flipped the blade down, and, with another crazed smile, drove them into the mountain floor.

Callen's eyes expanded in surprise as Silas's intentions settled in his mind. As if the world had suddenly slowed, he watched the blades pierce the ground in slow motion, and he jerked into action. Callen twisted to Averie, wrapped her in his arms, and spun them back into the hall as errant, lashing strikes ripped apart the ground. Final shrieks and roars threatened eardrums before everything went suddenly, deathly silent.

Averie's breath, slow and steady, sounded harsh against her bruised ears. "Is it over?" she whispered.

ACCEPTANCE

Lifting a finger to her lips, he shut his eyes once more and pushed his senses. *Not a single movement.* Carefully, Callen guided them to the end of the hall, his heart pounding in his chest as he held Averie close, and cautiously looked around the corner. Surrounded by the aftermath of destruction, a solitary figure knelt in a cloak of ash, blending into the scorched landscape.

"Silas?" Callen called.

Silas's head popped up, his eyes erratic and unfocused. His hands still flexed against the grip of the slightly popping blades, and his shoulders rose and fell in quick succession as he forced himself to his feet.

"Calm down. It is Callen and Averie. We are your friends."

Silas's steps faltered. The foreboding glow in his eyes flickered, its erratic dance coming to an abrupt halt as it disappeared into darkness. His shoulders slumped and body grew heavy from overexertion. The blades slipped from his hands, their angry clattering resonating through the broken ground.

Averie broke free from Callen's hold, her adrenaline surging as she rushed to Silas's side. Tossing one of his limp arms over her shoulders, she led him to one of the remaining chairs and helped him into it. "Are you alright?"

Silas's lashes fluttered as he forced his eyes open at the soft voice. "You're awake." He panted, a ghost of a smile curving his lips. "I knew you'd wake up."

Averie smiled and shrugged. "How's a girl supposed to sleep with all this racket?"

Silas's answering laughter quickly dissolved into a hacking cough. Averie flinched at the sound and held her palm over the cracked earth and curled her fingers. With measured, slow movements, she opened and closed them again and again until a thin strand of pale blue rose from its depth and into the air. "Here, drink."

Silas arched a brow at the casual display and leaned forward to drink. Surprise arched his brow as the cool liquid coated his parched mouth. "It's cold," he said lamely.

Averie chuckled. "Why wouldn't it be?"

Silas leaned to drink more and caught Callen's eye. An unspoken question lingering in the air between them. *Is she alright?*

Callen rolled back his shoulders. "We have to keep moving."

With a nod, Averie released her grip, and the water cascaded down to the ground, creating a delicate splash. "Are you up for more?"

Silas smiled, the haunting glow illuminating his eyes once more. "Can't stop now."

Callen looked at the broken, scarred earth and felt a surge of anger. The soft rainbow of light that had greeted every step was tarnished with the sacrifice of war. His hands fisted at his sides. How dare they enter this mountain and destroy what was *his*? His sanctuary, his *home*.

"Uh-oh," Silas whispered.

Averie raised a questioning brow before following his eyeline. Callen's body shook with repressed rage. His eyes glowed unnaturally bright as his veins pulsed with liquid platinum. A bored sigh tumbled free. "Let's get this over with. I think he might explode," she giggled.

CHAPTER THREE

Silas frowned but had no time to respond. Callen surged forward, his arms raised high above his head, before he brought them down with a ruthless blow against the cracked ground. The stone cratered at his impact and rolled like a wave, casting any in a twenty-yard radius hurdling through the air and out of the mountain.

Averie's eyes brightened, their luminescence captivating the eyes of Shadowed. "I think this is gonna be fun."

Averie glided into the depths, hands encased with blades of light. Silas watched in awe as, with a simple flick of her wrist, each creature that approached her was instantly immobilized.

"What have we done?" he whispered.

Chapter Four

Membrane — Thane

Thane's eyes widened. "I'm sorry. I think I misheard you. Did you just say this place is a *prison*?"

"Are you breaking the rules of the game?" Dar asked.

Thane blinked several times to clear his shock and shook his head. "Nope, just thinking out loud. That, however, was your question. Now answer mine."

Dar narrowed his black whirlpool eyes and lifted a long, black-tipped finger in warning. "I will let that pass just this *once*. Yes. The Membrane, as we call it, is a prison. One that was created to contain the uncontainable and has done so for eons. Or at least most of us."

Thane opened his mouth and snapped it shut once more, a question burning for escape on his tongue. "Your turn."

"What did you do to end up here?"

Thane shook his head. "I have no idea."

Another narrowed gaze.

Thane lifted his hands. "I swear. One minute, I was in the Seam, or Purgatory as I called it, the next, Averie and Karen are Mcflying before my eyes. Are we the only people here?"

Dar frowned. "You are the only *person* here. What do you mean, Mcflying?"

Thane crossed his arms. "It's from a movie. You wouldn't understand. How can I be the only person here if you are here, too?"

Dar smiled. "I am not a person."

"What are you?"

Dar stiffened. All ease gone from his stance. "I am afraid I cannot answer that."

CHAPTER FOUR

Thane arched a brow. "Why?"

Dar's head jerked to the side, an unnatural twitch that both amused and worried Thane. "I cannot answer that either."

Thane filed the train of thought away for the time being and moved on to the reason he had agreed to this game. "You asked me what I would do to see Averie again. Does that mean there is a way out?"

"Averie," Dar rasped, the familiarity in his tone making Thane stiffen. "Fascinating."

It was Thane's turn to narrow his eyes. Thane abruptly cut off his question with a swift snap of his jaw.

Dar smiled. "There is no way out."

"That doesn't make sense! You said—"

"I asked a question. Call it a curious mind. I never said there was a way out, because there is not."

Years of training in self-control were slipping through Thane's fingers like sand in an hourglass. Needing a moment to calm his bristled nerves, he turned away from Dar and stared up into the moonlit, pale version of his and Averie's childhood home. "She needs me."

"Why?"

Confusion furrowed Thane's brow. "What do you mean?"

A deep growl rumbled Dar's chest. "Follow. The. Rules," he hissed.

Thane whirled back to face Dar. "Then clarify your question!" he snapped.

Dar tilted his head in contemplation, his eyes shifting somewhere off into the distance before returning. "Alright. Why does Averie need you?"

Thane ran his fingers through his hair in frustration. "That is the same question!"

"You are not hearing me. Why does she need *you specifically*?"

"I'm her brother. It's my job."

Dar shook his head with a knowing smile. "No, you are not."

Thane took a daring step forward. "What is that supposed to mean?"

"You are not of any relation to her. If anything, you were put into her life for a purpose, that it seems you have fulfilled."

Like a gun going off, Thane's control snapped as he launched himself at Dar. Fury and ire seared its way through his veins with each angry thump of the organ in his chest. His fist flew through the air, powered with every bit of loathing, fear, and panic he had felt over the last months. The collision, however, made him instantly regret the impulsive reaction.

The instant his fist met Dar's flesh, two things happened. First, Dar quirked a brow, oblivious and unmoved by the blow meant for his jaw. Second, as soon as the blow landed, Thane was consumed by searing pain that shot through his body from contact so visceral it brought him to his knees.

Dar sighed and lowered into a crouch. "That wasn't smart. This place is different from anything you have ever known. Pain and fear are living things in this place. Tangible beings that wait in the shadows to attack."

ACCEPTANCE

Thane glared back. His loathing was palpable in the air between them as he clung to his hand.

"It would do you well to remember this moment and to know that every attempt to do harm, to defend yourself, or to leave is thrown back on the assaulting party. Now, would you like to continue?"

Thane waited to speak until the pain radiating from his hand dulled to the tingling ache of a sleeping limb. "For one last question," he grit. "What did you mean when you said I could see Averie again?"

"Much like the consequences of the Realm, there is a price for everything on this plane. You can see her again *if* you are willing to pay the Membrane back in kind."

"Show me how."

Dar nodded and rose to his feet. "I will meet you here tomorrow." Dar hesitated. "I feel as though I should warn you. You will face many ... others while you are here. Choose carefully who you reveal yourself to."

Thane watched the man clothed in polarity walk away and, for the first time since his death, felt hope blossom. "I'll do it, Averie. I'll find a way back."

Battleground – Averie

If true freedom existed, Averie was sure this was what it felt like. To fully unleash oneself in the defense of the people you cared for most was the most liberating and healing thing she had felt since... Averie frowned. *Since when?*

She shook herself free of the second puzzling thought of the day and focused on the task at hand. Abominations were slithering their way across *her* land and terrorizing *her* people *again*. Fury gnashed her teeth as she purged the being in front of her. Golden light burst from its melted eye sockets and ripped open its mouth before crumbling to the ground as a steaming corpse.

"Averie!"

Averie turned to find a battle-marred Radnar fighting his way toward her. His armor held even more scratches and dents than it had before. Ash was smeared across his cheek. Shadowed ichor and Abarimon blood mingled down the sides of his face to darken his beard. Sweat-slick hair matted the sides of his head. As Radnar lifted his sword to deflect another's serrated arm, Averie stepped forward with a decisive slash, severing the creature in half.

"What is it?" she asked.

Radnar reached behind his back and withdrew a familiar pair of blades. "I figured you would need these when you woke."

Averie stared down at her old battle companions. "I don't need them."

CHAPTER FOUR

Radnar frowned. "Take them anyway. They might come in handy," he urged, pushing them toward her once more.

Averie grabbed the blades in one hand and shoved Radnar to the side with the other, to sink the blades into the side of an eyeless Shadowed. A death gasp burst from the stitches that sealed its mouth as it crumbled to the ground.

Averie looked at Radnar and shrugged. "You were right," she conceded and worked her way to the hole in the mountain.

Radnar watched her go in a mixture of awe, concern, and wonder. Gone was the remorseful, grief-stricken girl he had left, and in her place stood a warrior. Fearless, unrelenting, merciless. Movement caught the corner of his eye. There was no more time to dwell on what she had become, as the tip of a blade sliced across his cheek. White consumed his eyes as pain flared.

"There!" Lucas called.

Sera pulled her arms to her sides, snatching the shadows back to her side, and looked to where Lucas pointed his sword. Averie stood at the mountain's opening, her deep wine hair shining like freshly spent blood in the morning light. Or was that her light?

Sera narrowed her eyes. Something had changed. Something that shook the air and rattled the shadows clinging to her side. "Take over here."

Lucas cursed as Sera stepped back into the shadows and disappeared from sight. A flash of white brought his smile back as an old acquaintance attempted to dislodge his head from his shoulders.

"Marcus!" He grinned, blocking the man's sword with his own. "How have you been?"

Marcus smiled a smile that did nothing to warm the icy darkness that claimed his eyes. "Good, considering you two left me to rot!"

Lucas frowned in mock sorrow. "Did we? Or did we just take out the trash?"

Marcus glowered at the smirking child and heaved his weight forward, sending Lucas back a step. Twirling his sword over his hand, Marcus circled. "You think you have favor because you know who she was in your Realm." He tsked. "You have no idea the things she will do. The memories she will rewrite, take away, and taunt you with. You are a pawn, dear boy."

Lucas leaned forward. "And a willing one at that."

"Then shouldn't you be one for the man that saved you?"

Lucas dropped his head back in exaggerated laughter. "I choose my savior, Marcus, and it certainly isn't you."

Swords clashed in rapid succession, each man struggling to get the upper hand on the other. One seasoned in battle with decades of training. The other enriched with youth, stolen power, and a drive to surpass those that doubt him.

ACCEPTANCE

When at last they separated, a familiar caress brushed Marcus's nape. With his focus on the barely panting youth before him, he felt a smile stretch across his face as he caught sight of what Solara tried to show him.

"It appears you chose wrong."

Lucas narrowed his eyes and studied the battle grounds, searching for what Marcus was speaking of. When he found it, unnatural panic consumed his body, widened his eyes, and quickened his breath. Without further thought, he plunged his blade into the awaiting shadow and let it carry him away, a taunting chuckle following him on the breeze.

Averie spun the sai up to settle the length of her arms and punched the hilt into one of the human traitors before kicking him from the ledge. Satisfaction lifted her lips at the broken thump of his body below. Callen fought feverishly at her back, his rage at the invasion and desecration of his home stretching far beyond the battle at hand. She could sense his discomfort at having his home destroyed, but this ferocity and anger stemmed from something more. The seasoned warrior he was wouldn't let something as trifling as a few invaders bother him so. Even if they had infiltrated his sanctuary.

It was on the tip of her tongue to ask what was bothering him, when the shadows in the mountain shifted unnaturally, and steel glinted in the morning sun. Averie lifted her blade. The clash echoed above all others and momentarily stilled the room as past friends were brought face-to-face.

Callen growled, his eyes swirls of liquid as he took a thundering step forward.

"No!" Averie snapped and smiled at Sera. "I've got this."

Callen wanted to fight against her words but was given no time when a half tiger, half vulture flew toward him with talons flexed and fangs dripping. His arms lifted to defend when a familiar slate bulk lunged and caught the creature between its mighty jaws.

"Seiko!" Callen called out in thanks.

"Pay attention!" Sera chastised, slicing at Averie's abdomen and smiling when she didn't move quickly enough.

Averie narrowed her eyes at a thin red line. "You aren't worth my attention."

"If not me, then who?" she demanded, unleashing a web of slithering shadows.

Averie slammed her foot against the ground, sending a spear of stone hurtling in Sera's direction. Sera easily sidestepped and shook her head when a Shadowed was pierced in her place.

"This Realm and these people."

"You're fighting for a world that doesn't deserve it!"

"You don't get to make that decision," Averie retorted, throwing her weight forward and shoving Sera back.

CHAPTER FOUR

Sera rushed forward. Metal clashed. Steam rose from their blades as fire met ice. "Do you think they care about you? They are using you!" A humorless laugh tumbled free as they circled. "You fight against me, when you should be fighting *with* me. You fight for people who don't deserve the air they breathe, and for what? Some warped vision of peace?" she said with another laugh and a shake of her head. "You can't be that stupid!" Sera threw the blade from her hand, the metal slicing Averie's cheek before embedding into the stone wall.

Averie wiped the blood from her cheek with the back of her sleeve. "And what do you fight for, Sera? To rule a Realm plagued with fire and death?"

Sera jerked back. "Who said I wanted to rule it? The Realm needs a reset, and I am the one who will flip the switch."

Averie felt her body begin to tremble in disgust. "You want to kill countless people in an attempt to 'reset' the Realm? What the hell do you think will happen then?!" A burst of energy flew from Averie's body and slammed against Sera's, throwing her reeling back onto the ground.

Sera climbed to her hands and knees and spit the blood from her mouth as she looked up with violence in her eyes. "Those that are left will learn!" Shoving from the ground, Sera used the shadows' power to bring the thrown blade back into her grasp as she lunged for Averie.

Averie lifted her sai, blocking Sera's blow. "Learn what, Sera? That the punishment for imperfection is death?"

"Learn that there are consequences for their actions! Consequences for what has been done!"

Averie snorted and kicked Sera back. "You haven't delt with consequences a day in your life."

Sera's crystalline eyes narrowed. "You don't know me. You only know what I have allowed you to. What I have shown you." Sera tossed out her hand, sending another round of shadow hands in Averie's direction.

Averie grit her teeth and easily deflected the hand of shadow with a burst of light. "You ruined me! Locked the Heart inside me, dragged me into this war, and condemned me to death!" The air crackled with electricity as a dazzling burst of light accompanied each word, obliterating the shadows that lay in between.

"It wasn't supposed to be you!" Sera seethed.

Averie stalked forward with a humorless smirk. "What wasn't? You've made it pretty clear I was the key to getting everything you want."

Sera shook her head. "*Quen* was the key. You were never supposed to be here. You're just a castaway. Sent away by your own mother. You were never meant to save this Realm, Averie. That path wasn't yours to walk."

Averie pursed her lips in false consideration. "If not me, then who? Why plunge an entire Realm into war?"

Sera's lips parted in a bloodied, toothy smile. "You don't honestly think this is the only Realm at war, do you?"

Averie lifted her chin, the only answer she was giving.

ACCEPTANCE

Sera clicked her tongue. "Avi, Avi, Avi. Poor naïve Avi. This Realm is just the beginning. The first domino to fall. Across all time and space, the Realms are fighting to be together, while the people within them wage war against each other. Trying in vain to keep them apart. The Realms were always meant to be one. All you are doing is delaying the inevitable."

Averie narrowed her eyes and flexed her hands against the grip on her sai. "Tell me, Sera, why did you start a war? Why drag me into it? What the hell do you want from me?!"

Sera dropped her head to the side and sat back on her heels. "You think mighty high of yourself. You are nothing but a tool. One that is starting to get on my nerves."

Averie's hand darted out, captured Sera's chin between her fingers, and pulled her close. "And the only thing you are doing is annoying me."

Sera's eyes widened as the light in Averie's eyes blazed to rival the sun. *Why can't I move?!*

Chapter Five

Sera clenched her eyes shut against the brilliant light and held her breath, waiting for the inevitable pain it would wash over her frozen body. Only it never came. Slowly, she cracked her eyes and gasped at the sight. Lucas hunched over her body, his face pale, even for him. His snow-colored eyes lacked nearly all their haunting light. His haggard breath puffed in the space between them.

"What did you do?" she asked.

Lucas quirked a broken version of his signature smile. "Saved you," he croaked, with ichor-tainted blood seeping from his paling lips. "Now … you … owe … me."

Sera's face pinched at the suffering gap in words. The feeling of warmth soaked through her ensemble. A quick glance revealed the black-tinged blood seeping from his body. Hands clenched, she moved herself from beneath Lucas and tossed his arm over her shoulder. "Call a retreat," she hissed to her shadow. Obediently, the thing slinked from her side and bounced between all the remaining members of her army. One by one, they halted their attacks, turned from their fights, and receded to the hills.

Confusion and disbelief crashed like a wave over the Rebellion. Washed over the men, women, and beast with shock as their enemy made no effort to fight, maim, or kill those they passed in their retreat. Instead, they wandered off as though there was never any battle to be had.

Sera glared at Averie. The arrogant curve of Averie's lips punctuated the silence that stretched between them as Sera waited for her shadow's return. When it finally did, she lifted Lucas to his feet and promised, "This isn't over," before dropping them both into the waiting arms of her shadow.

Hex and Snip stepped to her side. "What happened?" asked Snip.

Averie shrugged. "She gave up."

The twins exchanged nervous glances. "Are we going after them?" Hex asked.

ACCEPTANCE

Averie shook her head and moved to the large opening. "No."

Murmurs and unease spread through the crowd as the Shadowed, beasts, and nightmarish creatures continued their trek. "Let them pass," Averie called, gathering curious glances.

"Today, victory is ours!" she called, her blood-stained sai piercing the sky.

The battle was over, but the war was just beginning. Sera and Lucas had been sent running for the hills with the tattered remnants of their abominable army. They had won, if only for the moment. Fatigue was forgotten as cries of victory filled the midafternoon air the instant the last creature limped from sight.

Pride flared in her chest as she watched the celebration. Friends turned to each other, hugging and congratulating one another on a job well done, and for a single moment, Averie let herself revel in their victory. She inhaled deep, slow, even breaths through her nose and felt the steady thump of her heart as it slammed against her ribs when she exhaled. For the first time in weeks, she felt *alive*.

Then a painful moan caught her ear, and her eyes fell from the distance to the mangled assortment of limbs. Grotesque creatures were littered among the wounded men and women of the Rebellion. Their poisonous, black ichor streamed from their corpses to pop and sizzle like acid against wounded flesh and killed the fertile earth below.

She watched as one woman struggled beneath the weight of a strangely pale creature with twisted feet. Her eyes stayed locked on the strange creature as she lifted a hand and freed the woman from its burden.

"Maddox," Averie called. Her voice, while not raised, carried high above the cheering crowds.

The victorious cries evaporated as the man in question jogged free of the crowd. His blond hair was damp against his scalp when he stopped a step below. "How can I serve you, my Queen?" he asked.

Averie watched the woman rise on quivering legs. Blood poured from a deep cut on her thigh and another on her ribs. But that wasn't what drew Averie's attention. What caught her eye was the thick, pulsing, black lines that stretched from each wound and traveled upward. "See to the wounded. Drain their wounds of the diseased blood before it reaches their hearts and they lose their lives."

Maddox clasped his fist hand to his chest and bowed his head. "Yes, my Queen." He turned back to the stunned crowd. "You heard her! Gather the wounded and bring them inside. Trite!"

"Yes, sir?" asked the blond man.

"Gather as much healing tonic as you can, then get Agnus to show you where she keeps her new cleansing potion."

"Cleansing potion, sir?"

CHAPTER FIVE

"Yes. She devised it after…" His words trailed as he peeked at Averie from the corner of his eye.

Averie crossed her arms with a smirk. "After…?"

Maddox cleared his throat. "After you were stabbed by The Shadow."

Averie pursed her lips at the reminder and looked at Trite. "You heard him. Get the cleansing potion."

Trite nodded and ran up the steps to find Agnus.

"Is there anything else that has been done that I don't know about?"

Maddox frowned as Radnar, Callen, Hex, Snip, and Silas went deathly still behind her. "I don't believe so."

Averie nodded her head. "Good. Now get going."

Maddox shot Radnar one last curious look before descending the stairs to help move the wounded. Averie watched the Rebellion's choreographed movements with growing interest. Something about the precision appealed to her. The teamwork and camaraderie reminded her of family. *Family?*

Averie internally shook herself and, with her gaze fixed on the bustling crowd, continued. "Radnar, see that the Shadowed bodies are taken far from here and burned. Callen, fix the mountain. We need to seal these holes up before they come back. Hex, I need you to redo the barrier. Snip…" She paused and tapped her chin in thought. "Do you know of any way to hide us from prying eyes? Something that would keep us hidden, even from those that have been here? Something to stop Sera from sneaking up on us with another surprise attack?"

The stretch of silence had Averie turning to the group in question. "What?" she asked, confused by their stunned expressions. "Is something wrong?"

Snip cleared his throat and stepped forward. "I think I may know of … something that can help. For a price." He added the last in a whisper.

Averie's frown deepened. "And what would that price be?"

Snip scrunched his nose. "Let's just say the creatures aren't known for their beauty. Or their tastes. But they are reliable and can keep any you don't want far from you."

"The price, Snip."

Snip shrugged. "To be haggled at another time."

After a moment's consideration, Averie nodded. "Have it here tonight."

Snip snapped his body to attention and lifted his hand in mock salute. "Yes, ma'am!" With a flick of his wrist, a gaudy, glittering blue portal sparked to life.

Hex leaned back; his face scrunched in distaste. "Where in Fornax does that go?"

Snip smiled and draped an arm around Ryan's shoulders. "Why, this is my super amazing, everyone wishes they had it, portal to my bestie's house!"

Ryan shrugged himself free of Snip's grasp. "We are not friends, let alone '*besties*,'" he said with air quotes.

Snip popped his bottom lip out in a pout. "Are you saying that you don't want to go home? Because this portal only goes to my best friend's house. However…"

ACCEPTANCE

Another wave and a frightening, electrified black mass appeared. "There is always this one."

Callen and Radnar peeked over Ryan's shoulder in curiosity as loud pops and snaps of electricity sparked from within. Ryan didn't hesitate in deciding and took several steps toward the black, electrified mass before Snip grabbed his arm. "Stars, man! Would you rather face the pits of the underworld over admitting to our friendship?"

Ryan pursed his lips.

"Well?" Snip ground out.

"I'm thinking!" Ryan snapped.

Snip scoffed and snapped his fingers, closing the dark portal. "Come on, *Orion*. I have things to do." Pout firmly in place, Snip slipped through the glittering portal without a backward glance.

It wasn't until Ryan stepped forward that Hex stepped in his path. "You say nothing," he warned.

Ryan lifted a brow. "Didn't I warn you about secrets? Have you learned nothing?"

Hex narrowed his eyes as Ryan inched closer. His lips moved with words spoken too quietly for anyone else to have heard; then, he vanished into the ostentatiously decorated portal.

Hex glared at the space long after it popped from existence. "What did he say?" Silas asked, stepping to his side.

"Nothing. You need to get back to X. Things are not going well for him, either."

Silas stiffened, his hands tightening against the hilts of his blades. "Nicodemus?"

Hex lifted a hand, his eyes flashing bloodred as the air shifted. Silas stared at the space, reminiscent of the air rising from stone on a hot day.

"Leaving without saying goodbye to your own father?" teased a deep voice.

Silas clenched his jaw and slowly turned to face the man that had shaped him into the monster he was. Even after a bloody battle, Marcus still had not a single strand of hair out of place. The only tell that he had actually taken part was the mosaic of red, black, and green that covered his face, neck, and white robes.

"Every chance I get," Silas snarled.

"Silas," Hex urged.

Silas glanced over his shoulder and let his gaze linger on Averie as she spoke with Callen. "Keep me updated."

Hex didn't need to ask to know what, or rather *who*, he spoke of. "It'll never work."

Silas smiled and fixed a glowing glare on his father as he said, "I've beaten greater odds."

Hex released a heavy breath and narrowed his eyes before shoving Silas through and snapping it closed behind him.

"Care to share what the other one whispered?" Marcus asked.

A mask of nonchalance slid over Hex as he faced the man in white. The one that had caused so much pain and misery throughout the Realm. The one that was now standing on the same side as he was. "Nope."

CHAPTER FIVE

Marcus clasped his hands behind his back and chuckled. "Come now, do you think I don't know a warning when I see one? You don't get as far as I have without getting a few yourself."

"Strange to call what you've done *far*. I don't know a single thing that you've done that has been done on your own merit."

Marcus shrugged. "It isn't about how you get there, just what you do when you're there."

"Like fall?"

"You call it falling. I call it choosing the winning side."

"Actually, I call it destiny. What is it they say? Oh yes, the higher the rat climbs, the greater its predator."

Marcus clenched his jaw. "Careful not to make an enemy out of your enemy's foe. After all this *Time*, haven't you figured that out yet?"

Externally, Hex was calm, his face an unemotional mask. While inside, the beast raged against its chains. "Figured out what, *Betrayer*?"

Marcus took a daring step forward, his obsidian eyes boring into Hex's rubescent pools. "How this is all going to end, of course."

"Marcus," came a voice as musical as wind chimes. "That's enough."

Hex flicked his attention over Marcus's shoulder and spotted the dark-haired, golden-eyed woman that had called. His lips curved in an empty, humorless smile. One filled with the promise of something terrible to come when they clashed with Marcus's once more. "Sleep well, Marcus."

"Marcus," Solara beckoned once more.

Something flashed in Marcus's eyes. Something so dark and so fast that any other person would have missed it before his smile was back in place. "Duty calls," he declared.

Hex was watching Marcus and Solara walk away when he felt the wet touch of a nose against his hand. Hex looked down to find the great black wolf, its fur ruffling in the breeze and expectant frost-colored eyes fixed on him. "I know, I know. But we can't do anything about it, can we?"

Echo snorted.

Hex rolled his burgundy eyes and turned on his heel. "Come on, we have a barrier to repair."

Averie watched Hex hold the single-sided conversation with Echo with growing curiosity. "Can he speak to Echo?" she asked, interrupting Callen.

With a deep-set frown, Callen watched Hex assess the damage to the barrier before beginning repairs, Echo following dutifully by his side. From the distance, he could not make out more than the movements of Hex's lips and the slight twitch of Echo's head. "It is possible. They are bound to the same deity."

"Deity? What deity?"

Callen's eyes jerked to hers, his mouth drawn into a tight line, as though he had spoken too much. "Are you going to listen to what I am saying, or are you going to continue to ask questions about things I have no right to speak about?"

ACCEPTANCE

Averie rolled her eyes with a sigh. "Continue."

Listening but not truly hearing, Averie nodded along to their words. Her mind wandered and her eyes traced over the remnants of the battle surrounding them as their words droned on. A sigh puffed her cheeks. "Why don't you guys do that, and I'll check the mountain to figure out the full extent of the damage?"

Callen frowned. Nothing they had said was an action, just a simple recap of what had transpired and additional theories on how to hide themselves. "Averie, were you list—"

Radnar cleared his throat loudly, interrupting Callen's words, and fixed him with a stare. "Sounds great. We will let you know what we find."

Averie nodded, her eyes distant and body already turning toward the mountain. "I'll be back soon."

Callen took a step forward but stopped when a hand caught his elbow. He turned to meet Hex's piercing gaze and Echo's warning growl. A frowned wrinkled his brow. "How did you... What are you doing? She was not listening to what we were saying."

"Give her time. Now that the adrenaline of the battle is over, it is possible that her mind is struggling to fill in the gaps," Hex explained.

The urge to follow Averie's shrinking form was strong. Indecision warred, before Callen relented and turned to Radnar. "The sun is nearing its apex. If you are going to go, now is the time."

Radnar looked up at the sky and nodded. "I will be back soon."

Hex and Echo exchanged an indecipherable glance before turning their attention back to Callen.

"What would you have us do?" asked Hex.

Callen sighed and ran a hand through his sweat-dampened hair. "We prepare the pyres and clean the area, and you must get back to the barrier. Make sure we cannot be found."

Hex nodded and exchanged another glance with Echo. "Snip should be back soon with his ... acquaintance." Hex lingered for a moment longer.

"What is it?" Callen asked, feeling the weight of the man's stare.

Red clashed against blue as the two faced off for several silent, tense moments. "Every action has consequences. Are you prepared for yours?" Hex wondered.

Callen's jaw ticked, and his eyes hardened. "I did what was best for Averie."

Hex pursed his lips and lifted his shoulder. "What you think is best and what is truly best are often not the same thing."

Callen narrowed his eyes and fisted his hands. "If there is something you are trying to say, then say it."

Hex smirked and snapped his fingers. A whirling portal appeared, sucking the air from around them and pulling at their clothes and hair. "You have made a mistake, Callen. When it will show itself is still unknown, but a single fact remains."

Callen closed the space between them, his eyes illuminating with molten power. "What fact is that?"

CHAPTER FIVE

Hex slid his hands into his pockets and rocked back on his heels. "Decisions made with emotion are not the wisest ones to make."

"It was her only chance for survival."

"Ah yes, I remember thinking something along those lines many years ago and paid dearly for it."

"This is different," Callen seethed.

Hex quirked a brow, his lips lifting in amusement. "Was it? Or was it just *easier* for you to take away the source of her suffering instead of helping her through it?" Hex leaned forward. "You miscalculated, Eternal One."

Callen's hands balled at his sides, shaking in anger, but when he opened his mouth to speak, Hex had already disappeared into the portal.

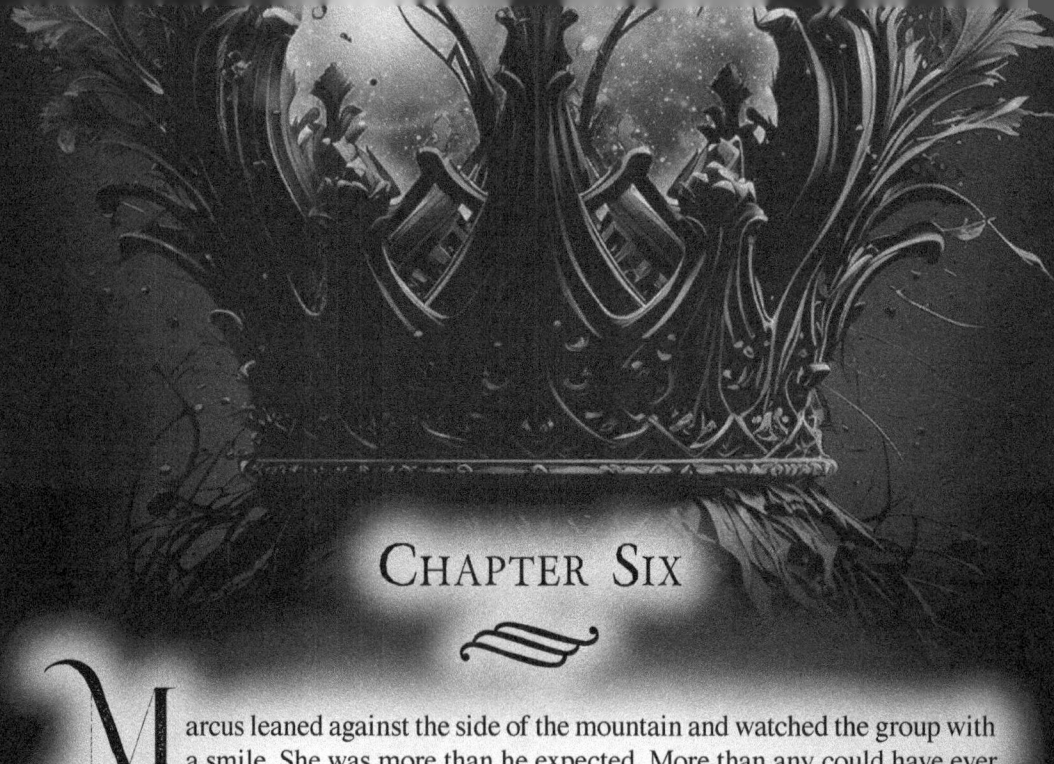

Chapter Six

Marcus leaned against the side of the mountain and watched the group with a smile. She was more than he expected. More than any could have ever imagined. *More than she was a week ago.*

Marcus narrowed his eyes at the last thought. He had been watching her since… What was his name? *Thane.* Marcus nodded to himself. He had watched her since Thane had died. Watched her grapple with herself, her guilt, and her grief. He had stalked the shadows and followed her night after night as she attacked the Shadowed. Watched her futile attempts to hide from her pain with a mask of merciless brutality.

While hidden, he studied every nuance of her movements, every tiny twitch and outburst, until he understood her. Until he could mimic and predict her imminent steps.

But what he had witnessed today was something he never expected. The raw power she unleashed and the glimmer of excitement that shone in her eyes with every kill… That was new. The empty void of grief in her gaze began to burn with a newfound intensity. "But how? Why?" Marcus whispered.

Averie stood amongst her loyal horde. Her spine was straight, and her chin was held up high. Her arms hung at her sides while her hands mindlessly flexed on the sai still in her grip. She stood with an air of satisfaction, as if the oppressive load that she had been shouldering had abruptly vanished.

A faint, victorious smile spread across his battle-splattered face. He felt a rush of satisfaction as the pieces of the puzzle started to snap together in his mind. Marcus looked over at the group with fresh, eager eyes. Radnar stood to her right, his brow furrowed and arms crossed over his chest as he watched her. To the untrained eye, he appeared relaxed. Casual even. But to those trained, to those that knew him and had seen him in action, he was anything but. His crossed arms were merely a divergence to the real thing. His fingers were tracing the hilt of his blade from beneath

CHAPTER SIX

his arm, and his eyes constantly inspected Averie from head to toe, as though she were a bomb and he was chosen to deactivate it.

Marcus shook his head in dismissal. *He may have the skills, but it wasn't him.*

He looked to Averie's left and felt another satisfying snap in his mind. The abominable twins. Hexius and Snip, Princes of the Sixth Realm, also known fondly as the Realm of Seasons. The very same Realm they had single-handedly emptied of every living soul in a mindless dispute. *The pair that shouldn't exist.* A pair that knew too much, could do too much, and always seemed to be everywhere but where they were needed, unless it suited them.

Marcus let his attention drift to the jester of the pair, Snip, and immediately dismissed him as too jovial, not serious enough to have done what had to be. Marcus slid his gaze to the next in line, Hex. The genius. The unpredictable, manipulative, all-seeing one. Externally, he exuded to all that he was, with a cool, dismissive demeanor. But Marcus knew better. Even so, he knew he was missing something, and while he couldn't eliminate the misleading twin from his list of suspects, he couldn't definitively say it was him, either. *Dead ends. All dead ends.* Marcus sighed as he found himself at a loss.

At least he was until he moved on to Callen and, like dominos, everything fell into place, and he could see it all.

Callen was stiff, too stiff even for the man made of stone. His eyes were locked steadfast and straight, unblinking, even when Averie's name tumbled from his lips. *Guilt.* Marcus knew of the feeling. Not from experience, of course, but he had seen it on many of his subject's faces during their ... questioning.

"Got you," Marcus whispered with a knowing curve of his lips.

The words were barely loud enough to be considered being said out loud, and yet Hex turned his unsettling, bloodied gaze on him. Breath stopped in his chest, and Marcus felt death's icy grip tighten around his body. Terror raced through his mind when his body started to twitch and shake uncontrollably. Darkness loomed at the edges of his vision, a menacing force intent on stealing away all the light and life, when Hex's attention was pulled away and back to Averie.

Marcus collapsed against the stone and inhaled sharply as his body filled with heat and his lungs filled with fresh air. The desire to retaliate had his hands clenching into trembling fists at his sides. Until a flash of red forced his attention from avenging himself. Averie turned from the group. The twirl on her heel lifted her wine-colored hair as she made her way around the crumbling mountain.

As the four huddled together, their heads dipped close and their whispered words laced with irritation, a plan began to form in his mind.

A flutter of air ruffled the white hair from his face. "What are you planning, Marcus?" Solara demanded.

Marcus looked at her with wide-eyed innocence. "Whatever do you mean?"

Solara narrowed her golden eyes. "I know you too well to fall for your false charm."

"What makes you think my charm is false?"

ACCEPTANCE

Solara narrowed her eyes. "Do not do it, Marcus. Whatever you are planning, leave Averie out of it."

Marcus turned to face her head-on, all mirth gone from his face. "I think you have forgotten the dynamic of our relationship, dear Solara. You do not tell *me* what to do. I tell *you*, and you do it regardless of how you feel because that is the deal you have struck."

Solara stiffened, irrevocable hostility pulsing from her iridescent body. "There was no deal in what you did, Death Walker," she hissed.

Marcus lifted a hand and roughly cupped her cheek. A being of both worlds, his touch would be the only one she could feel until the day he released her. "Be warned, I have let your past misdeeds go unpunished." Solara scoffed, and Marcus tightened his grip to painful levels. "Oh, I have, whether you choose to believe it or not, your sentence can be much, *much* worse. Are you going to be good and help me or would you prefer your … chambers?"

Fear flashed in her golden eyes far too fast for any to have seen, except for him. "I will help," she whispered.

Marcus smiled and brushed her cheek lovingly. "Good. Now go see where Radnar is running off to."

Solara stepped back from his reach and pinned him with a glare that could kill if such a thing existed, then disappeared. Marcus turned his attention back to what remained of Averie's tight-knit group and felt himself smile once more. Callen and Hex were fixed in a heated sparring of words. When Hex disappeared, his decision was made. Without sparing a single glance at Callen, he slipped into the shadows and followed Averie.

Averie wandered away from the bustle of people, nodding at those that sang her praises and thanked her. But the smile was stiff and the nod heavy. "Heavy is the crown," she whispered to herself. Her shoulders slumped as she stepped around the side of the mountain and disappeared from lingering sight.

Strength fled her body as the mighty formation blocked the expectant stares. Her body sagged against its chilled black stone. Resting her head back against it, she inhaled a shaking breath that lifted her shoulders. Wind lifted and pulled at her wine-colored strands, cooling her warmed skin and washing the stench of blood and death from her nose. It was at times like these, in those silent moments following a battle, that she felt the Realm's genuine life force. Its desire to cleanse itself of the stench and blemishes of battle and death, always proceeded with a cool breeze that smelled of wildflowers.

Averie swallowed through the lump in her throat and shoved from the mountainside. Her fingers lingered upon its surface as she continued her walk, the soft pads of her fingertips brushing between the jagged and smooth divots of the ancient

CHAPTER SIX

landmark. The farther her steps carried her, the more she felt it. Something was *wrong*. Something was *missing*. Only she couldn't place what it was.

Her free hand rubbed absently against her chest as she struggled to place what was missing. The world around her appeared almost dim, as if covered in morning fog. Her mind felt cloudy, as if it was packed with cotton, making it difficult to think clearly. It felt like her thoughts were trapped in a haze. Averie shook her head, deciding to leave it for another day. She needed to focus on the task at hand before Sera and Lucas decided to double back and strike again.

Her fingertips continued to brush along the jagged rocks of the mountainside and, as though it knew her plight, the mountain sent a calming sensation to brush her mind, granting it true peace for the first time in what felt like ages. The only thing was, she couldn't remember why her heart had been so heavy or why her mind had been so troubled in the first place. It was true she was a queen without a castle, but she had her people, their support and appreciation. She was strong, reliable, and capable of nearly anything her heart desired. Nevertheless, she had the vague memory of being in distress. Like a word she struggled to find that lingered on the tip of her tongue—there, but out of reach.

"Beautiful, isn't it?"

Averie spun on her heel, her eyes blazing as bright as the sun as she dropped into a defensive crouch. Surprise, for the second time in as many moments, made her stop and straighten her stance. Blinking to clear the golden haze from her vision, she frowned. "Marcus? What are you doing here?"

Marcus shrugged and clasped his hands behind his back as he rocked back on his heels. "Just out for a walk."

Averie narrowed her eyes. "Out for a walk?"

Marcus nodded.

"And that walk just so happened to bring you to me?"

A shrug and a coy smile. "Coincidence."

"Mmm. I've learned, mostly because of you and Sera, that coincidences don't exist. They're planned by one side to catch the other off guard."

Marcus dropped his head back with a laugh, the breeze slipping through his hair as if it had fingers of its own. "I suppose you have me there."

Averie narrowed her eyes when Marcus took several preemptive steps forward. "What do you want, Marcus?"

"To offer you an impartial ear when you need it."

Suspicion crawled down her spine, raising the hair on her arms and on the nape of her neck. "Why would I do that?"

"I saw the way they looked at you. Have seen the way they treat you and have heard their dismissal of your thoughts."

"You don't know what you're talking about. My friends look at me with worry because every battle takes a new piece of my soul and puts my life at risk."

Marcus quirked a brow as humor teased his lips. "Risks your life? You and I both know that isn't possible, therefore they have no reason to worry."

ACCEPTANCE

"They worry because that is what friends do. They worry. My thoughts are never dismissed. Radnar, Callen, Hex, and Snip are my most trusted consultants, and that is what they do. They consult me. They have decades of experience while I have none."

Marcus shrugged and looked up at the sky. "The weight of ruling is heavy, but being betrayed by someone you thought was a friend and losing your castle, your *home*, is an even heavier burden." Marcus's eyes settled back on Averie's as the last syllable was carried away.

"I don't need your help, Marcus. And I never will," Averie declared. With one final glare, she turned on her heel, intent on finishing her inspection.

"Never say never," he called.

Averie hesitated at the ominous words, her steps slowing, before she shook herself free of his words and disappeared around the side.

Chapter Seven

Averie stopped walking and peered down at the evidence of war painted on her hands. Black, red, green, and grime mixed into a nauseating and sticky mess. Any attempt to completely stretch her hands was hindered by the mix gluing the appendages together. She felt her skin prickle as the sudden urge to shower ran through her body, warring against the need to fix their broken safe haven. A quick glance around showed Marcus hadn't followed her. Averie stepped closer to the side of the mountain, placed her hand against its cool surface, and closed her eyes. With a deep breath, she threw herself into the magic veins that covered the Dark Mountain.

There was something freeing about leaving her mortal coils and following the steady thrum of power through the ancient dwelling. Streams of every color lifted and rose through the mountain, colliding in its heart in a blinding rainbow. Only, the streams were no longer smooth and free-flowing. They were broken and searching for their lost pieces. All they would need was a helping hand.

Averie smiled and withdrew back into herself. "Thank the Stars," she whispered, opening her eyes.

Averie pivoted away from the mountain and sprinted back to the spot where she had left Callen. When she returned, the scene was unrecognizable—gone was the evidence of battle. She stepped across the barrier, feeling its power surge through her, while the sound of construction echoed from the pyres being built in the distance. The tainted bodies had vanished, and all that remained was a stream of black smoke in the distance, signifying their eternal exit from the Realm.

Callen stood off to the side, huddled together with Hex and Snip, speaking in low, hushed tones.

"Why are you whispering?" she asked.

Snip jumped guiltily. "Fornax, Averie! Who just creeps up on someone after a battle? I could have killed you!"

ACCEPTANCE

Averie rolled her eyes. "Who isn't aware of their surroundings after a battle?"

Hex hid his laughter in a cough, earning a sizzling glare from his brother. "One who knows he is safe within a barrier."

Averie cocked her head to the side. "Then why were you scared when I came up?"

Snip opened his mouth to respond and frowned. "Well, now you got me."

"Good, then answer my question. Why are you whispering?"

"We are concerned about the progress being made," Callen answered.

Averie eyed the pair and felt the prickle of unease. *They're lying. But why?* Instead of questioning them further, Averie focused on the task at hand. After a quick clap of her hands and roll of her shoulders, she said, "No problem. Step back and I'll have the mountain back together."

Callen's eyes widened. "You cannot think to do it yourself."

Averie frowned. "Why not? I put the castle back together."

"And nearly drove yourself into an early grave!"

Averie waved her hand in dismissal. "That was then. This is now." Averie ignored Callen's disgruntled mumblings and took a couple of steps back. She gazed up at the majestic rock formation and felt the tension in her shoulders release as she lifted her hands, palms up. For a few moments, nothing happened, and Callen released a knowing scoff. Then her hands began to quake, and the rumble of dislodging stone shook the earth.

Callen and Hex turned to face the broken mountain and dropped their mouths in shock. Boulders, small and large, hovered just off the ground, shrouded in a golden glow. Averie shut her eyes and leaned her head to the side as her face pinched in concentration. Her right hand turned, palm down, and fingers danced like a puppeteer. One by one, the rocks were spun, twisted, and slipped into place.

Averie moved with swift, surgical precision as she followed the vein-like stripes of light that spread through each stone to set them neatly into place. Each one fell with a satisfying click, and as the last piece slid into place, the space between them blazed with golden light. Callen, Hex, and Snip winced against its radiance. Then, as if it had never been, the golden light vanished, leaving the mountain whole once more.

Callen's head jerked in Averie's direction, his body already moving to catch her if she fell. Instead, she stood with a satisfied smile on her sweaty face. "See," she panted. "Told you I could do it."

Callen's jaw clenched as he forced a wooden smile. "Yes, you did."

Averie's smile brightened as she straightened her spine and strolled toward the entrance. "Now, if you will excuse me, I need a shower, some food, and a nap."

Snip caught her wrist as she went to pass. "Are you sure you're alright?"

Averie patted her hand against his. "Of course. I'm not the same girl I was when I first got here." With that, she slipped her hand from Snip's grasp and disappeared inside.

As she turned to leave, Snip's clenched jaw revealed the mix of anger and sadness he felt in that moment. "I think we have a problem."

CHAPTER SEVEN

Averie strode purposefully through the mountain. She hadn't lied when she told Snip she wasn't the same girl she was when she first arrived, but she had when she said she was fine. The memory of reconstructing the castle played blurry and fragmented in her mind. The weight of the energy she had just released filled her with an exhaustion that threatened to overwhelm her.

The hall opened to the large gathering hall where men and women were carefully laid out on a long white mattress. Soft groans of pain sounded as the smell of the green healing tonic wrinkled her nose. If there was one thing she was grateful for, it was not needing the vile liquid. The smell of burnt hair, blood, and singed flesh grew with each hiss of use.

A quick scan of the area showed Maddox and Agnes had it all under control, allowing her to make her way through the crowd unnoticed and back to her room. The moment the door closed, Averie sank back against it and let her eyes close. Exhaustion was an old friend, but she couldn't let it take her just yet. After a moment, she shoved from the door and moved into the small alcove that would become her shower.

Averie lifted a hand against the smooth black stone and watched the spout shift from its place. Vines rose from the ground in a neat rectangle to protect her from sight. Averie stepped back and stripped the battle-stained clothing from her body as pink and purple flowers bloomed along the wall. Within moments, water poured from the spout in a warm rainfall. Averie stepped beneath the spray and let out a satisfied groan as the tension fled from her body.

Her eyes strayed to the floor, where a small grate carried the red and black traces from her skin. She watched, mesmerized, as the colors swirled with the water and yet never mixed. Averie shook herself free of the mosaic and crushed the flowers in her hands. Exhaustion crept in as she began to lazily mix the petal remnants between her hands, creating a fragrant lather that she used to scrub away the dirt and grime from her body and hair.

She sighed as she ran her hand against the wall, pushing the shower out of sight, and reveled in the feeling of being clean. Snagging a towel off the rack, she dried off and pulled on her favorite fuzzy sweatpants and off-the-shoulder top. Her feet slapped heavily against the stone floor as she crossed the room and nestled into the comfort of her bed.

"I'll just close my eyes for a minute," she promised herself.

"Averie? Averie, are you listening?"

Averie's eyes popped open at the stern question and frowned. Gone was the dark coziness of her bedroom. In its place, a field spread in front of her, filled with golden stems, vibrant wildflowers of all shapes, sizes, and colors.

"Where am I?" she asked, more to herself than anyone else.

ACCEPTANCE

"Averie, we don't have much time. I need you to focus."

Averie turned toward the familiar musical tone. "Who are you?"

A woman with long hair stood proudly before her. As she shook her head, the sun glinted off of the silver leaves that tied her hair back. The woman's cheek twitched as she strained to hide the smile. "Do you really want to your waste your question on that?"

Averie jerked back in surprise as a cold, wet nose brushed across her hand. Large honey eyes stared up at her from a face mirroring a bear. The dog barked excitedly and lunged for the stick in her other hand. Averie's frown deepened, but she did as the dog so desperately wanted and tossed the stick.

"Things are different now. When you go back, things are going to be ... difficult, but you must remain strong. Do not let the Darkness pull you under. Lean on those that lean on you. You are strong, little Avi, and you will be alright, especially in the moments it seems the least possible."

The words pulled the kernel of a memory and popped it free. "This is the place I went after Lucas." Averie turned on her heel and sucked in a harsh breath. The same plain door waited for her in the center of the field.

The woman, Solara, smiled. "Our time is up. Now ask your question."

Averie stepped forward. "How do I save the Realm?"

Solara smiled proudly. "That, my dear, is the right question. The Realm was destined for many things, but greed and deception destroyed its path and set it down another. To save the Realm, you must prepare the people for what is coming."

Averie frowned. "That doesn't make sense."

"I'm afraid our time is up."

"You didn't answer my question!"

The woman stepped to the side as the door swung open, and an unseen force began to pull her forward. Averie grit her teeth and dug her heels into the earth, to no avail. Catching the door frame, she looked at Solara. "Tell me."

The woman smiled. "To save the Realm, you must save yourself. The Heart wants what it wants."

A scream bubbled in her chest as the force pulled her into the depths of searing light.

Averie jerked upright in bed, her body slick with sweat and heart pounding against her ribs. Her eyes, unseeing and frantic, bounced through the low light in her room. The memory, forgotten once she had first awakened, blared like a neon sign in her mind. Tossing the covers from her body, she sprang from bed and raced from her room in search of the others.

By the time she made it outside, her veins thrummed with excitement. She scoured the terrain, her eyes searching for them amongst the smooth, repacked soil. Hex leaned against a tree, his arms crossed and eyes furious, with Snip at his

CHAPTER SEVEN

side, whispering into his ear. Callen and Radnar stood across from them, spewing heated words.

Snip met her eyes as she turned toward them, and he stepped back from his brother. Without a care for interrupting their conversation, she called out, "I've figured it out!"

Hex tracked her movements like a predator while Radnar jumped and cursed at her sudden proximity. "Figured what out?" asked Callen.

"I had a dream, or memory, or whatever. The point is, I remember what that strange woman told me when I was in the other place."

"The other place?" Radnar questioned. "What *other* place? What woman?"

Averie shook her head. "After the Lucas thing when I was sleeping—"

"When you were in a *coma*," Callen corrected.

Averie rolled her eyes. "Anyway, she said that I could ask a question, and she would answer it, so I asked her how to save the Realm. At first, she said a bunch of stuff I didn't understand, but then, when I was getting pulled through the door—"

"Pulled through what door?"

"She said the Heart wants what it wants."

Snip crossed his arms with a smile. "I didn't know she was a poet. Ouch!"

Hex shook his head and lowered his arm. "You deserved more than that. Be thankful it was one smack."

"Will you shut up!" Averie snapped. Taking a deep breath, she shoved her sleep-ruffled curls from her face and continued. "I think she meant the *Heart*. As in the thing inside of me."

The group looked at each other. Averie rolled her eyes. "I think to save the Realm, we have to give the *Heart* what it wants."

"Which would be..." Snip trailed.

"To be free."

If Averie had been expecting any type of praise for her deduction, she was sorely mistaken. After a few moments of tension, the group closed in on her, their eyes hard and unyielding as words erupted all at once.

"Have you gone mad?"

"Absolutely not!"

"Oh Stars, she's lost it!"

"Crixus!"

Averie's chest rose with a heavy sigh as the bombarding demands and questions continued.

"Do you have any idea what that would mean?"

"Did anyone check her for a head injury?"

"You are not thinking clearly."

"I told you this was a bad idea!"

Averie latched onto the last. "What was a bad idea?"

37

ACCEPTANCE

Hex shoved his elbow into his brother's side. Snip bent forward in a whoosh, his hands clutching his knees as he fought to capture his breath. It wasn't just a normal blow to the side, but rather one infused with power and anger.

"He is an idiot. Ignore him," Hex explained.

Hex gnashed his teeth and forced himself to straighten.

Callen stepped into her eyeline. "Averie, you cannot honestly be implying that you want to remove the Heart."

"Why not?"

"You will die."

She knew. Of course she knew, but hearing the words aloud seemed to add a different weight to the knowledge. "I know," she whispered, suddenly finding her bare toes interesting.

Callen placed a finger beneath her chin and lifted her eyes to his. "That is not an option."

"It could save the Realm. End this war and free everyone."

"No."

Averie jerked from his hold. "That isn't your choice to make."

"He's right, Avi." Hex shrugged when her glare fixed itself on him. "Right now, this is just a theory. An idea you got from a dream after overexerting yourself during battle. The mind is a complicated machine. We do not know if that is what she meant or what will happen to you once the Heart is removed."

"Wrong." Callen seethed, his eyes flashing a deadly molten silver. "We do know. It has been said a hundred times."

Averie lifted her chin. She knew when she was fighting a losing battle, and right now, that was exactly what she was doing. "Then find another solution. War Council meets tomorrow morning." With that said, she stomped back to the mountain with her hands fisted at her sides.

"Is she wearing fuzzy pants?" Snip chuckled.

Chapter Eight

Membrane — Thane

Thane paced a worn path at the foot of the stairs as he pondered his newfound existence and waited for Dar. Phantom tremors shook his arm as he remembered the impact, or lack thereof, when his fist met Dar's flesh.

"'I'll meet you here tomorrow,'" Thane mocked as he continued to pace. "Oh, will you? Because in order to do that, I would have to know when, but you didn't exactly tell me when you would 'meet me here tomorrow,' now did you!" he snapped to himself. Frustration made his body tense and his mind race.

"It'll be fine. Dar will show me how to see them again, and somehow, they will find a way to get me back, too." Thane dropped his head back at the absurd turn his life had taken over the last year.

"I am definitely not in Kansas anymore." He sighed and ran a hand through his hair.

"I told you, you're in the Membrane."

Thane turned on his heel, his hands lifted to prepare for defense, before he met the pure black ones of his newfound friend. Dar leaned casually against the stair railing, dressed exactly as heavily armed as he was the day before, with his eyes fixed on Thane's. Fighting against the burning instinct to keep his hands up, Thane forced them to his sides as he tipped his head in greeting.

"I know where I am. It's from a movie."

"A movie?"

Thane shook his head at the question. "Not important. Are you ready to show me how to see my sister?"

"Mmm, Averie, yes."

Thane narrowed his eyes. "Don't speak her name."

ACCEPTANCE

Dar smiled. The first genuine smile Thane had seen him make, and nothing about the sight made him want to smile in return. "Do not worry, Thane. I have no intention of hurting your sister."

Thane wrinkled his nose. "Don't do that. Saying it like that makes it weird."

Dar blinked several times and shook his head. "Would you like to see what is going on now?"

Internally, Thane froze. His mind, his breath, his hope. Externally, and only through the help of years of training, he remained calm and collected. "I don't like being jerked around."

Dar frowned. "I'm afraid I am not familiar with your turn of phrase."

"Lied to. Played. Tricked."

"I am not lying to you. If you would like, I can show her to you right now."

"Are you serious?"

"Of course."

Thane narrowed his eyes as he fought the wave of hope that threatened to pull him under. "Fine."

Dar nodded his head. "There is a cost," he reminded.

"And what would that be?"

He shook his head. "I am afraid I cannot say. It is different for every … being."

Thane bristled at the wording but pressed on with a nod. "Alright. What do I have to do?"

Dar smiled and turned on his heel. "Keep up."

Thane sprinted after the nearly flying Dar as he led him through the forsaken town and over the hill, before coming to an abrupt stop at the same swings he had used with Averie the last time he had seen her.

To Thane's surprise, even after the lengthy sprint, his heart kept its steady beat, and his breath came in even, unlabored puffs. To say he was uneasy with the development was supremely underrated. But now was not the time to dwell on his new existence.

"So? How does it work?"

Dar lifted a gloved hand to the swing Averie had used and, with a single finger, tapped against the air. Only, air didn't shift and wiggle like jelly when touched. Thane's eyes widened in surprise, and he couldn't have stopped his feet from approaching the strange space if he tried.

"What is this?"

Dar watched the wiggle slow and fade away. "A tear."

Thane frowned. "A tear? Like a rip? As in something you can stretch until you can slip through?"

Dar shook his head and lost himself in the distance. "If only things were that simple."

"What do you mean?"

CHAPTER EIGHT

Dar sighed and forced his eyes from the unknown and back to Thane. "It is true you can fit through, but you have no body to return to. And, even if you did, the Membrane is an incredibly possessive creature. It never lets you go for long."

"What do you mean, 'lets you go'?"

"The Membrane isn't just a prison; it's a living entity that feeds off the power of those trapped within."

Thane's brow wrinkled in confusion. "But … I have no power."

Another sigh. "No, you don't. Which makes your presence here all the more interesting. Another conundrum that has been added to the list since you have arrived."

"Then—"

"Not now. This tear will only remain viable for a small amount of time. Which means, if you want to see your sister, you need to go now."

"How will I find her?"

Dar lifted a finger and tapped the side of his head, while the other tapped against the air once more. "Think of her here. As hard as you can, and the rest will come naturally. Follow your instincts and nothing else. Ignore everything but the memories of her. The Membrane will do everything it can to veer you off your path. One wrong step and you will be trapped within the Eternal Circle."

"Well, that doesn't sound good," Thane mumbled.

"You will be fine. Just remember the rules. Now go."

Thane hesitated. His hope of seeing Averie threatened to overwhelm his reason. "How do I know this isn't a trap?"

Dar lifted a shoulder. "I suppose you don't. But you will never know until you try. After all, you are already dead. What else do you have to lose?"

He's right. What do I have to lose? Stealing his spine for what may come, Thane took measured steps toward the jiggling tear in the air and didn't stop until he stood an inch in front of it. "Any advice?" he asked.

Dar inclined his head in thought. "Prepare yourself. Things have changed since Death took you. Those you left behind may not be who you expect."

Thane frowned and opened his mouth with a question, when Dar's arm shot out, thrusting Thane through the tear with an ear-splitting pop. Thane's arms windmilled through the air as he attempted to right himself and failed. All the while, his mind raced with the desire to see his family again. His knees collided against the immobile and unforgiving black stone.

Thane blinked several times in disbelief before hope bloomed in his chest. He knew this stone. "The Black Mountain. I made it." He chuckled in disbelief and leapt to his feet. "Fox!" he called, his feet pounding against the stone as he raced through the familiar mountain until he caught the familiar flash of red. Twisting on his heel, he darted down the hallway, hot on her trail. Closer and closer until, suddenly, he was forced to a stop inches from her. A frown furrowed his brow as he lifted a hand to the space between them in confusion. "What in Fornax?" he whispered as his hand pressed against the cool, invisible barrier between them.

ACCEPTANCE

He looked around and found himself standing behind her chair in the makeshift war room like he had done so many times before. His eyes bounced around the room as his heart pounded with excitement in his chest. "Callen. Radnar. Snip. Hex. You guys are all safe."

"What in Fornax is he doing here?" Callen demanded.

Thane stiffened at the hate-filled words.

"Damn Callen, I know—"

"I was invited," interrupted a voice. Thane turned, and his jaw dropped in shock to see Marcus slip through the door.

"I invited him." Averie's voice cut through him and buried itself deeper than the blade that had claimed his life.

"Averie? Why? What are you doing?"

Thane stared down at his sister in utter disbelief. Words flowed like white noise around him as the world grew hazier and more distorted with each passing second. A nauseating sensation rolled his stomach as the feeling of being ripped back jolted his entire body.

When next he opened his eyes, he found himself kneeling at Dar's feet, once more in the Membrane.

"How did it go?"

Thane shook his head. Bile burned his throat, making his voice husky. "I have to get back." He panted and lifted his eyes to Dar's. "Something has gone seriously, seriously wrong."

Dar smiled. "Then I guess we have work to do."

Chapter Nine

Averie strode into the gathering with a bored expression on her face … and Marcus in tow. Each face displayed a laughable level of shock and amazement upon discovering the sudden partnership. Chatter stopped and jaws dropped when Radnar, Hex, and Snip noticed what Callen initially did not. The slight breeze of air that signified her entrance caused Callen's lips to curve into a soft, small smile. Then his eyes shifted to the man following her, his eyes darkening and lips twisting in disgust.

"What in Fornax is he doing here?" Callen demanded.

Marcus beamed. "I was invited."

Marcus looked up from his place along the wall in time to see Averie storm back into the mountain dwelling, irritation lining her face. He sliced another chunk from his apple and arched a brow in surprise when she spotted him and headed directly for him. He popped the slice into his mouth and started chewing as he watched the unfolding situation.

"Averie, how lovely to see you. What brings you to my corner of the mountain?"

Averie frowned and took a moment to scan the common area. Everyone congregated on the opposite side of the mountain, placing as much space as possible between them and Marcus. Averie shook herself internally and smiled.

"Are you busy tomorrow?"

Marcus popped another piece of apple into his mouth. "As a matter of fact, I'm not."

"I brought him here," Averie clarified.

"For what reason?" Callen pressed.

ACCEPTANCE

Averie shrugged dismissively and sat at the head of the table. "He is here because he knows more about how the Shadowed act and Sera thinks than anyone else."

Hex and Snip exchanged a blank glance. Radnar leaned across the table. "Are you sure that is wise? We don't know that he won't go running back and tell her what we have planned."

Averie eyed the older man. His salt-and-pepper hair was more salt now than it had been when she first arrived, and his eyes were lined with harsh exhaustion. "I am very sure. Marcus, do you intend to run back to the person who left you for dead?"

Marcus smiled, though it didn't reach his eyes, and stood at her side. "No."

Averie leaned back and looked over at the group with a smile. "There you have it. He has no intention of betraying us."

"And you intend to take his word for it?" Callen gasped.

Averie slowly turned her gaze to Callen. "Yes."

Radnar's throat cleared, the sound reverberating throughout the room and catching everyone's attention. "Averie, I do not think that is a smart move, lass."

"Why is he untrustworthy now, when you were the one that brought him along in the first place?"

Radnar's face blanched, and his jaw worked, opening and closing, as he struggled to find the words.

"Did he not fight on our side when Sera attacked at the Silver Rose Ball?"

"Well, yes."

"Did he not choose to fight with us instead of fleeing?"

Radnar ground his teeth, his jaw aching beneath the pressure, and nodded.

Averie leaned forward and clasped her hands on the tabletop. "Did he not aid in bringing our people to safety? Has he done anything to make you feel as though he has intentions of betraying us?"

Radnar's hand clenched into white-knuckled fists with each rhetorical question. "No." He grit his teeth.

Averie nodded, a satisfied smile curling her lips as she sat back. "Good. Now that we have settled that. Why are we here?"

Radnar scowled at Marcus's victorious smile. "We are here because we need to prepare for the time Sera inevitably strikes again."

"She won't be able to find us, which buys us more time. Snip's ... friend has made sure of that."

"That's true, but we should still be prepared. She will not take her loss gracefully."

Averie steepled her fingers, her mind riffling through the memories she had of her and Sera's friendship. *Had she ever lost?* The thought was troubling. She couldn't remember a single time she had. In elementary school, she dominated the playground playing kickball. In middle school, she made her mark on the spelling bee. When in high school, she took on the challenge of running for class president, just to prove a point, won, and then quickly stepped away afterward. "I think you're right. However, right now, we need to focus on healing and building our strength. It

CHAPTER NINE

doesn't matter if we plan an attack now if we do not have the necessary force behind it. We should give our forces some time to recover before we launch another attack."

"I agree," said Marcus.

Callen's chest vibrated with a deep, menacing growl, and his gaze locked on the man with a fierce intensity. "Who asked you?"

Averie lifted a brow in amusement. "I didn't know we had to be asked to agree or offer an opinion, Callen. Is something bothering you?"

His jaw muscles were tight, a telltale sign of his frustration as it visibly jumped in the corner of his cheek. "I feel as though you are being played a fool by the man that was so recently your enemy, your *prisoner*."

Averie leveled him with a golden glare. "I feel you have forgotten who the queen of this Realm is."

Callen's eye twitched.

"Now," Averie began, slicing through the growing tension with a soft smile as she looked over the group, "any suggestions?"

Several tense hours had passed within the great dark mountain. While tempers had flared and ideas had been shared, the sun had sailed across the sky and settled beneath the horizon. By the time Averie leaned back in her seat and stretched her arms high above her head with a long yawn, dueling crescent moons climbed the velvet sky.

"If that is all, I think I am going to get some sleep." Averie sighed.

Radnar rose from his chair and, after sending one last sweltering glare at Marcus, left the room without a word. Callen lingered, rising to his feet slowly. His eyes suggested he had something to say before he shook his head and disappeared.

Averie looked between Hex and Snip's silent, communicating stare and lifted a brow. "Is there something wrong?"

Hex looked at his brother and settled his dark red eyes on Averie's green ones. "I have a situation I need to take care of. I will be gone for a few days, a week at most."

Averie frowned. "Is it something I should know?"

Hex shook his head, his gaze briefly meeting Marcus's inquisitive stare before looking away again. "No. It has nothing to do with this Realm." With a flourish of his wrist, he disappeared from his seat.

Snip cleared his throat and rose to his feet to close the space between them. He clasped her upper arms and flashed his signature smile. "I'm afraid I must do the same, Princess, but I promise to return shortly." After a quick peck to her cheek, he, too, was gone.

Averie's frown lingered as she stared at the vacant space until Marcus's sigh pulled her free. Averie dropped her chin in her hand and fixed him with an irritated expression. "If you have something to say, just say it."

ACCEPTANCE

Marcus clasped his hands behind his back and rocked back on his heels. "I was just thinking, *wondering* really…"

Averie narrowed her eyes. "Out with it."

"It's just… Do you know where they go? Have they ever said?"

Averie schooled her features into a purposeful, blank mask as she thought over his words. *No,* she thought. *But I don't think that is a bad thing. There is enough going on here. We can't exactly help the other Realms right now.*

Marcus smiled inwardly, feeling a sense of satisfaction. Averie believed she kept herself locked away from prying thoughts, but for one such as him, it was easy to read the expressions someone thought they hid. Like a predator, he saw the inkling of doubt spark to life in the recesses of her eyes and pounced. "I just find it convenient that they are always a step from harm's way. That they seem to disappear when you need them most and never say where they have gone."

Averie clenched her jaw against the wash of a memory.

Marcus had just escaped. The ember of her anger, placated by having the man imprisoned, was being wafted to life with each passing second. He was absent from her clutches.

"*Averie! I have to talk to you," Radnar bellowed. His steps slapping against the stone as he raced to her side.*

"*I already know he's gone. Come on, Snip might have an idea."*

Averie frowned when pain shot through her head and the memory continued, hazy and distorted, before clearing once more.

"*What's the plan?"*

Snip cleared his throat and sent her a sheepish look. "We wait."

Averie tuned out the bickering between Silas and Snip as she tried to think of an alternative to Snip's very basic idea. Irritation raised the hair on her arms as their argument and insults grew louder. "That's enough!" she snapped, her chest lifting as she breathed a deep, calming breath.

A chuckle escaped Radnar's typical scowl and captured everyone's attention. They watched in shock as it grew until he was bent over, clutching his sides. He looked up at Silas and Snip and shook his head. "And you two thought I was mean."

Averie looked around the room as each, including herself, dissolved into their own peals of laughter. Until one came to an abrupt halt. Averie frowned and looked over to find Snip had disappeared. The moment she opened her mouth, the room exploded. Smoke and dust filled her lungs. A blaring ring filled her ears and shifted her perception.

Another pain flared in her head, causing her to wince. Determination took hold, and she delved once more into her mind.

CHAPTER NINE

"Where is Snip?" she called out.

Silas's words dissolved into a cough, leaving him to shake his head.

"Callen!" she beckoned. "Have you seen Snip?"

He looked around with a frown. "No."

Averie blinked away the memory and rose from her seat. "I trust them. Get some rest. It's going to be a long couple of weeks." Her words were laced with the steel of certainty and punctuated with her retreating steps.

Marcus lowered his eyes and dipped his head, a calculating smirk hidden behind the shadow of his white locks. "Of course, my Queen."

Chapter Ten

Several weeks later

Marcus watched, as he always did. While the others shifted the conversation to something more, to something deeper, he was the only one who saw *everything*. The eager flash of light emanating within one's dark depths, igniting the same light within the bloodied pools of the other. The subtle tipping of chins and twitching of fingertips.

He watched it all while his curiosity warred with the need to go unnoticed.

Averie's clear, decisive voice ensnared his attention. "We have two options. We either let this war continue to tear apart this Realm and all of us, or we end it once and for all."

Radnar's fingers strummed along the tabletop. "We have not been fighting for the love of it, but for necessity." His eyes flicked pointedly to Marcus, who smiled back. "If we could have ended it, we would."

Averie cocked her head. "But isn't that why you brought me here in the first place? The reason you sent Silas to find me?"

The thrumming of his fingers stalled. "What do you suggest we do?"

Averie smiled, and her eyes ignited liquid gold, as they so often did of late. "We take the fight to them."

Callen's brow furrowed. "That is a death sentence. Our people have just recovered from the last battle. If we surge ahead now, we risk losing everything."

"Not if we do it right. Not if we have a plan, the *right* plan."

Snip straightened in his seat and leaned his elbows on the table. "What do you suggest?"

CHAPTER TEN

Her smile grew, exposing her straight, gleaming teeth. "We take the fight to them. We lure them into a false sense of security and attack when they least expect it."

Callen's eyes bore into hers, a fog rolling over them as scenarios played in his mind before he shook his head. "We will never make it through the castle barrier."

"Who said anything about going to the castle?"

"If not the castle, then where?"

Snip's face lit up with his trademark smirk, and the room buzzed with anticipation as all eyes turned to him. "I think I know a place."

Averie leaned forward, her golden eyes shimmering with intrigue. "Where?"

"There is an old castle, nothing more than ruins now. But it sits on a hill and has a forest surrounding it, making it an easy enough place to defend."

Averie pursed her lips in thought, then finally nodded. "Alright. How do we get Sera to come?"

"Make it look like you have taken up residence," Hex supplied. Confused glances shifted his way. Suppressing his sigh, he continued. "If you make it seem like the Rebellion has moved their headquarters, her ego won't allow it to go unchecked."

"You seem to know a lot about her ego." Marcus smiled.

Hex dragged his eyes to Marcus. "I know a great many things, *Betrayer*."

"As do I, *Cursed One*."

"How do we get her attention?" Averie interrupted.

"Don't worry about that, Princess. I will take care of that. You just get your people in place," Snip chimed in.

Averie frowned as Marcus's words brushed her mind. *They disappear when you need them most and never say where they have gone.* "How are you going to do that?"

Snip shrugged. "Connections, Princess. I have spent many a year traveling the Realms, and I have found a few people that hold some unique power within their blood. I am sure some of them would be willing to lend a hand and share a few whispers."

Hex narrowed his eyes at his brother. "Have you now? And what price will we pay for this aid?"

Snip leaned back, an expression of mock hurt pinching his features as he clutched his chest. "You wound me, brother."

"Not as much as I wish to, I assure you."

"Hex is right. What is the price?" Averie interjected.

Snip shrugged and leaned back in his chair. "No price. I will call in a favor."

Averie chewed the inside of her lip before giving a brief, hesitant nod. "Fine. For now, we should get some rest. We have some long days ahead of us, and with a battle looming, we all deserve it."

Radnar and Callen locked eyes for a moment before they both stood up and left. Hex and Snip rose, glared at each other, and vanished into their own gateways.

The soft whisper of closed portals left Averie and Marcus alone in the silence. Relieved of her duties, Averie sagged against the back of her seat, her fingers tracing small circles on her temples. Marcus released a long, dramatic sigh.

ACCEPTANCE

Averie grit her teeth against the sound and asked, "What is it, Marcus?"

"Oh nothing. Just the same wonder as before rattling itself in my mind."

Averie frowned. "What do you mean?"

Marcus lifted a noncommittal shoulder and settled into Callen's vacated seat. "Where do you think they go?"

Averie groaned and dropped her head back against the seat. "I am not having this discussion with you again."

"You don't find it strange? Irritating? Secretive?"

Averie tensed at the implication. "What are you implying, Marcus?"

Another shrug. "Oh, nothing. I just find it convenient that…" He shook his head. "Never mind."

Averie's jaw flexed as she grit her teeth. "Spit it out, Marcus." She seethed as a wicked form of déjà vu played through.

"Haven't you noticed how quick their dispersal is? How they disappear moments before trouble arises but know the exact person you need to fix it all? Why do they keep their secrets until it is necessary for them to share? How do they arrive just when you need them?"

Averie pondered his questions once more as her finger tapped out a rhythm on the smooth tabletop. Questions that, as much as she loathed to admit it, she'd pondered more than once. Questions that had plagued her mind exponentially since he had first mentioned it.

Her shoulders rose with a deep breath as she rose to her feet and leveled him with a determined stare. "Hex and Snip have come to my rescue on countless occasions. They have given me advice and guidance when I needed it and when I wasn't ready to listen. Until they give me a reason not to, I trust them."

Marcus searched Averie's face for any hint of uncertainty, and when he found none, he nodded. "Of course."

Averie tipped her head in approval, then rose from her chair and headed for the door. Her hand lingered against the doorknob. Marcus looked up, curious about her hesitation. Averie cleared her throat and, staring at the dark stone door, spoke. "If anything should arise that seems suspicious, make sure you come to me directly."

Marcus smiled at her back. "Of course."

"And Marcus?"

"Yes?"

"We leave at dawn."

Marcus waited for the door to click shut before whirling around and catching the hidden party. His hand lashed out, catching the person's cool neck. A wave of white fabric fluttered in its own wind. "Solara," he growled. "What are you doing here? Didn't I give you a mission?"

Solara wriggled against his hold. Her golden eyes were full of fear even as they narrowed. "I have done what you asked."

Marcus smiled and stroked his finger against her smooth flesh. "Very good. Then everything is ready?"

CHAPTER TEN

Solara swallowed against his grip. "Yes."

Marcus leaned forward and pressed his lips to her forehead. "I will reward you, as promised," he whispered, then released her from his hold and turned to the door.

"Marcus," Solara called after him, halting his steps. The slight inclination of his head told her he was listening. "You promised to leave her out of your plan."

Marcus left the room with a smile she couldn't see and the noticeable absence of his agreement.

Chapter Eleven

Averie stormed down the corridor to her room and slammed the door behind her. Frustration trembled in her limbs as she threw herself on her bed and thrashed against the soft sheets. The meeting had gone as well as she could have imagined, so why was she feeling so anxious?

An angry growl rumbled in her chest as she forced herself to leave her bed and shower. Reaching forward, she twisted the knob all the way until steam rose and filled the warded area, saving her bed from its dampness.

Averie slipped free of her clothes and tossed them carelessly to the side before stepping into the steam-filled stall. As the warm water washed over her sore muscles, she felt them pop as they released, eliciting a moan as she dropped her head against the stone wall. With each pop of release, her body became more and more relaxed until she nearly fell asleep, wrapped in the warmth of the shower.

With pursed lips and more than a little bit of reluctance, she shut the water off and stepped from the shower. Quickly she dried and slipped into her favorite pair of fuzzy sweatpants and oversized shirt before falling onto her bed. With a satisfied sigh, Averie turned to her side and snuggled into the soft mattress. "Dreamless sleep," she pleaded as sleep pulled down her eyes. "Dreamless … sleep."

She felt her body jerk as if she had fallen from a tree and plopped onto the ground. Her stomach rolled as it took another moment to catch up, and the ground shuttered beneath her. The unexpected motion brought a rush to her senses and bile to her throat. Sound beat maliciously against her eardrums, eliciting a painful cry as Averie clutched her head.

Taking a deep breath, she filled her lungs and nose with the metallic smell of freshly spilled blood. Averie wrinkled her nose in disgust and scanned her surroundings, her eyes growing wider with each passing moment. Fire scorched its

CHAPTER ELEVEN

way across the earth, its ruthless warmth further tainting the air with acrid intensity. The brutal cacophony of battle filled the air with the sound of metal clashing and the final cries of the fallen and screams of the wounded.

Averie rose on shaking legs and circled, in complete disbelief, as her eyes soaked in the destruction of a live battle. She shook her head and felt the familiar heaviness of her sai slipping from her fingers. "No," she whispered on a groan, a sob catching in her chest. "No, no, no, no."

This isn't real. This isn't possible. I'm in bed. I'm sleeping…

"Watch out!" someone ordered. Averie frowned and turned toward the beckoning call as a large body slammed into her side. The unexpected impact forced her to the ground as a Shadowed Elite brought its smoking soul blade down in a deadly arc. Callen's enormous form slipped into her field of sight as he buried his blade into the soulless husk.

Averie looked up in disbelief. "What are you doing?" he demanded. His chest and face bathed in a warrior's elegance, tainted with streaks of darkness from the slain Shadowed.

"I don't understand," she whispered, more to herself than to him. Callen looked down with contempt as another figure rushed forward, dipping into a crouch as he pulled her to her feet.

"Are you okay?" he asked.

Averie swallowed a scream, her head shaking in horror as the faceless man lurched toward her. "I don't know," she whispered. This isn't real. This isn't real.

Against her better judgement, she couldn't stop herself as she scanned his blood-splattered, melted features. Lifting a shaking hand, she pressed it to the being's chest and felt her stomach drop at the solidity and warmth. "You're real," she groaned.

The melted-faced man shifted to Callen's direction, but Callen just shrugged as he plunged his blade into another attacker. Stomping against the ash-charred ground, he forced a large pillar to tear free from the wall and collide against several impending attackers.

The melted man gave him a double thumbs up before turning his haunting head back in her direction. "Yeah, Averie. Of course, I am."

Averie shook her head at the graveled voice and squeezed her eyes shut. "You don't understand! This isn't possible!" she shrieked. Her chest heaved with rapid, confused breaths. "I was just in bed with…" Averie frowned. With who? Why does this feel so familiar?

"Woah, Fox." The melted-faced man stepped back, the swirl of melted flesh where his eyes should be stretched into thick lines. "I don't need to hear about your private life."

"Don't be stupid," she snapped. The words came out unbidden. As though she were once more playing a part in a play she couldn't remember being a part of. The words continued to come out, unbidden from her lips. "I don't understand!" she panted, gripping her head. "We just got home after spending the last couple of

53

ACCEPTANCE

days chasing Marcus. We lost him, and we went home. I was exhausted, and Silas took me to my room. I remember falling asleep and then..." Averie shook her head, her hands pulling at her hair. "This doesn't make sense!"

"Averie!" The melted man lurched forward and caught her wrist. In one fluid motion, he tossed her onto the cracked floor and into safety as a blade slammed against the stone where she once stood.

The clang of his sword matching another's rang in her ears as a flash of white caught her attention. Nausea fisted her stomach once more as she croaked out, "Mom?"

Karen stared back, a smile on her soft features, her finger pressed firmly to her lips, before she turned from the battle and disappeared around a smoking, broken building. Averie didn't hesitate. In an instant, she was shoving from the ground, ignoring the desperate outcries of Callen and the melted man, and dodging her way through the ravaged battlefield. She followed the chocolate strands like a lifeline.

Her feet slapped against the broken ground, and her heart raged against her chest as her lungs heaved at her pace until a large, familiar, broken frame loomed before her. Memories tickled her mind as she slinked through a thin opening and made her way through the endless rubble. Her steps faltered as phantom pain bunched her muscles.

Averie stopped and narrowed her eyes. "I know you're in here. I remember what comes next, and you won't get me this time," she called out.

A soft chuckle echoed off the fractured stone as her mother stepped from the shadows. She lifted her hands and began to clap. Averie watched as her mother's skin began to bubble and stretch, her hair twisting and turning, fading into a golden blonde. The rich honey of her eyes twirled until a vibrant, crystal blue looked out.

"Are you sure?" Lucas asked.

Averie kept her face carefully blank as she spoke. "Sure of what?"

Lucas smiled, the curve of his lips pulling at the pale pink scars on his face. "That you remember. That you truly remember."

"This is the dream Sera planted in my head. In about three minutes, Hex is going to swoop in and take me from this place."

For a moment, Lucas did nothing. Said nothing. Then all at once, his shoulders began to shake, and laughter spilled freely. "You think... You think this is that time? That everything is going to happen the same way? Oh Averie..."

Averie stiffened as Lucas continued to dissolve into his laughter. Bending at the waist, he clutched his knees and shook his head. "Are you done?" Averie asked through clenched teeth.

Lucas slowly straightened and wiped an errant tear from his eye. "Oh, dear Avi. This may seem similar to that time, but Sera has no control over your dreams. In fact, she isn't even here. I'm not even here."

She shook her head, trying to dispel the queasiness that threatened to overwhelm her. "That's not possible."

Humor still colored his cheeks as he lifted a brow. "Isn't it?"

CHAPTER ELEVEN

"No, because I would never bring myself back here. I would never..." Averie frowned.

Lucas leaned forward and trapped her in his glowing, crystalline gaze. "Never what?"

"It doesn't make sense."

Lucas pursed his lips, clasped his hands behind his back, and rocked back on his heels. "What doesn't make sense, Averie?"

Averie's eyes fell from his face and fixated on the ground. Her mind was in a frenzy, considering countless bewildering scenarios.

"What doesn't make sense, Averie?" he asked. "What isn't quite right?"

Averie shook her head and pinched her eyes closed.

"Say it," he whispered, and though he hadn't moved, the taunting words brushed against her ear.

Tears burned behind closed lids. "This isn't real."

"Open your eyes and say it! What is missing?!"

Averie's eyes popped open at the grave demand. Pain seared through her mind as she struggled through the blurred memories until she could barely see through the tears in her eyes. Ice-cold hands gripped her face and forced her to look up.

A blood-curdling scream tore from her throat as she stared into the molted flesh where eyes should have been.

"I've got you," the voice promised.

Her body and mind raged against the touch as memories of falling asleep alone blared like a warning in her mind, only to be quickly washed away by the soothing warmth encompassing her fragile form. Her struggle slowly ceased as the conflicting chill of a hand covered her eyes. With one last sigh, Averie surrendered herself to the reprieve of blissfully dreamless darkness.

Chapter Twelve

FOREST — SERA

She failed. *Again*. Only this time, she couldn't claim ignorance. If she had listened to Lucas, if she had believed in what her instincts had told her and ignored those pretty whispers… No, it was too late for that. Now she had to face the truth—the Averie she was facing now was not the same as the one she grew up with or the one she had faced in the past. This Averie was someone different, someone new.

A howl in the distance threw her back in time.

Averie looked down from the crumbling keep with her wolfen beasts at her sides. Her golden eyes shone so brilliantly that they had an aura of their own. With a knowing smirk on her perfect face, she asked, "Ready to give up?"

Sera glared, her hand pressed against the wound at her side as blood pooled into her palm and dripped from between her clenched fingers. She hadn't expected Averie to turn her blast from the Shadowed to her at the last moment, and because she had once again underestimated her, she was again injured.

"No? Then, since you're nearly out of power from blocking yourself against me, how about I give you a head start?"

Sera's glare darkened as she called out, "It doesn't have to be this way."

Averie chuckled. The noise was unnatural and unlike the girl she had grown up with. "You have thirty seconds before you get very well acquainted with my friends, Seiko and Echo." Snarls and guttural barks punctuated the promise. "One…"

CHAPTER TWELVE

Three hours. That's how long it had taken Sera to escape Averie's unrelenting assault and those pesky wolves that had been sicced on her. Sera shuttered as the ghost of the heat of their breath and the hatred in their growls brushed along her skin and taunted her ears. They had been on her heels, nearly overcoming her too many times for her comfort. The memory was sure to haunt her dreams in the nights to come.

Pain radiated down the side of her body, faltering her steps and reminding her of the near empty well of power inside her. Another few feet and she was free of the forest and bathed in the soft glow of the castle. The magnificent building emanated the glow from the moons that hovered mockingly complete above her.

Movement fluttered in her periphery a moment before the question she knew was coming was asked. *What happened?* demanded the deep voice.

Sera bit back the lashing that burned her tongue and continued across the pristine courtyard. "She caught me off guard. It won't happen again."

Darkness fell into step beside her. His silence made her skin crawl.

"It was a mistake. I underestimated her and those *friends* of hers."

Hmm.

Sera stopped at the foot of the grand staircase that led into the taken castle and whirled on her heel to face the dark apparition. "Is there something on your mind?"

You are acting irrationally. Rash. Careless. We cannot afford to lose this one, Seraphina. We have come too far to fall now.

Sera's hands clenched into shaking fists at her sides. "What makes you think I'm going to lose?"

Darkness looked over the girl that had been his cohort for the last several generations. While her appearance was disheveled, with hair caked to the sides of her porcelain face in a mixture of blood, sweat, and ichor, her eyes burned with fierce determination. Though she favored her right side, giving way to the injuries she had accumulated, and her clothing was torn and ratty, she faced him without fear. Long gone was the broken and scared little girl he had found. Now she stood tall with confidence and had a furious air glittering around her.

It is not a fear of losing this battle that has my ire. It is the fear of you losing sight of our goal. Of losing you.

Sera blinked several times, the anger melting from her crystalline eyes. "You worry about losing me?"

Ah, so the insecurities are still there. He mused. *Of course. If our goal is to be met, I need you to keep a clear head and not react out of emotion over logic. We are running out of time. Things are progressing faster than we expected.*

Sera cleared her throat and tipped her head. "I understand."

Good. Go get cleaned up and rest. We will meet again soon.

"Where are you going?"

Something has shifted here. I am going to find out what.

Sera watched her ally fade into nothingness before she dragged her tired body up the stairs, through the castle, and into the old, familiar room. The door shut silently behind her, closing her away from the world and those that sought her out.

ACCEPTANCE

Sera closed her eyes and rested her head against the wooden door. Pain continued to radiate down the side of her body and grew in intensity with each passing moment. The feeling was a constant reminder of how close Averie had come to taking everything from her.

Anger clenched her fist and forced her from the door. Unsteady steps carried her into the enormous marble bathroom. In many ways, it was like the bathrooms she had grown accustomed to in the Unknown Realm. A toilet sat in its own small, closet-like space in the far-right corner while a stone, glass-encased shower consumed the remaining back lefthand space. Two sinks were nestled into a counter to her left, each topped with its own mirror, and an enormous claw-foot tub lay just ahead, beckoning her forward. In others, it was vastly different. There were no faucets to be seen. Not at the sinks, in the shower, or in the tub. Instead, golden vines, elegantly woven through the marble and stone, waiting for someone to pass and call forth the enchanted flowers.

Sera released a pent-up breath and lifted a trembling hand to peel the battle-soiled fabric from her body. A hiss crossed her lips as pain heated her skin at the simple movement. Thin, vine-like shadows separated from the walls at the sound of her distress and came to her aid. With precision and delicacy, they slipped between the torn fabric and her wounded body and forced the separation. Sera grit her teeth against the pain of wounds being reopened as piece after piece fell to the ground with a soft clatter.

A stray shadow slithered to the tub and ignited the enchantment that brought the water flower forth. Water poured from the rainbow-blue flower, filling the space with steam and the scent of fresh rain.

"Thank you," Sera whispered to the shadows and sank into the tub. She allowed herself a few precious moments of heated bliss before she wrapped her hands around the rim of the tub and nodded to the hovering shadows.

Instantly, they sank into her flesh, their darkness weaving between her torn flesh and stitching it back together. Screams lodged in her throat as agony parted her lips and ripped her voice away.

Sera stared over the replicated devastation that was their battle. Her features were carefully schooled into a mask, void of the emotion that boiled inside, as her eyes swept across the frozen reenactment once more. Something had changed in Averie. Something unexpected and terrifying in its magnitude. During their first battle two weeks ago, her army of Shadowed and tainted creatures had held the Rebellion at bay and verged on overtaking them completely. Then she appeared.

At first Sera had thought it a fluke, and after healing, Lucas had set out to put the next phase of her plan into action. Sera straightened her shoulders and waved a hand over the model. The pieces moved back to their original places before beginning

CHAPTER TWELVE

once more. A week had passed since their confrontation. She had granted herself a day of rest to recover from her wounds before forcing herself into action. Six days ago, Sera had entered this room, created the model, and began watching it over and over, like an addiction she couldn't kick.

It wasn't supposed to be this way. Sera grit her teeth at the emergence of the golden light at the top of the ruined castle. Her eyes narrowed slightly as it sent a jarring blast through her first line. The force of it shook the ground of the model. Sera leaned in, her eyes tracking the seared steps of the miniature Averie. Shadowed were eradicated by a single glance, their darkness washed away by the radiating light of her body. A small arm lifted, shaking the model and wiping out the entire force to the left. The other arm lifted, doing the same to the right.

Sera's jaw clenched as her attention dragged to the smaller version of herself, frozen in shock, standing atop the hill. *Move,* she growled in her mind, knowing what would happen next.

Averie advanced, her loyal group flanking her sides as she forced her way through the greater numbers without a care. A gloating smile curved her lips as her arms rose into the air. In an instant, she dropped to one knee, her arms slapping the ichor against the ground. A wave of earth rose from the tips of her fingers and washed over the land, sending hundreds of Shadowed flailing into the air. Averie jerked her arms back.

"Watching it again?" Lucas chuckled.

Sera tore her attention from the model, and with a wave of her hand, it froze in place. Her eyes clashed with Lucas's casual stance against the wall. "Something changed in her."

Lucas pursed his lips and shoved from the wall. His thoughts locked in his mind as he swaggered forward. "Did you expect differently? You took Thane from her."

Sera's cheek jumped. "I did nothing of the sort."

Lucas lifted a brow, the scar running down his face crinkling his eye. "No? It wasn't you that had Emma infiltrate their ranks and ultimately take his life?"

Sera lifted her chin and followed his eyeline to the miniature Averie. "She was growing unstable. Making rash decisions and—"

"Decimating your outposts."

"*And* playing into my hand."

"Now she has beaten you twice in as many weeks." Lucas ripped his attention off the model and settled his milky gaze on hers. "Watching this over and over isn't going to change the outcome. What's our plan?"

"The same as it always was."

"Which is?" he prompted.

Sera smiled. The curve of her lips was saccharine and unnerving. "To build an empire of Realms."

Lucas nodded; his eyes locked on hers as he dragged his fingers around the table until he stood towering above her. "And Plan B?"

"You don't need a Plan B when Plan A is successful."

ACCEPTANCE

"And is it?"

"The war has only just begun, and I have no plan of losing."

Lucas cocked his head. "The loser never does."

Sera's eyes flickered with hostility. Onyx washed over the crystal blue and spread like webs to the veins around her eyes. "Are you saying I'm going to lose?"

Lucas lifted a hand to the fallen strands against her cheek and tucked them behind her ear. "I'm saying you might need to reevaluate your plan given the new … Averie we are faced with."

"I'll let this Realm burn before I turn it over to her and those misguided miscreants she calls a Rebellion. They have no idea what's coming."

Lucas trailed his fingers across her jaw and traced her bottom lip with his thumb. "They took you once, Sera. There is nothing wrong with admitting they outmatched you. Even if it is only for a short time. Every game comes with the rise and fall of victory."

Sera bit down on his thumb and smiled when he jerked it away. "I let them take me. My plan will work. All the pieces are in place. One setback changes nothing." Lucas watched Sera turn and make her way to the other side of the table. Her palm hovered above the miniature version of Averie's golden form. "I want you to find him and tell him what's happened."

"And then?"

"And then we prepare for what's next." Sera slammed her hand down, extinguishing the light completely.

CHAPTER THIRTEEN

Membrane – Thane

Days, or perhaps weeks, had passed since Dar had begun to teach him about using the tears to his advantage. With no proper way to determine time in this hellscape Thane had found himself within, he instead began to use his brief glimpses into the real world as a way to track it. Since he had first seen Averie in the war room, Radnar's beard had remained more black than gray. Now, whether because of the insanity of war or age, his beard had grown more gray than black.

Slowly, and with much practice, Thane had learned how to extend his time in the Real Realm, as he called it. He had caught glimpses of Callen and Radnar raging at each other over what to do next. Of Hex and Snip whispering over some game they seemed fond of. And of Averie… Well, he wasn't quite sure what to call what she had been doing. Nothing about what he witnessed seemed to make sense.

But the one that had surprised him most had been the meeting between Callen and Marcus on the moonlit night. Thane stroked his beard absentmindedly as he pondered each interaction.

Each day he spent in the Membrane was getting stranger than the last. *I'm running out of time. I need to find a way back.* Thane's chest rumbled in frustration when Dar's words penetrated his consciousness. "Excuse me?" Thane asked, leaning forward and cupping his hand around his ear. "I thought I heard you say you wanted to follow me. But that can't be right, because what reason would you have to see Averie?"

Dar lifted a brow. "Who said I wanted to see Averie?"

Thane frowned. "Who else could you possibly want to see? And why now? You haven't come along any other time. What's so special about now?"

ACCEPTANCE

Dar tilted his head to the side with an amused smile. "Who said I haven't? Do you think you are the only one that has a desire to see the real world? I have been here a lot longer than you. Do you think I enjoy being trapped in an endless day?"

Thane ran a hand through his hair and considered Dar's words. "You know," he started, and fixed his eyes firmly on Dar's, "you never said what you did to get locked up in here."

"No, I didn't."

"And what of these others that you have claimed are trapped here with you?"

"What about them?"

"Why haven't I seen them?"

Dar's eyes grew impossibly darker. "You should count yourself lucky, Thane. Not all the people here are as kind as I am."

"Mmm. So, you say."

"Are we going to go, or are you going to continue to stand there glaring at me?"

Thane arched a brow. "Who said I can't do both?"

Dar rolled his eyes. "Come. This tear is growing increasingly unstable. If we are not careful, it will disappear before we get the chance to slip through."

That sent Thane into motion. It wouldn't be the first time that they had experienced a tear disappearing from them—a fun fact that Dar had conveniently forgotten to mention. The first had been a few days after the first time he had crossed. He and Dar had met at the swings, and just as Dar lifted his finger to tap against the strange Jell-O-like air, the ground began to shake beneath their feet, and Dar had leapt on him, shoving him to the hard ground as a mini explosion had ruptured horizontally through the air.

"What the hell was that?" Thane demanded as he shoved Dar from atop him.

Dar rose to his feet and dusted nonexistent residue from his clothes and shrugged. "That is what happens when a tear ruptures."

"They rupture?! Crixus!" Thane cursed and ran his hands through his hair. "When in Fornax were you going to tell me that? What would have happened if I were inside?"

Dar's lips pursed in thought before he shrugged. "I am not sure. I assume you would be fine. Best not to test it, I would say."

"Oh, no, of course. And just how do you know when they are going to … you know, weirdly explode?"

Another shrug. "I suppose you don't. I suppose we should head to the next spot."

"You… You don't know. Oh, this is just grrreeeaaat," Thane said with an exaggerated eye roll as he followed Dar.

Dar whirled back with fury igniting in his black eyes. "Did you think there would not be consequences to what you are doing? That there was no risk involved in crossing the planes of Life and Death?" Dar shook his head. "It's time to grow up, Thane. I thought your death would have already taught you that."

"Are you ready?" Dar asked.

Thane's jaw jumped at the idea of bringing Dar along but nodded. "Let's do this."

CHAPTER THIRTEEN

"Remember, keep her and only her in your mind. If you—"

"Yeah, yeah, I know. I've done this a time or two, remember?" Thane snapped and stepped up to the door of the small bakery. Another strange phenomenon Thane had noticed was that, when one tear ruptured, another would open somewhere he and Averie had spent a lot of time at. Thane kept that fun fact tightly to his chest. The last thing he needed was for Dar to turn his attention to Averie.

"After you," Dar urged when Thane hesitated at the entrance.

Thane turned and made sure Dar caught his eye roll before facing forward and letting his eyes close. *Averie,* he chanted in his mind and entered the tear. The familiar pop rippled throughout his body. *Averie.*

Wind tousled his hair and pulled his eyes open. Thane grinned at himself at another successful transition, then frowned. "Where the hell…" His words died on his tongue as he stepped forward, hindered only slightly by the barrier that separated him from everyone else, and took in the full sight before him.

Sera and Lucas were prominent on the ground below with a seemingly endless army of Shadowed and Tainted at their backs. "Sera," he growled, the burn of betrayal more vibrant now than in the few moments they had shared before his death.

"Know her?" Dar asked.

Thane jumped at the question and proximity. "I wasn't sure you would make it."

Dar lifted a brow and clasped his hands behind his back before running his eyes over the two factions. "It appears we have come at an interesting time. Do you have any idea what is going on?"

Thane shook his head and looked around. "I don't think I've ever been to this place before. They aren't normally here. Something must have happened—"

"Have you come all the way here to surrender?" Averie called out, severing Thane's train of thought.

Sera's laughter rang out in the still morning. "Not a chance, Avi. But I'll take yours and save you what remains of your '*Rebellion*,'" Sera taunted back.

The air shifted unsteadily. Radnar's and Callen's curses screamed in his mind, even though the words couldn't have been higher than a whisper.

"Averie, breathe," Callen warned.

Thane frowned and tried to step to her side when the barrier forced him back. "Averie? Averie, what's going on?" The air popped and sizzled around them—a sure sign of something terrible to come.

"Last chance," Averie warned. Her voice was mechanical and *wrong.*

"Fox," Thane pleaded, his desperation growing as the surrounding group shifted uncomfortably. His eyes shifted from his sister's stiff pose to Callen and Radnar, who appeared to be losing the very air they were trying to breathe while advancing alongside Averie.

"Averie." Radnar gasped.

"What the hell is going on?!" Thane bellowed, his hands clutching at the hair on his head.

"Fascinating," Dar whispered, the awe clear in his voice.

ACCEPTANCE

Ignoring Dar's comment, Thane struggled to find a way around the group so he could face Averie's unsettling gaze. "Come on, Fox. Whatever you are about to do, *don't*. Damnit, Callen, do something! STOP HER!" he pleaded. "HEAR ME!!!!"

"I will get the men into position."

"I'll take care of it." Averie smiled. The look that was once enduring and contagious was now unsettling and haunting. Thane watched in horror as she lifted her arm, and with a casual flick of her wrist and a determined glance, a decimating light shot forth and eliminated an entire gathering.

"Shit…" Thane cursed. His eyes were wide and stomach was clenched at the sheer devastation. His months in the Realm had taught him about war, but this… This was carnage. "Fox, stop!"

A gloating smile revealed the gleam of her teeth. In an instant, she dropped to one knee, her arms slapping the ichor against the ground. A wave of earth rose from the tips of her fingers and washed over the land, sending hundreds of Shadowed flailing into the air.

The familiar tug of the Membrane pulled at his body. Thane shook his head, fighting harder than ever before to remain imbedded in the scene playing out. His eyes shot toward Dar. "Stop her!" he pleaded. His words were lost as his entire body was ripped free of the Real Realm and thrust back into the Membrane.

The familiar roll of his stomach confirmed his worst fear. He was back in the hell between Life and Death, unable to control the pull that left him in the desolate, lonely place and the world he had come to call home. He fell to his knees in disbelief. "What… Who… Stars, Averie, what has happened to you?"

Thane stayed on his knees, his eyes lost in the maze within the cement as he collected his thoughts. "Dar." He sighed, then frowned. His head shot up as he searched the surrounding area. "Dar?!" he called. Thane clenched his teeth and rose to his feet. "Where the *hell* are you, Dar? And what are you hiding?" A new resolve stiffened his spine and straightened his shoulders. He wasn't just going to get back to the Real Realm; he was going to save his sister if it was the last thing he did, and everyone who played a hand in turning her into the thing she was now, would pay.

Chapter Fourteen

Averie lay awake long after the moons had passed their apex and neared the horizon. Her weariness was undeniable, yet it was the unsettling thoughts of potential consequences that prevented her from seeking rest. Over the last several weeks, images that played too closely to forgotten memories flashed within her sleeping mind while the melted boy/man haunted her during daylight hours.

Averie turned to her side and groaned into Echo's fur. Seiko lifted his head and peered at her with worry glittering in his green eyes. Echo let out a huff and shifted out from under Averie. "Where are you going?" Averie asked as the great wolf moved toward the door.

Echo turned her large head and pinned Averie with an unreadable stare before pressing her nose against the door and disappearing through the opening. A moment later, the bed shifted once more as Seiko dropped to the floor. Averie's brow furrowed as the silver beast copied his counterpart's look and disappearance.

"Screw it," she whispered and rose from the bed, her steps silent as she pulled the door wide and followed the disappearing beasts. "Where are you going?" she whispered. The whispered volume was natural in the depths of the night. "Seiko! Echo!" she beckoned, only to be ignored.

Averie quickened her steps, still trailing after the pair as they led her down one darkened corridor after another until, finally, they stopped at a cracked door. Light spilled from the small opening, like a beacon to an adrift ship after a storm, and like a moth to the flame, Averie was lost in its allure.

"You can't!"

Averie jerked back at the anger in Radnar's voice.

"Do not tell me what I can and cannot do."

Averie frowned at the returned venom. *What are Radnar and Callen arguing about so late?*

ACCEPTANCE

"She is not an animal, Callen. This is *wrong*."

"She is. But unlike her, I have shown mercy and given her enough to survive."

"You locked her *underground*. She is a prisoner, but we are better than them."

Prisoner? Who are they talking about? Averie wondered, her intrigue at Radnar and Callen's argument growing as her curiosity peaked. Another step and she was close enough to peer through the small gap in the door. Callen and Radnar stood in the center of what Averie could only decide, from her limited sight, was an office. A large desk sat at a strange angle with papers, books, and other indecipherable items strewn across its surface, as if the entire piece had been shoved to the side in a fit of rage.

"She may be a prisoner, but she is human, and what you are doing is inhumane! Emma—"

"Do not *dare* speak that *thing's* name here!"

Averie jerked back at the vehemence and loathing in Callen's tone. *Emma?* The name registered somewhere deep within her mind moments before images of the petite, smiling, blonde-haired woman with bright green eyes flashed through her mind and were followed by a twist of her stomach, the pounding of her heart, and the replaying of a sickening scene in her mind.

A man trembled in her hold, his blade inching closer and closer to her thundering heart. Panic hadn't had its chance to take hold before the sear of pain exploded in her chest ... just shy of its target.

Her jaw dropped in a mixture of disbelief and relief. "How did you miss?" she asked. "You are literally... You know what? Never mind." Her hands moved impossibly fast and filled the air with a sickening snap. A chill settled into the marrow of her bones as she attempted to pull from the well of power inside and found it lacking.

She pulled the blade from its place within her body and let it fall to the ground with a clatter. "Stars..."

Her head snapped up and eyes collided with worried crystalline. A laugh tumbled free from her lips as exhaustion pulled on her shoulders. The sound was a stark contrast to the carnage surrounding her. She swept her hands down the front of her ruined gown as the last of the near mortal wound zipped closed, leaving a thin, golden line behind. "Well, that was gross. This dress is beyond repair." She smiled, hoping the man would relax just a fraction, when time came to a stuttering halt.

Unable to move, she felt a wave of panic wash over her as her legs remained frozen in place. The sound of her mind cracking screamed in her ears as she stood frozen, unable to intervene, as an attacker approached from behind and mercilessly thrust a serrated blade through his back. The steel sliced through flesh and bone effortlessly, like a hot knife through butter.

A single syllable fell from his bloodstained lips and severed something vital inside her. "Fox?"

CHAPTER FOURTEEN

A petite blonde rose to the tips of her toes and peered at her from behind as she smiled against his neck. "Gotcha."

Averie snapped back to the present. One hand flew to her mouth to quell the burn of bile, while the other clutched her stomach as she sank to the ground. *What the hell was that?* Her heart slammed painfully against her chest as her mind replayed the scene again and again, fighting to clear the man's face. She wasn't sure why, but Averie knew she was missing something colossally important from the scene.

She forced herself to think of the night that Sera had cast them once more from the castle. *The Silver Rose Ball... What happened? The shadows. They came from everywhere. Hex and Snip... Falcon... Rose dying... Then ... who was it? Who came for me? Who led me to the Chamber of Peace?*

Averie's tormented and reeling thoughts were interrupted by heated, gritted words that seemed to tear through the air. "No one will enter. No one will visit, and *no one* will release her. Do you hear me? She is *mine*," Callen sneered. Her senses heightened as she braced herself for the approaching steps.

"Emma," she whispered to Seiko and Echo. "Bring me to Emma."

Seiko and Echo exchanged a knowing glance, their heads dipping in unison before they turned and disappeared into the enveloping darkness. Averie sprinted after the pair and disappeared around the corner as light filled the corridor in her periphery. Her heart thundered like anxious birds rattling a cage in her heart.

Weeks of confusion replayed in her mind. Broken conversations that ended upon her arrival. Strange dreams too real not to be memories. The blurred man haunting her night and day. *When did it start?* An angry whimper caught in her throat. How was she ever going to pinpoint the moment when it all changed if things were clearly being kept from her? How was she going to find out what it was? *Emma. Emma will know.*

Averie lost track of how many turns, hallways, and doors Seiko and Echo had led her through. All she knew was they were heading deeper into the mountain. Deeper and lower. Gone was the magically heated air, and in its place was a chill so frigid it sunk its way into her bones, freckled her exposed flesh, and left clouds of breath with every exhale.

"How much farther?" she panted.

Her answer was another turn and an abrupt stop at the end of a short hall. Averie frowned. "You brought me to a dead end?"

Seiko harrumphed and pressed his nose to the stone.

At first nothing happened. Then the sound of stone scraping and a soft hiss as air escaped and echoed in the empty hall. Averie frowned. *Why is there a hidden door?* Over the weeks and months that she and the rest of the Rebellion had lived within Callen's dark mountain, there hadn't been a single place that he had said they couldn't travel to. While most contained themselves to the makeshift gathering hall,

ACCEPTANCE

others had made themselves at home in the far reaches that Callen had carved out into rooms, bathrooms, and living quarters.

I suppose you wouldn't have to tell someone not to go in somewhere they didn't know existed... Averie's thoughts continued to whirl with prospects of hidden rooms and what they might contain as she slid her fingertips into the opening, heaved the door open, and slipped inside. Darkness lay before her. The only light was the small stream from the hall behind her. It wasn't until she was several steps inside that she noticed Seiko and Echo hadn't entered the darkness behind her.

"Not coming?" she asked.

The pair simply stared, content in their silence.

Averie shrugged and turned to the darkness ahead. Inhaling deeply, she wrinkled her nose at the damp smell. After another few steps, a prickle at the back of her neck told her to stop.

"Hello?" she called out. The cavern snatched her words and tossed them throughout the room. As her question faded from the air, the rustle of *something* sounded. Averie straightened, her eyes pulsing and body poised for attack.

Gradually, the shadows began to shift, fading into shades of gray, as a solitary figure stumbled and jerked forward. Averie waited with bated breath as she peered into the darkness, squinting to get a better look at the fuzzy figure as it stepped closer. Desperate for clarity, she summoned a small light orb and cast it into the space between them, revealing the endless pit that separated them.

As the light flooded in, vibrant green eyes blinked and then narrowed, filled with a fiery rage that pierced through Averie deeper with each encroaching step. A petite body, adorned in the grimy and tattered remains of a red dress, stepped into the light. Her long blonde hair was matted and clung to the sides of her face.

A crazed chuckle left the woman's smirking lips and echoed in the eerie cavern. "I was wondering when you were going to show. What took you so long, Averie?"

Chapter Fifteen

Emma's Prison – Emma and Averie

"Emma." Averie breathed. Scenes burned across her mind at a sickening speed. *Wide, vibrant spring green eyes stared into her own from tear-streaked, rosy cheeks.*

"I was going to tell you," promised the melted man as he stood proudly beside the sniffling woman.

Averie smiled. "T-ne, it's fine. I'm happy for you."

Averie flinched as she was thrust into another memory.

Lights, laughter, and banter rang against her eyes and ears as her own rang out into the mix. "How about we find everyone and take a vote?" she asked with her eyes bouncing from Callen's sudden eager expression to the melted man's somber one. "But that means—"

"Cake," Callen beamed.

"Don't worry, she promised to make something just for you," chimed a petite, honey-haired, green-eyed woman.

"Fox, this is Emma. Emma, this is Averie."

Averie's stomach rolled as her mind shot her into another memory.

She, Snip, Callen, Emma, and the melted man sat spread across the floor in her castle bedroom with a mountain of snacks at its center. "Where is Silas? Did he leave because you kissed Snip? Who's the better kisser?"

ACCEPTANCE

Averie's jaw dropped as words failed to come together. "Oh, um…"

Snip squeezed her knee and winked. "No need, love. Everyone already knows it's me."

Laughter consumed Emma's small body as the room fell silent at her peppered questions, until she collapsed against the large, leaning body of the melted man. He groaned. "You really shouldn't ask things like that around me."

Averie rolled her eyes, her own smile tugging her cheeks. "Says the guy who is making out with his girlfriend on his sister's couch."

Emma quirked a brow. "Were you expecting someone else?"

The simple question jerked Averie back into the here and now, with more questions buzzing in her mind than ever before. *The melted man is my … brother?* Clearing her throat, she asked, "Why are you here?"

Laughter burst from Emma's lips. The sound twisted and grated against the ear. Averie clenched her teeth and waited for the woman to stop. Slowly, she did. Confusion mingled with the deranged glint in her eyes. "You don't remember?"

"Remember what?"

Emma's eyes flashed excitedly before narrowing. Her tongue swept her dried and cracked lips as she searched the room with blatant suspicion. "Is this a trick?"

Averie tilted her head to the side. "Why would I trick you?"

"I already told Callen everything I know. I have nothing to tell you."

"Mmm. Well, I'm not Callen. So why don't you start at the beginning?"

Emma dipped her head in a slow nod as she settled herself onto a nearby boulder while keeping her eyes firmly on the unpredictable woman in front of her. "It all started on the day the Rebellion went to save a village…"

"Awaken."

The demand came on a chilled breeze that brokered no argument. Not that this being would argue if it could; it wasn't designed that way. The being's eyes popped open, and searing light burned into the newly formed retinas. And yet, it didn't blink. Not right away. Instead, it lost itself in the pain, welcomed it even. Anything, even this searing feeling, was better than being trapped in the nothingness where you were nothing.

When it could no longer take the pain, a soft sigh mingled with a twisted chuckle. "Blink. It'll help. I need you in full form for what I have planned, darling. Now, rise."

Instantly, the female body it was trapped in jerked upright and peeled her eyes open once more to meet the creator. A small body stood next to a much larger one. While both had light-colored hair, one was longer and the other shorter. One reeked of power, while the other had three pinched, pink scars running down the length of its face.

"Well," asked the smaller one. "What do you think?"

CHAPTER FIFTEEN

The one with shorter pale hair, white eyes, and the terrifying claw marks running down its face smirked. "I don't know. Do you think she will work? She seems a little empty ... up here."

The other rolled her eyes and smacked a hand to the taller one's chest. "Give me a moment." *The smaller being stepped forward, lifted a hand, and placed it against the newly formed flesh. Images, scenes, words, life poured into the shell that was now more than just nothing. It was something.*

Sera stepped back with a satisfied glint. "There, much better."

"Do you really have to name it?" *Lucas sighed.*

Sera rolled her eyes once more. "Of course I do. She won't work out otherwise, now will she?"

Lucas shrugged. "Amnesia is pretty big where I come from and totally realistic for what you have planned next."

Sera shook her head. "Callen would never believe it. Besides, he would see through something like that immediately."

"Fine. What are you going to call it?"

"How about ... Emma."

Another shrug. "Perfect. Can we go now?"

"You know Averie and I used to love **Beauty and the Beast** when we were kids."

Lucas frowned. "What does that have to do with Emma?"

Sera pursed her lips and focused back on the newly formed creature. "Are you ready?"

"What would you have me do?" *Emma asked.*

Sera smiled. "Play the damsel, fall in love, and then, when the time is right, tell me all about it."

Hours passed before Emma found herself being led from one room to the next, each growing more dimly lit than the last, before she stepped out into the world. Screams assaulted her ears, and putrid smells tainted the fresh, warm breeze. Emma scrunched her nose at the unpleasantness.

A chuckle sounded behind her, foretelling Lucas's approach. "The smell got you, huh? Yeah, it's not great. But something about the echoes of battle makes you feel alive, doesn't it?"

Emma sent him a blank look. "What happened to you?"

Lucas lifted a brow. "Excuse me? Are you actually asking about these?" *he asked, his long fingers tracing the marks on his cheek.*

Emma shook her head. "No. I mean, what happened to you in here? And where is the piece they took to make you what you are now?" *she wondered, her small fingers tapping the side of her head.*

Lucas narrowed his eyes and drew the deadly blade from his side. "Stay behind me. We don't have much time before the Rebellion shows up."

Emma watched Lucas tear through the crowd with a fluidity that was unnatural for a man. There was a glint in his eyes when he would turn, and the sun would die within his eyes, as if eaten by the empty space inside.

ACCEPTANCE

"It's time." The order was carried on a breeze that beckoned for Emma's attention. It wasn't until she turned that she felt fear for the first time. The nightmare they called The Shadow stood at the town's edge, its body dripping in slinking shadows that sucked the warmth from the air. "Follow Lucas."

Emma turned and found the man in question lingering beside a crumbling building. Hesitation wasn't a word she understood or an action that she participated in. The moment her eyes locked onto Lucas's position, her feet were moving and didn't stop until she was at his side.

Lucas watched her with a bored stare. "Are you ready?"

Emma nodded. Lucas leaned down and heaved a fallen chunk up from the side of the building and motioned forward. Emma frowned.

"Well, get down there. You can't very well be the only survivor and somehow be out wandering around a battleground now, can you?"

Without another word, Emma climbed between the wall, and Lucas let it fall back into place, shrouding her in darkness and the smell of earth. The next thing she saw was a pair of bright, crystalline eyes staring back at her.

"And the rest is history." Emma grinned.

Emma's last words reverberated through the cavern, leaving an eerie echo that matched the weight of the irreversible consequences of her fateful journey. Averie's breath stalled in her chest, held captive by a mixture of hurt, betrayal, and loathing for those she held close.

"Why?" Averie finally asked.

Emma frowned. "Why what?"

"Why … Thane?"

"Isn't it obvious? Because he was easy. His mother is dead, Karen just died, and you weren't here. Not to mention you didn't need him anymore, being the savior and all. He just wanted to mean something to someone again. He didn't matter."

"He meant something to me. He means something to Callen and Radnar. He matters."

"And what is the cost of letting someone matter, knowing in an instant they will be gone? To be driven to madness, to be pushed to the brink of insanity so harshly that those around you have no other choice but to take them away just so you can breathe once more." Emma shook her head. "Never have I been more safe in my indifference than witnessing the horrors people will do for those that have mattered and been lost. The rupture of a soul that has lost its heart becomes a greater monster than I, one who was born without one."

Reality washed over in a frigid chill. Weeks and months of sneaking out into the depths of night and hunting down the Shadowed played through with cruel intensity. Everything was so clear, all except for the reason for it all. What was the drive behind each blow and every splatter of ichor against her skin? *Was it him? Was it all because of him?*

CHAPTER FIFTEEN

"Yes."

Averie jerked in place, her eyes flying to Emma's. "What?"

"You're wondering if your madness was because of someone you cannot remember, and the answer is yes." Emma rose from the rock, her eyes shimmering beneath the light of the magic orb, blazing with realization. "If you are wondering if they took him from you, the answer is yes."

"How do you know?"

Emma smiled and sauntered to the cliff's edge. "Because if they hadn't, I'd be dead right now."

Words eluding her, Averie tipped her head in a curt nod and turned on her heel.

"I know it doesn't help, but if it were possible, I would have loved him."

"You're right; it doesn't."

"Wait!" Emma called.

Averie stopped, her foot poised for the next step.

"What are you going to do?"

Averie smiled to herself, lifted a hand, and snapped her fingers, extinguishing the light and plunging Emma into darkness once more. "Nothing."

Chapter Sixteen

Averie was spiraling. Her late-night conversation with Emma had done nothing to soothe her when she had returned to bed. If anything, it had kept her awake until the sun had nearly risen completely, and she had finally caved and forced herself from bed. Echoes of Emma's story and the memories that had pushed free at first sight had been slowly driving her mad. The lack of sleep was definitely not helping.

"We have her on the defensive! We should keep pushing," Radnar said, rising from his seat.

Callen pinched the bridge of his nose. "We have spoken about this before. We cannot attack when we do not know what she has planned."

"She has nothing planned! That last battle was proof of that. We had her running within minutes."

"*Averie* had her running. We just stood there and looked pretty," Snip interjected.

"She wiped out half of Sera's forces. We need to strike before she can make more."

Averie rolled her eyes and massaged her temples. Three days had passed since their latest altercation with Sera and, since that moment atop the ruins, they had done nothing but argue about what their next step should be. It was giving her a migraine. Or was Emma's story and the strange string of dreams doing that? Maybe the missing time?

"Every minute we give her is another minute she will use to undermine the progress we have made."

Averie nodded. Radnar wasn't wrong. *Or is he? What else are they hiding?* Averie bit back a groan at the endless circle she found herself trapped in.

Since she had awakened from her unexpected slumber and cast Sera, Lucas, and their haunting army from the mountain, they had regained nearly all the land between the mountain and the castle. But with every step forward they had taken, her

CHAPTER SIXTEEN

mind slipped another step back. She was losing control, losing moments. An uncomfortable feeling sank into her stomach as she thought about their latest confrontation.

 Callen stepped to her side and looked down to the massive Shadowed army encroaching on the ruins. "They are coming."

 "I'm not worried."

 "I will get the men into position."

 Her body moved of its own accord, spewing words she hadn't thought to say. "I'll take care of it." One moment she was standing next to Callen, and the next, she was at the edge of the ruined tower, her body vibrating with power. A single glance at the Shadowed gathered at the base of the tower and they disintegrated beneath her light. Her arm lifted and palm rose in a stopping motion. Power shot forth, devastating the entire gathering to the left.

 Averie jolted in place as the memory sent an icy chill down her spine. A change had started within her—something that both invigorated her and filled her with fear. Emma's words continued to plague her late into the night. Along with the ire she felt building each time she saw her "friends." *I need answers.*

 Her eyes clashed with Marcus's black ones. He lifted a brow and straightened from his casual stance against the wall. His mouth parted with an intent that was quickly subdued with a brief shake of Averie's head. Marcus's brow pinched questioningly, but he remained silent.

 "If we act without a solid plan, lives will be lost. How will that soothe your pride?" Callen retorted.

 Radnar's glare darkened. "We will lose more if we let Sera and the Shadowed regain their strength."

 Another good point, Averie thought.

 Hex sighed. "What do you propose we do?"

 Radnar settled back into his seat and took a deep breath, his eyes falling on Averie.

 Here we go.

 "We prepare the men and have Averie lead us in to take her and the Shadowed down once and for all."

 Hex steepled his hands. "You forget yourself, old man. Sera isn't just another warrior. She is The Shadow. The thing that haunted this Realm for decades. The thing that ripped power from countless souls. If it was that easy, we would have done that already."

 "And she is weak right now."

 Marcus snorted his disagreement and met Callen's disapproving glare with a smile.

 "Hex is right," Callen agreed, dragging his attention back to the group seated at the table. "We cannot rush this."

 Averie rested her chin on her hand and looked over the group with angry eyes. A quick shutter of her gaze and she trapped the anger back behind a wall. "Have any of you thought about asking the person in question what she wants to do?"

ACCEPTANCE

All eyes turned to her. Snip smiled as he leaned forward to copy her pose. "Avi, Princess, love, what would *you* like to do?"

"I think we should send her a message."

"What kind of message is better than the ass kicking she got a couple of days ago?"

Averie bristled, uncomfortable at the memory. "I know her. Or a part of her. We were friends for years. Sera is going to keep pushing until you give her what she wants."

Callen shook his head. "But what she wants is the Realm. We cannot give her that."

"What she wants is the *Realms*. Plural. She wants to put them back together."

Snip's eyes flared. Hex jolted in his seat. Radnar stiffened, and Callen scowled. "What makes you think that?" Radnar wondered.

Averie shrugged. "She told me."

Callen shook his head. "It does not matter. That is not possible."

"Actually, it is." Hex sighed, drawing all eyes. "What it's not is workable. If Sera gets what she wants and the Realm comes back together, there will be nothing but destruction and death."

Seiko and Echo wandered into the room, their sharp eyes briefly narrowing in on Marcus before they continued forward, oblivious to the ensuing conversation. Averie shifted in her chair so the two magnificent animals could settle in front of her and smiled. "Hey, you two, where have you been?"

Seiko sat first. His rich green eyes were more human than beast as he stared. Averie's brow pinched when Echo continued forward, her snow-colored eyes cloudy. "What do you have there?"

Echo trotted forward and dropped the small bundle she held in her mouth into Averie's lap before sitting. Averie swallowed through the lump forming in her throat and steeled herself for what the bundle may contain.

Radnar, Callen, Marcus, Hex, and Snip watched Averie peel back the cloth and jumped at an unexpected noise. Laughter bubbled and grew, pouring from her until she was clutching her sides and wiping the tears from her eyes.

"What is it?" Callen asked.

Averie bit down on her bottom lip in an attempt to stifle the giggles and failed. Sliding the bundle over, she watched as the men tried to find out what was so humorous.

Callen frowned and scanned the small box once more. "I do not understand."

"Open it." Averie giggled, wiping the tears from her eyes.

Callen flipped the top off the pink box, and they all collectively peered inside. "It… It is an invitation?"

Averie shook her head. "Not just any invitation. It is an *exact* replica of the invitation from my thirteenth birthday."

The guys dropped their eyes back to the pink, purple, and yellow pinwheel-shaped card that lay inside on a bed of rainbow glitter.

CHAPTER SIXTEEN

You're Invited!
to
Averie and Sera's Realm Truce Negotiations

Time: Tomorrow at 3pm
Where: Ruins

You can bring 1 guest.
No animals, traitors, or twins allowed.
Don't be late.
Kisses, your BFFE, Sera

One by one, they looked up from the tacky invitation and settled on Averie, who sat casually running her hands through the silken fur of Seiko and Echo.

"That's rude. Who wouldn't want us? Or me at least?" Snip pouted.

"Why pinwheels?" Hex asked.

Averie opened her mouth to answer and frowned. The reason lingered somewhere in her mind, there but indecipherable. Like trying to watch a movie through static and when she pressed, the familiar sting of pain laced behind her eyes. "I … I'm not sure."

Guilt flashed through an exchange of looks. Fleeting but not unnoticed. Marcus hid his smirk behind his hand, and Averie narrowed her eyes. These instances were growing with every passing day. "What are you hiding?"

Radnar and Snip looked at Callen, who watched her impassively. "We are hiding nothing."

"Then why do you all look like you are about to tell me you killed my cat? And no, Callen, I don't have a cat. It's an expression."

Callen nodded in appreciation of her explanation. "We are not hiding anything."

Averie's eyes flicked to Marcus, who dropped his head to the side with a small shake. Frustration clenched her jaw. "Alright then."

"'Alright then'?" Snip repeated slowly. "What does that mean?" he wondered, glancing from his brother to Radnar, both of whom shrugged in answer.

"You cannot be thinking of going," Callen pointed out.

Averie rolled her eyes and stood. "Why not? What else do I have to do?"

Radnar sighed. *I am too old to be dealing with these reckless children.* "Averie, lass, you are not thinking clearly."

Averie's eyes narrowed at the older man. "I'm not?"

Radnar scrubbed a hand down his face. "I meant no offense." His voice dropped to barely above a whisper as he spoke more to himself than anyone else. His eyes absently searched the air and shoulders fell as his mind struggled to comprehend his mistake. "I don't understand. This should have worked. You have not been acting or thinking right since we lost—"

ACCEPTANCE

Averie frowned. "See, there it is again! Lost *who*?" Her gaze drifted from one man to the next, her curiosity growing as each one failed to meet her eyes. All except Marcus. He stared back, his eyes glittering with either knowledge or curiosity. She just couldn't figure out which.

"No one that you would know," Callen answered, capturing her attention.

Unnoticed by the pair, Snip and Hex exchanged a knowing glance before slipping to either side of Callen. Seiko and Echo rose to flank Averie. *Tension*, Marcus thought, *the precursor to spilled secrets.*

"Why does it feel like everyone is keeping something from me?"

"Perhaps you are paranoid? I have found that war tends to create such feelings."

The reaction to Callen's words was a physical one felt around the room. Snip sucked in a harsh breath, Hex pinched the bridge of his nose, Marcus failed to cover a laugh, and Radnar grumbled about the stupidity of Eternal Ones beneath his breath.

Averie's eye twitched—a tick that she had been developing over the last several weeks that also upset her further. "I'm not *paranoid*, Callen. I can tell something is different. Every time you stop talking when I come in or whisper in a corner of the mountain. The way you stop halfway through a story. You are keeping something from me."

"Have you thought for a moment that maybe it is for the best?"

Averie scoffed and spoke words she once more didn't understand. "Because keeping secrets has worked out so well in the past?" Stiff silence descended. Averie's lips curved into a humorless smile. "Get some rest, because with or without you, I'm meeting Sera tomorrow."

Radnar, Snip, and Callen watched Averie leave with Seiko and Echo trailing close behind, while Hex watched Callen. His arms crossed over his chest, and an angry light shone in his red eyes. He also wasn't surprised that, the moment the door clicked shut, Callen whirled on him, hauled him up by his shirt, and slammed him into the wall.

"What did you do?" Callen growled.

"Callen," Snip warned. His voice was low and protective.

"I did what you asked me to. I removed Thane."

Callen's grip tightened. "And put him where?"

A slow, dangerous smile cracked Hex's face. "Deep enough to give her time to deal with her pain."

Callen released Hex with an irritated growl and ran his hands through his hair. "Do you realize what you have done?"

Hex straightened his shirt and leaned back against the wall. "Do you? Do you see what is happening before your eyes?"

Callen stiffened. "Enlighten me."

"Averie isn't Averie! The Heart is bleeding through more and more with each passing day. Its influence is like a shield around her. Did you see what she did in the ruins? That shouldn't be possible. No one can unleash that much power and survive."

"She is fine," Callen said through clenched teeth.

CHAPTER SIXTEEN

"If she's fine, then I'm the next King of the Realm."

Marcus waited in the shadows until each person had filed from the room before he dared to step out. When the confrontation between Callen and Averie had begun, he had put his plan into action. While everyone was focused on Callen's callous words, Marcus had cloaked his body in the slivers of shadows and removed his presence. It surprised him to find how well it had worked. They had forgotten his presence entirely and had revealed the very thing he had been questioning since Averie had awoken.

Marcus smiled, shoved his hands into his pockets, and strolled from the room with a cheery tune on his lips.

Chapter Seventeen

"I had not realized you were the spying type. Though I suppose I should have, given your fondness for secrets."

Marcus stopped at the snide remark and turned to find Callen glaring at him from his position at the wall. "Is it spying when you were there from the beginning?"

Callen straightened from the wall. "Did you think I would not notice your poor attempt at shielding yourself in shadows?"

Marcus cocked his head to the side and smiled. "You knew, and yet you did not stop the truth from being shared." He leaned forward with his hands clasped behind his back and whispered like they were two friends sharing a secret. "It's almost as if you wanted me to know what you miscreants have done to dear Averie."

Marcus withdrew slowly as a small group of Rebellion members passed. Each member bounced their eyes between the unlikely pair before disappearing around the corner, leaving them locked in a battle of wills in the form of an icy glare and knowing smirk.

"Have something to say?" Marcus asked.

"You are feeding on her. Using her to further whatever twisted plan you have rolling around in that rotten mind of yours."

Marcus chuckled. "Tell me, Eternal One, just what is it that you think I am doing?"

"You look at her and see her insecurities, and you feast on the chaos of them. I will not let you continue. I will not let you use her."

Marcus smiled and rocked back on his heels. "Is that so? If you are right, and I am not saying that you are, just how do you plan to stop me? Are you going to spill your secrets? Hmm? Tell her what you have done? Do you think she will forgive you if you tell her why?"

Callen stiffened. The movement would have been imperceptible to any other but the hunter that stood before him. "You do not know what you are talking about."

CHAPTER SEVENTEEN

Marcus threw his head back with a boisterous laugh and slapped a hand to his chest. "You wound me, Eternal One, by thinking that I am anything like the others. To believe that I don't see what you and your merry band have done." Marcus leaned forward with a dark gleam in his eye and the smile fading from his face. "That I didn't hear what you did."

"You misheard."

"Mmm. Perhaps I did. However, I have run this Realm since the Fall. Kept it on its toes for decades, and you dare to stand there and think that I haven't noticed the change in its Heart?"

"What are you talking about?"

"She doesn't remember, therefore, she no longer is. You took the one that imprinted her soul. The one that gave her the strength you have so admired. She does not know of the person who gave her morals. The one that taught her to think and to rationalize through the turmoil of emotion. You thought you were saving her, but all you did was dim the light that blazed with determination and ferocity. She doesn't know who she is, so how can she know what she fights for?"

Callen's hands fisted at his sides. With an intense, determined look in his eyes, he leaned forward and stared into the dark, demented ones opposite him. "You think you will win, but none of us will survive your plan. None of us will survive the devastation you have *always* left in your wake. Averie will see through your plan and persevere because she is greatness, while you are mediocrity. While you think of only of your victory, she continues to think of salvation for all."

Marcus chuckled and shook his head. "You are confused, Eternal One. I am not looking for salvation; I am only looking to survive what is destined to come."

Callen's brow furrowed with confusion. "What are you talking about?"

Marcus's eyes widened for the briefest moment before he shook his head in awe. "Oh, Eternal One. How far have you strayed that you do not see what is coming? You paint me as corrupt and evil, but all I have done is to prepare for the end, while you have fought for a world that is already gone." Marcus turned from Callen and whispered his final warning. "The Realm is falling. I was never your true enemy, only the one you saw before you."

Callen paced along the Black Mountain's barrier, wracking his brain for a solution, an answer to his restlessness. All the while, knowing exactly what haunted him. For days, Marcus's last words rang in Callen's mind. Had he truly strayed too far from the essence that had brought him into being? If so, how did he get back? Was Marcus merely spinning tales and making up things in order to guide attention away from himself? Callen grumbled beneath his breath as the warning prickle of the barrier raised the hair on his arms.

"Something bothering you, Eternal One?"

ACCEPTANCE

Callen stiffened. "You are early, Betrayer."

Marcus stepped from the mountainside with a pout twisting his lips. "You know I always preferred Death Walker to Betrayer. Dealer's choice, I suppose." Callen stood stiff and silent. His mask was firmly in place, his eyes burning into Marcus. Finally, Marcus lifted a brow. "Do you care to share why we are doing the old cloak-and-dagger routine?"

Callen frowned and glanced down at his simple attire, t-shirt and pants.

Marcus sighed dramatically. "It is a saying, Eternal One. Why am I here sneaking around with you?"

Callen lifted his chin and, with clenched fists, said the words that tasted like ash on his tongue. "I need you to do something for me."

Marcus's smile gleamed beneath the moon. "You have captured my attention, Eternal One. Do tell."

Somewhere in the Heart Realm – The Man

The wind slipped over his body like a gentle caress as he soared high above the slumbering Realm. In the weeks since his emergence back into the Heart Realm, he had learned a great many things. The Fall hadn't just ripped the land apart; it had separated families, generations, and power. When the Seven Kings died, they left a devastation that had gone unchecked in their absence. The Man shook his head and flattened his wings to his back, letting himself plummet toward a viciously scarred section of land.

When he was several feet from the ground, he spread his wings wide and let them lift him higher before closing them entirely so he could land. The moment his feet touched the ground, he knew he had come to the right place. A crumbling structure with a hidden door he knew led to an underground hideaway stood off to the left, while the remnants of a funeral pyre lay to the right.

The Man crouched down and placed a hand into the deep rivets that had been engraved along the surface. "A battle took place here," he whispered to himself. "One that cost more than just lives."

Rising to his feet, he allowed his emerald eyes to scour his surroundings. From the blades of grass to the bent and broken tree limbs, his eyes carefully examined every inch until, finally, they stopped on a single purple blossom. With great caution, he approached the seemingly innocent bud. But he had lived too long to let something even as simple as a flower lower his defenses. He wouldn't get trapped by such frivolous things, not again.

His eyes swept across his surroundings once more before he crouched down and cautiously tapped his finger on the top. Only the flower didn't bob beneath the

CHAPTER SEVENTEEN

weight of his touch. In fact, his finger never got the chance to touch the petals before the air shifted and wiggled before his eyes.

"I was wondering how long it would take you to find me." He smiled, a humorless curve of his lips.

"How did you escape your personal prison?" rasped a deep voice.

The Man rose from his haunches, and his smile broadened as he watched the apparition dust off its haze. "It's nice to see you again, too, Darkness."

"You didn't answer my question," said Darkness.

"And here I thought it was all part of your meticulous little plan. Didn't you know? Your pet freed me. Along with six others." The Man leaned forward. "Jealous?"

Darkness stiffened, the haze surrounding him shifting and trembling with emotion. "We don't have time for your gloating. Do you know what is coming?"

The Man sighed. "It's a tale as old as time. Of course I know."

"Have you gathered your pieces?"

The Man narrowed his eyes. "People are not *pieces*."

Darkness chuckled. "Always so sentimental. I thought an eternity alone would have beaten that out of you." Darkness's head jerked back to The Man. "Unless…"

The Man lifted a brow. "Unless what?"

After several moments, Darkness shook his head. "Never mind. Our focus needs to be on the future. The time is growing near, and we need to be ready."

"I'm ready. The real question is, are you? How are you going to be a part of this fight if you are still trapped?"

Darkness smiled. "We all have our methods. Take care. When next we meet, I might just make some time to settle an old score."

The Man watched Darkness fade anyway into nothing with more than one new question bouncing around in his mind. How long did they have? Was Darkness really going to make it out? If so, did that mean the others would too? Where are the other six? And most of all, where was Averie?

Chapter Eighteen

Prison – Emma and Solara

A meaningless tune thrummed in Emma's throat. Meaningless because it wasn't a song she had heard before or one with any other meaning than to simply fill time. The tune stopped. *I suppose nothing is truly meaningless, then*, she pondered to herself. A bored sigh passed her lips and echoed in the hollow cavern that was her prison. Boredom was her only companion these days. Though, by any other scale, she should count herself lucky. There was no torture or demand for answers. No starvation or dehydration. There was simply nothing.

Three meals a day arrived from the stones, along with a steady stream of water that trickled in the far corner. But in the end, the silence and the boredom proved to be far worse than any torture that could be inflicted. The worst fate for anyone to face was being trapped within the confines of their own mind.

The soft scrape of stone echoed in the otherwise empty room. Even in the darkness, Emma looked to where she knew the door was and waited. When silence continued to weigh heavily in the air, Emma smiled.

"Two visitors in as many days. It appears I'm becoming quite popular," Emma taunted. Perched on the flat stones, she dipped her fingers into the water, feeling its coolness against her skin as she absentmindedly traced patterns on its surface.

No steps sounded in the endless cavern that would have confirmed her assumption of a visitor, and that, in itself, was a confirmation. For there was only one that was capable of true and complete silence of movement. As the silence continued to stretch, Emma began to briefly wonder at her own sanity when, finally, the soft whisper of fabric brushing stone and a shift in the air released a tension she hadn't realized had built up in her shoulders. *Solara.*

CHAPTER EIGHTEEN

Light burst into the air, severing the darkness and temporarily blinding Emma, as Solara's voice echoed between them. "Who else has come to this prison of yours?"

Emma blinked through the sudden burn of light and tucked her teeth between her lips before placing a finger to them.

"Emma," Solara chastised. "Was it Callen? Has he finally come back? Or did Radnar take pity on your situation and try to offer your freedom in exchange for ... something? What did you tell them?"

Emma chuckled and shook her head. "I'll never tell," she said in a singsong voice. "But you will, Bound One. What have you come for this time?" she taunted.

Solara bit her tongue on a retort until the taste of metal filled her mouth, and she forced herself to breathe deeply. She knew Emma spoke the truth. If she said she wasn't going to share who had visited her, there was nothing she or anyone else could do to make her speak. *I came to this stone prison for a reason. Focus on the reason. I can't leave here without knowing what is to come.* "When last we spoke, you mentioned overhearing The Shadow's plan for—"

"Seraphina's plan," Emma corrected.

Solara suppressed a growl of frustration. Decades forced to be at Marcus's side had nothing on being forced to deal with the creature that sat across the cavern. "They are the same person, are they not?"

Emma smiled, and Solara ground her teeth.

"What is her plan for Averie?"

"Who said she had a plan for Averie?"

"You did!" Solara snapped.

Emma laid her head back against the stone and tapped a finger to her chin. "I did? Are you certain? Perhaps it was another prisoner who said such silly things."

"Emma," Solara warned. "The first time I came here, shortly after your imprisonment, you thought your life was going to end, and you mentioned that the Sha—that Sera had a plan for Averie. Now I need you to tell me what that plan is."

Emma peered over the cavern with interest glittering in her eyes. "If you wanted to know then, why didn't you ask?"

Solara hesitated, then let her thoughts spill. "I didn't ask because, at the time, Averie had Sera in her clutches. I thought her demise was imminent, and I was mistaken. So tell me, what is her plan?"

Emma shook her head. "That doesn't sound like me."

Solara fisted her hands at her side as her anger threatened to boil over, when Emma snapped her fingers. "Ah-ha! I remember now. I said I heard about a plan for what's *in* Averie. Not Averie herself."

Solara's stomach clenched as remorse and guilt over the past washed over her once again. "What did she say? What is her plan for the ... for what's inside of Averie?"

Emma snorted. "Oh please, as if anyone in any of the seven Realms doesn't know that girl has the Heart locked away inside her. How else would she have survived for so long and so well?"

ACCEPTANCE

"My patience is running thin, Emma."

Emma pursed her lips in false contemplation. "What will you give me for that bit of information?"

Solara looked down her nose at the petite, dirty woman that leaned against the stone walls. Her hair, once glossy with health, was stuck to the sides of her face from weeks of neglect. Dirt and grime covered her body, giving her a displeasing scent. She rolled her eyes and lifted the small package in her hand. "Fresh food, soap, and clothes, as promised."

Emma tried to suppress her excitement at consuming something other than the chunk of bread and side of carrots but failed miserably. Even the thought of cleaning the grime from her body sent a tingle along her skin. "Well? What are you waiting for? Send it over."

Solara lifted the bag and let it rise from her fingers and drift to the space between them until it came to a sudden stop and hovered above the endless ravine. Emma narrowed her eyes at the irony between mother and daughter.

"You see that I've brought what you wanted, now speak."

Emma narrowed her eyes but did as she was ordered.

Solara flew through the halls of the Black Mountain at such speed her body appeared to be more mist than humanoid. Her mind raced at what Emma had revealed. Her heart and mind were at war with reality and hope. "It's not possible. It can't be. I would know if there was a chance…" Over and over she spoke the same sentences like it was her new mantra.

Her hand slammed against Marcus's door, sending it back against the wall with ferocious force. Marcus didn't even bother to flinch from his place on his bed. "Can I help you?" he asked.

Solara narrowed her eyes at his relaxed expression. Only that wasn't what angered her the most. No, that would be the casual way he lay atop the smooth blankets with his legs crossed at the ankle and his hands behind his head. "What are you doing?! Shouldn't you be helping Averie and the others?"

Marcus rolled his eyes and looked back at the ceiling. "The meeting is complete. Where have you been?"

Solara fisted her hands at her sides and forced herself to breathe. "I was visiting Emma."

"Oh really? How fascinating. And just what were you hoping to accomplish by doing that?"

"She said that Sera wants to release the Heart."

Marcus snorted. "Of course she does. That has been her plan from the start. Why are you acting like this is new information?"

Solara stomped a soundless foot against the ground. "You did not let me finish!"

CHAPTER EIGHTEEN

Marcus's eyes shot to hers as he slowly rose to a sitting position. "Didn't I? Then please, Solara, continue."

Solara swallowed the whimper of fear. Even though Marcus had a calm, charming outside, she knew of the devil that lurked just beneath the surface. She also knew that he hated being defied, lectured, or snapped at. Something she had just done in full force. *I have to be careful.* "You're right. I do know that Seraphina has always planned to release the Heart, but what I didn't know, what neither of us knew, was that she is searching for a way to remove it *without* ending Averie's life."

Marcus's eyes flared with dark interest. "Is that so? It appears as though things are getting more interesting by the minute."

"Don't you understand? This means that there could still be a way for Averie to be saved!"

Marcus smiled a smile that brought chills to Solara's arms and a sickness to her belly. "That's right. I think we should prepare to share this information with the group. But first … you do something for me."

Solara nibbled on the inside of her cheek until she felt her nerves calm. "Alright. What do you need me to do?"

"Don't be so worried, Solara. I just need you to go to the Tavern at the edge of all Realms and deliver a special message for me."

"You don't mean—"

Marcus moved in a flash, perching at the edge of his bed one second and towering above her the next, with his finger pressed firmly against her lips. "I do, and you will not speak a word about who or what or where you are going. Once you get back, we will share what you have learned with the rest of the group, but until then, you will not mention *a word*. Do I make myself clear?"

With wide, frightened eyes, Solara nodded.

"Very good."

"What is the message?"

"The countdown has begun."

Chapter Nineteen

A night of tossing and turning had done nothing but raise Averie's ire. Frustration bubbled just beneath her skin and raised the hair on the back of her neck. Although Averie knew what she could walk into, her entire body was screaming, trying to tell her something that her mind couldn't grasp. Something that Emma's story and her own memories were fighting to shake free.

A groan rumbled her chest as she pulled her pillow over her face and opened her mouth to scream out her frustration when an echo of soft whimpers and light scratches sounded at her door.

A small smile tugged at her lips as she tossed the pillow aside and climbed from her bed to open the door. "Hey guys, just in time."

Seiko and Echo brushed past her and jumped onto her bed before fixing her with their expectant eyes. Averie rolled her eyes and shut the door before climbing back into bed. Seiko settled at the foot of her bed while Echo took up the place at her side. Wrapping her arm around the enormous wolf's body, Averie smiled into her soft, black fur. "Somehow, you always know what I need."

Seiko huffed at the foot of the bed, eliciting a soft laugh from Averie. "You too, Seiko," she promised.

The sound of Echo's steady heartbeat and the feel of her silky fur against Averie's skin soon sent her into a peaceful slumber.

"Are we there yet?"
A soft chuckle. "No, honey, not yet."
Averie frowned at the intrusive voices. What are they doing in my room?
"Do you think he will be excited?" chirped a girl.
"Of course he will be."

CHAPTER NINETEEN

He? *Averie blinked her eyes once, twice, three times, then gasped when she woke to find herself in a familiar old car.* "No," *she whispered.* "Please, not again." *Averie pinched her eyes shut, hoping beyond all hope that when she opened them again, she would be back in her room. Only, the old, rumbling car turned and hit a particularly deep pothole, and she smashed her head against the cold glass. Averie groaned in displeasure and rubbed at the soft throb.*

Resigned to her fate to relive yet another muddled and confusing moment of her life, Averie focused on the moment unfolding before her eyes.

A younger version of herself was practically bouncing off the passenger seat, her eyes locked on an old building as Karen put the car in park. Averie frowned as she watched her younger self go still until a shadow passed in front of the tinted glass, and she threw the car door wide. "T-e! T-e, look what Mom brought home!"

The blurred figure turned from the older man to Averie as he stepped into the afternoon light. Averie stepped from the car and watched her younger self crumble at the graveled words. "Those are for babies, Fox."

Averie huffed and fisted her hands at her sides as she glared at the blurred figure. Rage shook her body as her younger self dropped the pinwheel to her side with a nonchalant shrug. "Oh, yeah, I suppose you're right."

The older man at the boy's side growled disapprovingly, and the boy flinched. "Actually, hold it up for me."

Both Averie and her younger self jerked in surprise. "Really?"

The blurred boy shrugged as he nodded to the car. "Yeah. I think the lack of light from the gym made it hard to see." The older man at his side barked out a laugh, then unconvincingly covered it with a cough into his fist.

Averie smiled as her younger self lifted the pinwheel, determination pinching her face as she waited for the boy's approval. The boy leaned in, his eyes narrowing as he inspected the toy. Averie suppressed a breath as the younger her held her breath so tightly in her chest that her cheeks puffed out. Finally, the boy leaned back and nodded his approval. "You're right. They are pretty awesome."

Averie's chest squeezed as her younger self smiled, lighting up the world around them, like the first sunbeam parting the clouds after a heavy rain—vibrant, warm, and full of hope. Averie cleared her throat and stiffened, worried that she would be noticed, then frowned when she wasn't. The moment was so familiar and yet ... not. Pain seared through her temple, drawing a hiss from her lips.

"Averie." Her mother calling out her name skipped her heart and jerked her head up. Only she wasn't talking to her, not really. "Why don't you grab the others from the car and show Th-e? I need a moment with Jak."

Averie frowned. Jak? Averie stepped closer to the adults and felt a tickle of recognition. Th-e? Despite her mother and younger self both saying the name, it was muffled and difficult to hear compared to the other words. Just like the boy was blurred while everyone else was clear. Like the melted man...

ACCEPTANCE

"There's more?" the blurred boy groaned, earning a quick slap to the back of his head. "Hey!" He gasped, rubbing at the tender spot.

The adults began to talk, but Averie didn't care. Her attention was locked on the younger version of herself and the blurred boy that seemed so familiar. She moved unconsciously, both seeing and hearing the children's exchange while ignoring it all the same. Averie leaned forward as the two looked into the white plastic bag and began discussing their next steps.

"So, what's the plan, Fox?" he asked with false enthusiasm.

Young Averie ignored his tight words and collected the bags in her arms. "The wind is coming from that way, so if we line them all up, we can make a rainbow."

Averie stepped closer to the blurred boy as his head turned to find a better spot. He stopped, his image clearing until Averie saw crystal blue staring back at her. "Remember what I told you, Fox. You can't give up. You can never give up."

Averie jerked awake. A chorus of worried whimpers and the touches of cold noses against her hot, clammy skin pulled her from the echo of his last words. Seiko and Echo stared at her with knowing, worried eyes. Averie swallowed through the lump in her throat and ran a shaking hand through her sleep-tangled hair.

"It's okay. I'm okay. It was only a dream. It was only a dream." She repeated the words like a mantra until her heart stopped its tirade against its cage and her labored breaths returned to normal.

A quick glance at the clock told her there was no use in going back to sleep, not that she would or could. Not after another strange memory/dream still swam in her mind. A reluctant sigh puffed her lips as she tossed the covers from her body and stepped from bed.

"Today, we find answers."

After a long, contemplative shower that bore no answers, Averie dressed in a comfortable, reinforced, black long-sleeve shirt and skinny jeans. Her mind continued to replay through the collection of disturbing and real-feeling dreams when her door burst open and slammed against the mountain wall.

"Hello, Callen," she sighed. Collecting her shoes from beside the dresser, she sat on the edge of the bed and slipped them on as she waited for Callen to begin.

"This is a trap," Callen proclaimed, his arms clenched at his sides as he stormed further into her room.

Averie's fingers deftly tied her laces as she shrugged. "Probably."

"And still, you are going?" he demanded.

Averie pulled the freshly sharpened blades from beneath her mattress and slid them into her boots. "Why not?"

The sound of Callen's teeth grinding together was enough to earn a curious glance.

CHAPTER NINETEEN

Averie lifted a brow and fought a smile. "Is something wrong?"

"I—We cannot afford to lose you. Not now," Callen explained.

Averie nodded and pressed her lips into a thin line as all humor fled. "So, when is a *good* time to lose me, then? When this is all over? Tomorrow, next week, next year? I just want to know so I can star my calendar." She smiled to herself at the imagery.

"This is not a joke!" he snapped.

Th-e would have found it funny. She chuckled to herself, then froze with her fingers wound in her hair. *Who would have found it funny?*

"You are willingly walking into a trap, and for what? The potential of a truce?" he continued.

Averie shook herself free of her inner confusion and finished tying her hair into a high ponytail. "You and I both know there will be no truce."

Callen threw his hands into the air as frustration got the better of him. "Then why go?!"

"Look, I get you are concerned, and really, I appreciate it, but we both know she can't kill me. If she could, she would have by now. I am going because I think there is still another way to end this."

"There is not!" Callen roared. "The only way to put a stop to all of this is to put a stop to her. If you cannot do that, then I will."

The glimmer of gold consumed Averie's eyes until they shone with a dangerous glint. In an instant, the space between them closed, and Averie glared up into his eyes. "Do not *ever* think I can't or won't end this. She has taken *everything* from me. And when I have done the same for her," Averie nodded, "*that* is when *I* will end this." With her final piece spoken, Averie turned on her heel and stormed from her room and down the darkened hall.

A chill settled into Callen's bones at the visceral reaction and display of power Averie had unknowingly released. The moment the Heart had colored her eyes, all the air had been sucked from the room and his lungs until she slipped from the room. Air rushed into his lungs as she disappeared into the hall. His mind raced with what to do next while his mouth and feet were already moving.

"I am coming with you," he called out, his steps echoing against the stone floor.

Averie clenched her teeth and fisted her hands at her sides. "Fine," she hissed. The pair stormed through the mountain in tense silence, both oblivious to the way people flattened themselves against the walls or stepped back to give them more space.

The moment they stepped free of the mountain, Averie felt the stress seep from her body. The fresh mid-morning air filled her nose with the scent of flowers and pine as a soft breeze cooled her cheeks ... and brought a whisper of harsh words. Averie frowned and scanned her surroundings. Snip stood just outside the mountain barrier, glaring at his brother as they spoke in harsh, hushed whispers.

"Problem?" Averie asked.

The twins shared one last glare before separating. "Nope," Snip chirped, his signature blazing smile in place.

"Good. What's the plan?"

ACCEPTANCE

"We will open a direct portal to the meeting spot. You will have ten minutes to talk, negotiate, or kill each other before we come and drag you both out."

Averie nodded her head. "Perfect. Let's get going."

Hex caught her wrist as she went to step by. "Believe nothing she tells you and only half of what you see."

"What's that supposed to mean?" Averie tracked the tick in his jaw and leaned forward. Her eyes bore into his. "What aren't you telling me?"

Hex opened his mouth to answer and snapped it shut.

"Are you doing this?" Snip asked.

"Yes," she answered, though her eyes stayed on Hex. Slipping her wrist free of his grasp, she stepped to Callen's side.

"Are you ready?" he whispered.

"As I'll ever be."

A snap of Snip's fingers and the scenery went hazy. "Ten minutes," he reminded.

Averie nodded, steeled her spine, and stepped through.

Chapter Twenty

Stepping through the portal was like stepping into another world. Averie knew she was still in the Heart Realm, and yet the battle had twisted the beautiful lands into something out of the apocalypse. The land was scarred from the battle that had taken place just days before. Deep gashes spread out from the ruined castle, leaving endless lines of destruction accented by the cracked and fallen trees and decaying flowers and dead grass. The air still held the acrid smell of blood and dead Shadowed.

Averie scrunched her nose at the smell. *The Realm hasn't even tried to heal itself…*

Averie looked over the aftereffects of battle and felt … nothing. *A means to an end,* she promised herself.

"Are you having second thoughts?" Callen asked, a glimmer of hope lining his question.

Averie shook her head and took a step toward the ruined dwelling, the chill of what transpired sending shivers down her spine. It didn't take long before they were crossing the tattered threshold.

"Averie, I wasn't sure you would come." Sera's voice echoed in the empty room as she slipped from the shadows. Lucas smiled at her side.

Callen stepped forward, his body placed strategically in front of Averie's, while Averie stood in rigid silence. Her hands flexed, itching to grab the deadly blades in her boots. "Why would I ever turn down such a thoughtful invitation?"

Sera stepped deeper into the light, her hands clasped behind her back and teeth shining in a malevolent grin. "I thought it fitting. It is your birthday, after all. And what is a birthday without gifts?" Sera leaned forward conspiratorially and whispered, "I think you are *really* going to like it."

ACCEPTANCE

"I'm not here for gifts, Sera." Averie's words brought a chill to the dampened, crumbling structure. Water droplets froze in their descent and crashed to the ground with tiny clinks. "I am here to discuss business."

Sera frowned, her pink painted lips pushed into a pout. "Be nice, Avi. I put a lot of thought and work into this one."

"She is planning something," Callen whispered, his eyes already heating to molten steel.

Averie's gaze narrowed. "You said if I came, we would discuss a truce. So, either you state your terms, or I'm leaving."

Sera held a finger in the air. "Oh, come on, Avi. Just one gift, and then we get down to business. I promise. You know I always give the best gifts."

Averie slid her attention to the bleached version of the Lucas she had known. Nothing about his demeanor showed any hint of attack. In fact, he looked extraordinarily calm as he leaned against one of the remaining pillars with his arms and ankles crossed. Feeling the weight of her gaze, he met her stare head-on and smiled his signature flirtatious smile. The pinched pink scars crossing the side of his face hardly dimmed the effect.

Hands fisting at her side, Averie tipped her head in the slightest of nods. "Fine."

Sera's eyes flared, her grin beaming in the darkness as she excitedly clapped her hands together. "You can come out now," she called in a cringy, singsong voice.

Averie slipped the blades from her boots. She had felt no one else in the ruins. Either she was losing her touch, or Sera had found a new way to conceal her men. Neither option was good for her. "What are you playing at, Sera?"

Sera waved off her concerns and held her smile. "You'll see."

"Slow and steady breaths," Callen whispered from her side.

They waited, each slipping into their own defensive stance as the echo of heavy steps grew closer and closer. With each step, Sera's eyes shone brighter. Her excitement was palpable as she continued to stare unblinkingly. Averie felt Sera's eyes scan her face over and over again, cataloguing every twitch, flicker, and emotion that crossed her features, but refused to tear her own attention from the nearing steps.

Averie adjusted her grip on the hilt of her sai and shifted her stance as a tall, broad, muscled shadow stepped from the darkness and into the light. Averie straightened, a frown creasing her brow as she looked from Sera's eager expression to the empty one on the man beside her. *What is going on?*

Averie inched closer to Callen to voice her question when he stumbled forward, his breath coming in frantic pants as he stared at the emotionless man in front of them.

Averie's jaw dropped in shock at the visceral reaction before she swiftly recovered and closed the space between them. "Callen? What is it? What's wrong? Do you know him?"

"It is not possible," he whispered. "It is not."

Averie wrapped an arm around his waist before turning a golden glare to the newcomer. He was tall, rivaling Callen, and broad, with light brown shaggy hair

CHAPTER TWENTY

and empty, soulless blue eyes. Eyes that seemed so familiar and yet not. Her dream from the night before tried to sneak its way into the forefront of her mind. Before it could come to fruition, Callen let out a harsh breath. "I do not know what game you are playing—"

Sera had watched Averie with victory shining in her crystalline eyes. Only she hadn't gotten what she expected. Averie had remained calm, cool, and collected while staring straight into the eyes of her recently deceased brother. The only time she had shown any type of reaction was when the one at her side had nearly collapsed from shock. The very reaction she had expected from Averie.

Sera fixed her expression into a more causal one and glided to Thane's side. "Avi, do you know who this is?" she asked and skimmed her long pink nails down his bare arm.

Averie lifted a brow and bounced her attention between Sera, the newcomer, and Lucas. "Should I?"

Lucas dissolved into disbelieving laughter, claiming the attention of all parties. "I'm sorry, but this is just... I mean, she doesn't even... And he's just... Oh, this is *good*."

Sera and Callen watched Lucas fall further into the pits of his own laughter while Averie kept her attention on the tall, blue-eyed man. *Those eyes... It couldn't be... Is he the one from—*

Sera flew down the first two stairs and bared her teeth as inky darkness consumed her eyes and stretched to her temple. Averie dropped her head to the side in wonder when Sera stretched out her arm and pointed to Callen. "What did you do?" she demanded.

Callen stiffened at Averie's side. "We need to leave. Now."

Ignoring Callen's warning, Averie allowed her curiosity to move her from Callen's side until she stood directly below Sera and the strange man.

"Averie," Callen growled.

"What did you do?" Sera demanded once more.

Who are you? Averie pushed forward, her eyes seeking answers from the man's empty gaze as Sera continued her tirade.

Lucas pushed from the wall but took no further steps. "Do you want to know?" he asked. His voice pulsed with his eagerness to reveal a hidden truth.

Averie clenched her jaw against the desire to give in and demand answers. For the first time, she was thankful that Lucas enjoyed the sound of his own voice as he continued. "That's what you're thinking, isn't it? Who is he? Why does Callen care? Why is Sera so angry? Why don't I know?" The soft click of his approach tightened her stomach until his breath tickled her ear. "I'll tell you. He's—"

"This is your fault!" Sera shrieked, her body shaking in anger as the shadows separated themselves from the walls and flocked to her side. "I should have known you would do something. None of what she has done has made any sense. But now it does. She's not Averie!"

ACCEPTANCE

Averie jerked in place. The screeched words that spilled from her former best friend ripped at her own insecurities and reminded her of the haunted words Emma had spoken. Insecurities she wasn't ready to face now. Averie shoved Lucas from her side and leapt down the stairs.

Callen sucked in a breath, his body trembling with indecision as he called out, "Averie, wait!"

But he was too late. He watched the moment pass with a sickening slowness. The Heart's signature gold consumed the rich emerald of Averie's eyes as she lifted her arms high above her head. A callous smile curved her lips as her arms trembled and forced their way through the air in a downward motion. The ancient stones cracked and groaned as they were ripped apart and sent plummeting down upon the three unsuspecting people.

Bile boiled in his stomach, burned its way up his throat, and filled his mouth as the gruesome crunch of bone resonated in his ears. Callen bent at the waist, no longer able to fight back against the sickness in his stomach as it forced its way free.

Averie looked over at the sound of retching with a confused frown. "Callen? What's wrong?" she asked and rushed to his side to place a comforting hand on his back.

Callen shook his head and wiped his mouth with the back of his hand. His eyes burned with unshed tears as they stayed glued to the bile-covered stones. "You killed him."

Averie jerked back. "What? Killed who? Sera and Lucas? They'll be fine." As if to prove her point, the crumbled remains shifted once again and revealed Sera's black gaze.

Averie's attention jerked to the moving stones before shifting back to Callen's bent form. A soft growl shook her chest as she threw Callen's arm over her shoulder. "Time to go."

Snip shifted his stance as his mental clock continued its countdown. "Come on, Averie," he whispered.

Hex stood frozen in a casual lean, his outward appearance drastically different from his internal one. On the outside, he was calm, collected, and patient in his wait for Averie and Callen's return. While on the inside, the beast inside ripped and tore at its chains, making his skin crawl with the uncomfortable urge to release him.

"That's it, times up." Snip stepped forward just as a large, heavy body was shoved into his chest. The unexpected weight and surprise sent both parties to the ground with a resounding *thud*.

"What in Fornax?!"

CHAPTER TWENTY

A second later, Averie stepped through and lifted a brow. "Want to close that before someone else slips through?" she asked, a hand motioning to the air that shimmered behind.

Hex lifted his hand, his fingers poised for a snap, when his brother's dramatic plea split the air. "Get him off! Get him off! He's suffocating me!" Snip cried.

Hex and Averie exchanged eye rolls before Hex moved forward to help remove Callen from his brother. "If you were suffocating, you wouldn't be able to speak."

"What the hell happened?!" Snip demanded as he climbed to his feet.

Averie fixed an empty expression on Callen. "I don't know. Why don't you three tell me?"

Hex looked up with a frown, his hands still holding Callen's bent form in place, while Snip's eyes widened. "How would we know? You two were there! How do you expect us to—"

"Snip. Stop." Callen pinched his eyes shut and prayed to the Stars for strength as he straightened. "We do not have time for this. We have to get back to the mountain. *Now*."

The twins exchanged a worried glance. "How bad?" asked Snip.

"Sera has found a way to reanimate the dead."

Hex cursed under his breath, and Snip stepped forward. "How animated?"

Hex narrowed his eyes at his brother.

"Soulless but mobile."

Averie frowned at the exchange, the action deepening when Snip asked his question, excitement in his words, only for his shoulders to fall in defeat at Callen's answer.

The echo of Hex's snapping fingers signaled the closed portal and their departure. "You guys go ahead," she whispered, earning worried glances from all three. "I'm fine. I just, I just need to clear my head."

Hex's jaw jumped as he clenched his teeth but nodded. Snip sent her a sad smile. "Alright, Princess. Make sure you don't stay out too long. The protection of the barrier doesn't reach this far."

Averie chuckled and turned her back on the trio, her steps already carrying her away. "I don't need protection."

"Averie!" Callen called, stopping her. "Be careful," he stressed.

"Yeah, sure."

Chapter Twenty-One

~~~

Sera panted beneath her Shadowed shield, her breath pushing against the worn stone and sending dust up to brush against her nose. If it weren't for its quick reaction, she would have been seriously injured beneath the castle's remains. A disgruntled growl left her lips as she pushed against the shadows and forced them to lift the stones that had threatened to crush her moments ago. Her growl grew as she used all of her energy to free herself from her stoney grave.

The fresh air she had hoped was waiting to greet her was clogged by the dust that clung to the air, heavy as fog only not as thick, which allowed her to make out the distorted shapes of Averie and Callen as they fled.

Sera pushed her hand forward, her finger lengthening to point at their disappearing forms. "Follow," she wheezed. The word, immediately followed by hacking coughs, was obeyed before the syllable died on her tongue. And not a moment too late, as Averie and Callen disappeared into the awaiting portal.

Sera sagged against the stones at the sight and attempted to catch her breath. The clack of shifting rock brought her attention to her side as a dirtied hand plunged free of its hold. Sera chuckled at the horror movie cliché playing out before her eyes and regretted it instantly as more coughs rattled her chest.

"Damn it!" Lucas cursed as he heaved himself free. "Who knew death would hurt so much and come so often?"

Sera rolled her eyes and climbed from her shadow's protective hold to stomp down the stairs, leaving a trail of dust in her wake. "You aren't dead," she snapped. "Not yet, at least."

Lucas shrugged and followed her to the grassy knoll lingering by the ruins. "Tomato, tomahto," Lucas quipped, his finger brushing the dirt from her nose as he passed her and dropped himself to the grass. Leaning back onto the cool surface, he stared up into the vibrant blue sky and let his mind replay the fascinating scene

CHAPTER TWENTY-ONE

they had just survived. "Well, that didn't go as expected." He sighed and tucked his hands behind his head.

Sera released a noise halfway between a growl and a snort as she joined him on the ground. "That's putting it lightly," she answered, hugging her knees to her chest.

Lucas nodded, his eyes catching on a large bird soaring across the sky. "What are we going to do with him now?"

Sera sighed and rested her chin to the tops of her knees. "The shadows have him."

Lucas frowned at the non-answer. "And Averie?"

Sera turned her head to the side and eyed him with a quirked, perfectly arched brow. "What about her?"

Ignoring her stare, Lucas followed the bird until it disappeared from sight. "Yes, exactly. What about her? What did they do to her?"

"Tied to this Realm, and yet you still can't see," Sera mumbled. "It's obvious, isn't it? They took him away. Though I suspect she knows that already. She's probably just finding a way to process the information and plan her next steps."

Lucas's frown deepened, his eyes blazing with shock as his head whipped to the side to meet Sera's sure gaze. "Why would they do something like that?"

She shrugged. "Survival."

Lucas arched a brow. "Theirs or hers?"

"Is there a difference?" she asked and stretched her body down by his side.

Lucas shrugged and looked back to the sky. "I suppose not. I guess, knowing that, everything else makes more sense. The erratic shift in her fighting and use of power."

"Mhmm."

"You shouldn't have done it," he whispered.

"Mmm."

Silence descended between them. Neither tense, nor comforting, nor contemplative. But rather still. As the sun began to descend toward the horizon, Lucas rose to his feet with an outstretched hand. "Ready?"

Sera breathed deeply and placed her hand in his. "As I'll ever be."

Lucas watched the world around them with admiration. From the way the breeze danced between the branches and leaves to the playful sway of the blades of grass. His eyes tracked the clouds as they continued their endless race across the sky and admired the birds as they soared high above.

Sera was dusting the rubble and grass from her clothes when Lucas asked the question that had plagued his mind from the moment he had opened his eyes after Averie had nearly killed him. "Is there any other way?"

A sad smile curved her lips. "No. No, there's not."

Lucas squeezed her hand in his and smiled back. "Alright, then. Let's begin."

ACCEPTANCE

Somewhere above the Heart Realm – The Man

Weeks threatened to turn into months before he found what he had been searching for. The sight was so surreal he had to double back twice, circling like a vulture above its decaying prey, as his mind struggled to catch up with what his eyes had found. But when it did, he moved faster than lightning. His wings flattened against his back, plummeting him to the earth faster than he originally expected. At the last moment, he stretched out his gray-tipped wings, thankful for the sudden uplift before settling on his feet.

There she stood. An arm's length away. Her green eyes glittering with curiosity, and her deep red hair lifting as it was swept up in the wind announcing his arrival. She was thinner than he remembered. Her cheeks were slightly more gaunt, and her body was clad in green armor so dark he had to blink to see it wasn't black. Electricity popped between them and pulled his eyes back up to hers, only to find they pulsed golden.

"Averie," he croaked. His voice was deep and husky with indecipherable emotion.

Averie blinked several times in surprise, then clapped her hands across her mouth in her own disbelief. She shook her head and took an uncertain step back. "This isn't possible," she whispered, glancing around her surroundings and pinching her cheeks. "You can't be here."

The man lifted his arms in a placating manner. "It is, because I am here."

"But … how?"

He shook his head and, with a brilliant white smile, slowly closed the space between them until he could cup her face. Happiness shone in his brilliant eyes when his skin touched hers, and their warmth mingled. "It doesn't matter. All that matters is that I am here. That I will always be where you need me."

Tears filled her eyes, washing away the gold and leaving behind fields of green. "I've missed you, Feliks."

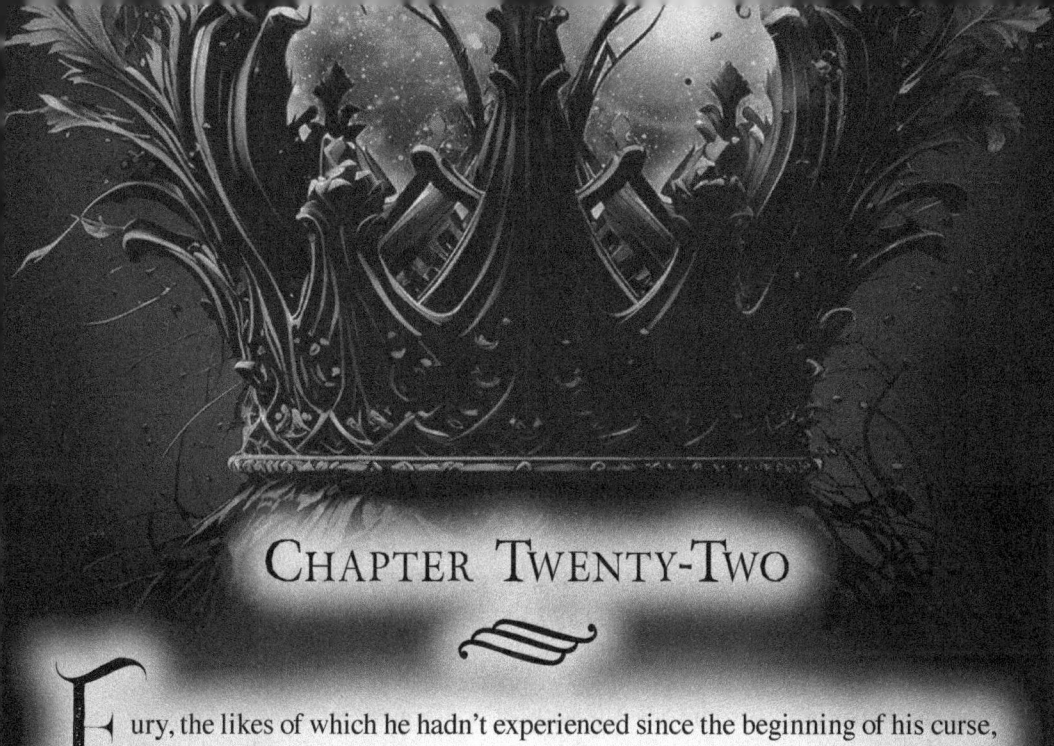

CHAPTER TWENTY-TWO

Fury, the likes of which he hadn't experienced since the beginning of his curse, rushed through Feliks's veins with searing ferocity. The Black Mountain loomed in the distance, there one moment and gone the next. His roar rumbled in the air like thunder, announcing his presence and warning those inside of his ire.

His body tightened as it prepared for impact when, much to his surprise, the barrier thinned. Unsure of what awaited him but willing to take the risk, he pierced through to the other side, with only the soft pop in his ears telling him he had gone through anything at all.

Unspent energy thickened his muscles as Feliks burst through the Dark Mountain's entrance and instantly homed in on the man he knew had a part to play. He had woven through the inner mountain and entered the gathering area before he decided to place his feet on the black stones. Ignoring the outcries, smell of fear, and startled shrieks at his sudden, and unannounced, arrival, he charged down the halls in a direct path toward the door that held the culprit he sought.

Stone cracked as the door ricocheted off the wall from his kick, laced with all the anger of a pent-up beast. Feliks's chest heaved while his mind battled for the rational, while his body longed for destruction. Three thunderous steps brought him to the center of the room, where four shocked people stood staring, mouths agape, at him.

"What. Did. You. DO?!" he roared.

Callen swallowed through the guilty lump in his throat and stared off with the fuming, winged man. "How did you get in here? Who are you?"

Hex and Snip exchanged an unreadable glance before flanking the raging Feliks. "Hey, buddy, how did you get in here?" Snip asked, his voice as placating and sweet as a pleading babysitter to a screaming child.

ACCEPTANCE

Feliks dragged his glare from Callen to the approaching jester of a twin. "Answer me."

"We took her pain away," Hex answered.

"How?" he growled, his body shaking with his anger. Why?"

"She was out of control. She was *losing* control," Radnar explained.

"Who in Fornax are you to make that decision!?" Hands clutching at his head, he pinned the Eternal One with a glare. "Do you have any idea what you have done?!"

Callen's chest clenched with shared agony as he swallowed through the growing lump in his throat. "I did not have a choice."

"There is *always* a choice!" Feliks raged.

Callen shook his head with growing intensity. "You are wrong. You do not understand—"

Feliks swung back with a fury, setting his eyes aflame. Closing the space between them, he clutched his shirt and dragged the barely shorter man from his feet, barreling toward the wall and slamming him with such force the mountain shook. "No. *You* don't understand. Because of your weakness, you have destroyed *everything*. You can't take pieces from someone without consequences!"

Hex stepped forward, rubbing at the mark searing his skin. "I told you."

Callen glared over the man's shoulder, his gaze piercing into Hex, before sliding to the blazing ones a mere inch from his own. "Who are you?"

"The one you thought was your destruction."

He snorted in derision. "Instead, you are what? Salvation?"

The man released the smirking man and twisted away, clenching his perfect, gleaming, straight teeth as he ran his hands through his hair.

Callen straightened, rolling his shoulders as he watched the display. "You weren't there. We did what we had to. Maybe instead of hiding away, you should have been here."

Hex slowly shook his head, letting out a heavy breath as Snip sucked audibly through his teeth. The man froze. "Excuse me?"

Callen stepped forward, his chin lifting with confidence. "You heard me. You stand there wanting to judge a situation when you were nowhere to be found."

Slowly, so slowly, the man turned. Hex and Snip exchanged a knowing glance before taking several steps back. "Are you pushing your mistakes onto me?" The words were low, deep, and menacing.

Callen stepped forward, a steady tick pulling his cheek. "If you knew something we didn't and refused to share that knowledge, then you have no right to judge the actions of the unknowing."

"There is no shortcut to grief! There is only a beginning and the sickening twist and turns that haunt life. Do you have any idea what you have done?"

"We thought we were helping her. She was … is … dangerous if she isn't stable. In Quen's current state, neither would have been in control of what their abilities did."

Feliks shook his head in disgust. "You are making excuses. The moment you took Thane from her memory, you erased everything he taught her. Including control.

CHAPTER TWENTY-TWO

The Heart isn't locked away; it's standing in front of you. There is no more Quen and no more Averie. Only the Heart."

"What do you mean there is no more Quen? Quen is the Heart."

"Quen was a shell, Callen. Just as you and Senan are. We are all shells for the power that courses through our veins. The moment we cease to exist, the power seeps from our pores and waits for its next host. Magic is a parasite, and we are its willing victims."

Callen shook his head. "That is not possible. Quen would never do that. She would never intentionally harm Averie."

Feliks snapped his fingers. "Intentionally. But Quen has been locked away for a long time, her body long since gone, leaving only a will to fight against a creator. Would any of you like to make a wager on who wins in that battle?" The group stayed silent as Feliks's angry eyes met each of theirs. "No one?"

"What do we do?" Callen asked.

Feliks dropped his head back in a boisterous laugh. "What do you do? Well, the first thing would have been to let her grieve and not treat her as a tool for you to play with. To not remove the only people in her life that truly meant something. But seeing as how you have already done that, I would say your best option is to run. Run as fast and as far away as you can, because when the Heart gets that last piece to snap into place, we are already dead."

"There has to be a way," Callen snapped.

Feliks shook his head. "You still don't understand. Quen no longer *exists* and without her, there is no one to hold back the Heart's single-minded thought. Why do you think there were THREE OF YOU?!"

"That's enough!" Radnar bellowed. "We have not got the time to bicker over nonsense when Averie's fate hangs in the balance."

"You still don't get it. Averie's fate has already been decided."

The group went deathly silent as, one by one, they lifted expectant eyes to Feliks.

"What do you mean?" Callen asked.

Feliks lifted sad, resigned eyes to the group. "The moment you let Hex remove Thane from her memory, the Averie you knew began to die. And the moment she opened her eyes, she ceased to exist."

CHAPTER TWENTY-THREE

Feliks trembled beneath the weight of self-restraint. His anger was palpable in the air with audible snaps and pops cracking the silence of the room. His hands clenched into white-knuckled fists. The loose, fluffy appearance of his wings darkened as his feathers flattened, giving the appearance of wicked armor.

Callen's shoulders drooped as he struggled under the weight of his own crushing guilt. "It was not supposed to be like this."

Feliks narrowed his eyes as every other person in the room involuntarily stiffened. Radnar's eyes snapped to Callen, a flare of panic igniting the gray of his eyes. Hex and Snip, his jailers, shared an unreadable glance before the trio forced themselves to appear nonchalant.

Feliks took a menacing step forward. "Go on."

"Callen," Radnar warned beneath his breath.

A sad smile carved his lips. "She was not supposed to survive."

If Feliks had believed himself angered or enraged prior to Callen's words, he was the embodiment of the emotions now. "Excuse me?"

Callen swallowed through the emotion lodged in his throat and ignored the imploring stares to stop. "We have always known that the Heart was still locked inside of Averie."

"How?"

"When Quen did not return, and the Realm continued to stray, it was the most obvious conclusion." A devastating storm brewed behind the winged one's eyes, but Callen pressed on. "After much deliberation, we found only one solution to ending this war and protecting the people of all the Realms. To bring Averie home."

Feliks narrowed his eyes. "That was always the plan."

Callen flinched. "Yes, and no. Bringing Averie home was indeed always the plan. She is one of the keys needed to restore a modified version of the Seven Kings

CHAPTER TWENTY-THREE

Bond. However, when time continued to pass and Quen did not come home, the plan was altered."

"Altered how?"

"Callen," Radnar warned. His eyes, having never left the imposing creature before them, had noticed the shift in his demeanor. Gone was the tremble of rage that quaked his body, and in its place was an eerie calm. A calm that Radnar had spent too many years in battle cultivating a sixth sense of danger to have missed. Callen was too preoccupied with relinquishing his own guilt to notice the shifting situation unfolding before him.

"Our belief that Averie still held not only the Heart but Quen inside her, as well, presented us with a new theory and opportunity. A soul, even one as exceptional as Averie's, can only contain an Eternal for a short time. Add in harboring a Creator, and her time was cut exponentially." Callen ran a hand through his hair and shook his head. "The fact that she has lasted this long is astounding. Unheard of."

"Get on with it," Feliks urged.

Callen cleared his throat and met Feliks's gaze. "We assumed the moment she stepped from her Realm into this one, she would cease to exist, freeing both Quen and the Heart. We believed we were right when Averie's power exploded across the Realm the night she appeared."

Three things happened in the span of a single blink. First, Snip and Hex took several steps back, leaving plenty of room between them, Feliks, and Callen. Second, a shadow stepped from the opened door. Third, Feliks released a furious, guttural roar that threatened the integrity of everyone's eardrums before charging into Callen. His essence collided with Callen's so fiercely that Callen was thrown into the mountain wall before disappearing entirely.

Callen felt every snap, pop, and crack of his bones as Feliks's parting fury imbedded him into the Dark Mountain. Soul-wrenching pain burned through him for agonizing moments before the reprieve of unconsciousness pulled him into its abyss.

Words, distant and without full appreciation, filtered into his groggy mind as he drifted in and out of consciousness.

"This is your fault."

"You knew the cost."

"This wasn't supposed to happen."

Somewhere deep within, Callen felt the echo of pain begin to draw him to the surface. A part of him itched to recede back into the safety net of darkness, while the whispered slips of a conversation he wasn't party to scraped against his ears and drew his curiosity, pulling him closer to the surface. The intensity and weight of the context behind the words were fleeting as his pain grew too fierce to be ignored.

"It wasn't supposed to be her!"

"This isn't a game!"

"She isn't a puzzle…"

Callen groaned as the angry voices grew into a louder hush and became closer, punishing him even more than the pounding in his head. The conversation stalled. A throat cleared, and a familiar voice beckoned him.

"Hey, buddy."

Another groan mingled with a whimper at the vicious pain as the words repeated themselves, this time straight into his ear. Callen flinched from the voice and forced his eyes open, the horrid action reminiscent of sandpaper sliding across his cornea. His vision swam as red-and-black pits swirled before him.

"There you are." Snip grinned and pulled back into his eyeline.

Callen's tongue darted out to wet his chapped lips as his eyes slipped shut once more. "What happened?" he croaked.

Hex chuckled. "You really messed up, antagonizing a god."

His eyes shot open, the pain bringing water to his burning gaze. "God?"

Snip shrugged. "I mean, we don't know what he *really* is, but god is the best word we can use."

"How do I not know of him?" Callen pondered.

Hex cleared his throat. "Let's call him a first draft."

Callen forced himself into a sitting position and narrowed his eyes as the memories became clearer. "How did he get in?" Callen demanded.

Hex sat back on his heels and smirked. "I let him in."

"Why would you do that?"

Hex shrugged. "Because you deserved it. I told you I didn't agree with what you wanted to do in the first place."

"And yet you went along with it."

"At least with what I did, there is a chance that she survives."

"At least one person wants me alive."

One by one the group straightened and snapped their heads to the side. There, Averie stood staring, her arms by her sides and fists clenched, as she held a searing and molten stare on Callen, with Feliks at her side.

With placating hands lifted, Callen carefully rose to his feet, and before he could finish uttering her name, for the second time in one afternoon, Callen was thrown into the Dark Mountain wall.

Chapter Twenty-Four

"Stars, Averie!" Radnar gasped. "What are you doing? We cannot turn on each other now!"

Averie swung back with hate in her eyes. "We can't turn on each other *now*? Where was that mentality when you were hoping for my death? Or when you ripped me away from my life for this crumbling world!?"

Radnar jerked back at the loathing in her eyes and the venom in her words. "Averie…"

Averie lifted an expectant brow as she waited, nearly begging for him to give excuses. When none came, a disgusted sound left her lips before she turned and slipped through the tunnel she had created with Callen's body.

"She will never forgive herself if she kills him," Radnar whispered.

Feliks eyed the older, war-ragged man with surprise. "She may not have in the past, but she is not who you have known."

"We were only trying to help. We didn't know what else to do. If she lost control…" Radnar shook his head. The outcome was too much to bear even thinking about. "She will never forgive us."

"We are all far beyond forgiveness now."

Radnar watched Feliks follow Averie while his haunting last words echoed over and over again in his mind. "What have we done?" Radnar asked himself once more.

Callen burst through the mountainside and rolled head over foot across the ground, leaving large craters where his body hit. When he finally came to a stop, he had nearly uprooted a tree from his impact. He hissed a breath through his teeth and quickly took stock of his body. Warmth began to trace the sides of his head, his left leg was bent at a strange angle, his arms were heavy, likely broken as well, and his back was covered in deep gashes with twigs and stones embedded deep within, at least if the bone-deep burn was any indication.

Gritting his teeth, he forced his hands through the Realm's rough surface and let the healing properties that birthed him enter the twisted and torn flesh of his hands. The thump of angry steps told him Averie had left the mountain and was striding purposefully toward him. With no other choice, he forced along his healing process and barely managed to hold back his outcry as his bones snapped back into place. With his newly restored arms mobile, he closed his eyes and used his abilities to peel chunks of the rich soil from the ground to crush against his torn back.

"Would you like to explain yourself before or after I have ripped you limb from limb?" Averie asked, her voice shaking with repressed emotion.

"Averie wait," Snip pleaded. His hand reached out to catch her arm and was quickly batted away by Feliks. "Let us explain."

"You have done enough," Feliks ground out.

Callen peeled his eyes open and sighed as the last of his flesh stitched itself together, leaving only the familiar tingling behind. "Snip, stop. She deserves the truth."

"Yes, *she* does," Averie grit.

The twins flinched, their eyes anywhere but on her. Callen swallowed through the lump in his throat and spilled the whole story.

By the time Callen had stopped speaking, Averie was quaking with rage. Her vision was covered with a golden haze, and her teeth were gnashed so tightly she feared for their integrity. With each word, he uttered the reality of Emma's story, and Averie's dreams unfurled. The tightening in her chest made her words rumble. "You did *what?*" she bit out.

Callen flinched at the venom in her words. "We thought we were helping."

Hex cursed under his breath. "Get Orion," he ordered Snip. Snip sent an apologetic look in Averie's direction before stepping back and disappearing.

"HELPING?!" she shrieked. "Helping is *talking*," she spat and shoved her hand forward, launching a nearby boulder toward his chest. "Helping is screaming, fighting, *loving* someone through it." Averie twisted her hands until both palms were facing up, and slowly, shakingly, they rose, and so did a sizeable chunk of the ground that separated them. "Helping is being there!" With her arms now quaking above her head, she flung them forward and cast the earth hurtling toward Callen.

Callen grunted beneath the weight as he pushed his own power against hers to avoid being crushed. By the time he forced the earth to the side, Averie had launched herself into the air and was descending upon him with every bit of hurt and fury she felt.

She was merciless. Her movements were calculated and executed with vicious precision. Like a cat toying with a mouse, she ripped and tore her way through his quick defenses. At first, Callen was willing to let her vent her anger. He only blocked fatal blows but accepted the others. But a well-placed punch in his gut followed by the slice of her blade against his cheek was the final straw. Gone was her anger, and

CHAPTER TWENTY-FOUR

in its place were the familiar, frantic movements that belong to a single devastating character. *She is letting the Heart take control.*

"Enough!" Callen bellowed. A burning blast of raw power accented his outcry and sent her reeling backward.

Averie's feet slid along the ground, her heels digging into the grass and leaving dual trenches. When at last she stopped, she dropped her head back and caught his eye.

Averie narrowed her eyes as an unnatural shadow attempted to slither from sight. Without conscious thought, she lurched forward and separated its wispy form from the ground and forced it into a more solid state. Gone was the formless shadow, and in its place was a thick, snakelike body with four short arms that ended with three taloned fingers.

"How long have you been following us? What have you heard?" she asked.

The creature squirmed in her hand, eager to be free but silent in answer. Averie tightened her hand until black liquid seeped across her fingers. "I'll give you one more chance to answer. Are you going to take it or die here and now?"

Silence was the poor stitched creature's continued response. Averie growled and hissed as her nails dug into the stitched flesh. A gargled cry slipped from the wiggling creature in her grasp as her victim's hands clawed at her own. Disgust distorted her features as she sneered into the bulging, empty pits of its eyes. A quick jerk of her wrist sent chilled liquid splashing across her chest and face as the being crumpled in her hold. Revulsion pulled a scoff from her throat as she let the corpse drop to the ground.

Callen stood stoically and watched Averie's futile attempt to shake the liquid from her hand. "This is not you," he said into the silence.

A warped smile pulled her cheeks as her hand tightened on the struggling form in her grip. "What's wrong, Callen? You don't like what you've made me?"

Callen shook his head. "We did not turn you into this. You did."

Averie sighed. Whether from Callen's words or in acceptance of the tar-like substance covering her skin, he wasn't sure. "What did you think would happen when you took away the largest pieces of who I am?"

Callen stiffened, his mask of concern flashing with shock and understanding.

Her smile grew. "Did you think I wouldn't figure it out myself? That I wouldn't notice the way you all watch me? The names you whisper or stories you change when I'm around?" She tsked and shook her head. "You cannot be that naïve, *Eternal One*. You may have finally come clean, but I have always known something was wrong. Emma was the only one brave enough to be honest."

Callen's jaw jumped at the sneered title, and his heart stuttered at the name. "We were trying to help you. She is the reason we needed to at all!"

Averie chuckled and spun on her heel to face him. "You weren't trying to help *me*, Callen. None of you were! You were trying to help yourselves. You couldn't take watching someone so lost in their grief when you needed a weapon! So, you fixed it. Fixed *me*."

ACCEPTANCE

Callen shook his head as he closed the distance between them, his fingers circling her arms. "No, Princess, we were trying to help *you*. You were falling apart. Acting erratic and crumbling beneath the weight of your own grief. Every day you were growing more careless and daring. We were afraid of losing you." Callen's hands slid to hers. "We—*I* wanted to stop your pain."

Averie's stare bore into his, her eyes bouncing between the cerulean pools as she searched for the truth in the depth of his words. She dropped her chin to her chest, but not before Callen noticed her sinking her teeth into her quivering lip. His chest tightened as her shoulders shook.

"Averie…" Callen stopped short as an unexpected sound rang in his ears and bent his lips into a frown. Dark, mocking laughter rumbled in her chest, shaking her shoulders and threatening to draw tears into her eyes. "Averie?"

She shook her head and slipped from his hold to grip her knees as the force of her laughter grew. The sound spilled unrelentingly from her lips. Shaking her head, she straightened and brought a hand to her lips. "I'm sorry…" She chuckled. "But who are you trying to kid right now? Me or yourself?"

Callen shook his head. "I do not understand."

Averie's laughter came to an abrupt halt as her face fell into an unemotional mask once more. "Isn't it obvious? You guys took a shortcut and called it helping. When you took him away from me, *again,* you took who he made me. Wiped away every lesson he taught and the lessons I'd learned." Averie stepped back and spread her arms wide. "You didn't help, Callen. None of you did. You took the easy way out, and now I'm paying the price."

Chapter Twenty-Five

Unease bunched the muscles in his abdomen, a warning a moment too late, as Averie sent a powerful blast, slamming into his body and throwing him from his feet. Callen flew across the scarred lands. His mind stuttered, rebelling against his newfound reality, while his body leapt into conditioned action. The muscle memory of centuries of training, battle, and war moved him with no thought.

His body twisted midair, his stomach inches from the ground when he dropped his feet onto the battle-laden soil. His hand plunged into the surface, slowing his retreat. Sweat beaded his brow, and air lashed at the burnt flesh on his chest. An angry roar tore from his lungs as he pushed himself against her blast. His breath was heavy and labored by the time he managed to stop himself completely.

Slowly he rose to his feet, his legs threatening to buckle beneath his own weight, and he dragged himself to his full height. When he lifted his head, the soft cerulean blue that had consoled Averie was gone, replaced by the liquid silver of war.

Averie charged again, the ground shifting with every step, and threw her arms forward. Spikes of rock shot out, ripping the ground apart and attempting to impale Callen. Jumping back, he threw his body backward, twisting between the rising pillars before landing in a crouch.

Averie dropped her head to the side as Callen straightened. She was surprised he could move at all, considering the force behind her blast and the fact that she had caught him off guard.

"Stop this, Averie."

"Or what? What could you possibly do to me?! I have nothing left for you to take, Callen!"

"Mistakes have been made! We have lived every day in remorse for what was done, but we believed we were helping you!"

ACCEPTANCE

Averie pulled her arm back and pooled the power of the Heart into her hand before launching it like a baseball in Callen's direction. "Then you talk!" she screamed, winding up for another. "You don't take pieces of someone away!"

Callen lurched to the side, expertly dodging the first ... or so he thought. The moment the golden ball hit the ground, it detonated, reminding him of Thane's misdeed with the Dragon's Ash. Callen cursed under his breath as the second came flying toward his head. Taking a chance, Callen prepared himself to catch the golden ball and sent a silent thanks to the Stars when it didn't explode. His feet dug into the earth as the force propelled him backward. His arm reeled back, the strain pulling in his shoulder, and with a loud grunt, he thrust it forward.

"We tried!" he snapped. "You were not in your right mind!"

Unprepared for Callen's full counter, Averie cursed under her breath and dropped her body to the ground. The air burned the tops of her arms as they rose to shield her head. Debris and Shadowed parts rained down upon her, covering her in grime, dirt, and the unthinkable.

The still air shifted, and Averie rolled to the side a moment before Callen's body collided with her own. As she rolled onto her back, his hand circled her ankle and pulled her forward. Anger thrummed in her veins, washing away the sting of rocks grinding against the exposed skin of her back.

Callen was on her in a moment, trapping her between his powerful thighs and binding her hands to the ground. "ENOUGH!" he bellowed into her face.

"Never," she seethed.

"I am sorry! If I had known what you would become..." Callen looked away, disgust for himself blazing in his molten eyes.

The pounding of footsteps slapped against the brutalized earth and drew their attention a moment before Radnar rammed Callen from atop Averie. "What in Fornax is going on?" he demanded, his chest rising with hasty breaths as he glared between the pair. Averie stared listlessly up at the pure blue sky while Callen slowly rose to a sitting position.

Callen ran a hand through his hair and looked off into the distance as Snip and Hex rushed to Averie, each holding out a hand. "Averie?" Snip asked as several still moments slipped by.

Averie shook her head, her eyes lost in the rich blue sky. "I knew something was missing. From the moment my eyes opened, I could feel it."

Callen flinched. Radnar hissed, and the twins remained immobile. "The worst part is, I'm not even angry at you, at any of you. I'm angry with myself. I'm angry that someone that was so important, someone that was such a big part of my life, was taken away, and I feel *nothing*. I don't miss his face or the sound of his voice. I don't miss his laugh or his touch or even care that he isn't here right now, and if I'm being honest, *that* is what hurts." Forcing herself to her feet, Averie brushed herself off. "The truth is, if you cared about me, any of you, you would know, without a doubt, I would never have chosen this path. I would have rather died than let you take away someone that meant so much to me, regardless of how much it hurt." With her last

CHAPTER TWENTY-FIVE

words ringing in the air, Averie turned and disappeared into the forest. She ignored the outcries of protest and pleas for her to stay.

"Damnit!" Feliks snapped. "We cannot let her go."

"No," Callen said with enough force to stop each man in their tracks and turn their attention back to him. "What she said is the truth."

Radnar shook his head. "Callen, you did what you thought was right. We all did. It was a decision we all made. One that *I* originally brought up."

Callen shook his head. "You are mistaken. I always knew it was an option. I just did not want it to be."

Hex stepped forward with a frown as Radnar spoke the words that clung to the tip of his tongue. "What have you been hiding from us, Eternal One?"

For the second time that day, Callen spilled another secret.

Chapter Twenty-Six

Before the Battle at Black Mountain — Callen and Averie

"You cannot keep doing this, Averie." Callen's voice severed the silence of night and ended what Averie thought was an unnoticed entrance back into the Black Mountain and into her room.

She sighed. "What do you want, Callen?"

Callen stepped from the shadows with pity in his eyes. "I want you to stop putting yourself in danger."

Averie released a humorless chuckle. "Danger implies that someone has something to lose. A life, a loved one. But not me; I have nothing left. Not even a life."

"That is not true, Averie. You still have so much to lose."

"Do you believe in revenge?" she asked, changing the subject he so desperately wanted to finish.

Callen sighed and ran a hand through his tussled tresses. "I do."

"Thane used to watch a movie—I can't remember the name of it now—but one of the lines keeps repeating over and over again in my head."

"What is it?"

"'*I roared, and I rampaged, and I got bloody satisfaction.*'"

"And have you? Gotten your satisfaction?"

Averie shook her head. "No. But now I have a purpose."

Callen stiffened, not liking the direction this conversation had taken. "What purpose is that?"

"Revenge."

Callen shook his head. "That is a dark path to walk."

CHAPTER TWENTY-SIX

"Mhmm. They say those that seek revenge should dig two graves. Do you think that is true?"

"Depends on what the reason for that revenge is."

Averie lifted a brow. "Is there any better reason than the loss of a loved one? What other high honor can you offer them?"

"Sometimes, there is honor in revenge. Others, it is to serve a selfish purpose."

Averie nodded and bit the inside of her cheek to stop the sudden wave of emotion as her eyes watered, and she fought against the burn of tears. "And how do you know when it is honorable and when it is selfish?"

Callen watched as something dark began to build within her emerald eyes. Flashes of purple flashed and cracked like lighting across the glowing surface. A storm was brewing inside her, one so fierce she began to clench and unclench her fists to remain in control. Callen took her hand in his. "Revenge is honorable when it is to right a wrong, to teach a lesson, so the wrongdoer learns the most valuable consequences of their actions. It is wrong when it, too, is done in darkness."

"Thane is dead," Averie whispered.

"I know."

"Someone *will* pay, Callen. Someone *has to* pay for taking him away!" Averie screamed into the night, her pain a physical manifestation in the world around them.

"Averie, you need to breathe," Callen soothed. Taking her arms in his hands, he turned her to face him. "Averie, look at me."

Averie shook her head, her eyes clenched tightly closed. "I can't do this without him. He promised. He promised he would never leave me."

"He has not left you, Averie. His appearance may have changed, but he is always with you."

"We left him back there." Averie's broken sob had her trembling in his arms.

Ah, it is more than Thane's death. She feels guilty for leaving him behind. Callen's chest ached at the memory.

Tears were flowing like never-ending streams down her cheeks, leaving bright red trails in their wake. There were no sobs or hiccups, no tremors in her shoulders or stutters in her breath, only tears and the gentle rustling of her breeze in the room.

"I know it hurts. Every breath and beat of your heart. But life is not over. Your life is not over, and I promise that one day the pain will lessen, and you will live more deeply than you ever have before. Because you will be living for yourself and for Thane."

Averie shook her head, a humorless chuckle passing her lips. "That's where you're wrong. It doesn't hurt, Callen, but Stars how I wish it did. This feeling. It's not pain. It's something that cuts so much deeper than any pain ever could. It's something darker than any agony and more consuming than any other emotion. It doesn't hurt, Callen. It is a void that is slowly devouring any trace of soul that I had left. I pray for the pain to come because pain shows you that you are still alive. That you exist. But this, what I *feel*, only shows me what I have lost."

ACCEPTANCE

Callen's brow furrowed as he struggled to put the pieces of what she was feeling together. "So, to feel something, you go after the Shadowed. You use the adrenaline of battle to replace the emptiness you feel."

Averie shrugged and dropped herself to her bed and pulled her feet free of the ichor-covered shoes. "It's easier."

Callen smiled as he watched her perform the simple, *normal* action. "Sometimes choosing the path that appears to be smoother is not always the best choice." He lifted his eyes from her destroyed shoes to meet Averie's jade. "Sometimes you need the misery to understand the joy that you once held so carelessly so that you may seek it out once again. It is okay to be mad. It is okay to be sad and miserable and to hate the world that you have been brought into, but it is not okay to give up and let it swallow you whole. Embrace your agony, Averie. Wallow in it. Let the despair drag you into the endless depths of grief, and know that when you cannot breathe anymore, we will be there. Know that *I* will be there to pull you back. Look up and realize that we are here for you. You are not alone."

Averie closed her eyes against the assaulting wave brought on by his words and swallowed through the pain.

"There is no cure for grief, Averie. There is no shortcut. Only time and its cruel game. You are not alone in this loss. You are not the only one who feels his loss like a pit in their soul. The pain you feel, I feel it, too. The pain eats me, like acid in my veins, creating a cavernous void." Callen dropped to one knee in front of her and drew her hand into his.

"I'm alone," she whispered. "I'm walking this path alone. Living this life alone."

Callen squeezed her hand. "Everyone is alone. Whether it is when you are surrounded by a crowd or sitting alone in your room. That is what grief does to you. That is what grief makes you feel. It corrupts your mind and twists your insecurities until you are suffocating. Grief is having to swallow the love you can no longer show to the ones you have lost. To live each day knowing the experiences you dreamed of will never come. But that does not mean you give in to it."

"I don't know if I can do this anymore."

Callen leaned forward and tipped her chin until their eyes met. "When you cannot go on anymore, draw strength from me. When you feel like the weight is too heavy to bear, I will carry it for you. You are strong, Averie. Stronger than what has happened to you. You were made for this."

"You're wrong. It's not that I can't survive this. I don't want to."

Callen sucked in a vicious breath and let his eyes close against the implication of her words. When he had finally regained control, he caught her eye once more. "If there was a way to take away the pain, would you do it?"

Averie sniffled and wiped the tears from her cheeks. "What do you mean?"

"If I could find a way to make the pain stop, a way that would give you the chance to live on without the weight of your grief, would you take that chance?"

Averie looked off and lost herself in the depths of the Dark Mountain walls. She remained in silent thought for so long Callen had begun to wonder if he overstepped.

CHAPTER TWENTY-SIX

If he had pushed too far, too fast when, finally, she met his eye and shook her head. "No."

Callen blinked back his shock and frowned. "No? I do not understand. Why would you choose this pain over being free of it?"

Averie looked at him with a sad smile. "Because the only way for the pain to stop would be for me to have never loved him at all, and nothing, not even knowing that this would be the end result, would ever make me regret having him in my life."

Chapter Twenty-Seven

Present

As Callen's confession came to its devastating conclusion, a hushed stillness settled over the world, and anticipation hung heavy in the air. Reality weighed down with a crushing force so fierce not even the wind dared to blow. Birds remained silent in their nests, and predators froze mid-flight.

"You bastard," Hex fumed. His words spurred the breath of those around him. "You knew. You knew the whole time, and you manipulated everything to what you wanted. To what you *knew* she didn't want."

Callen shook his head. "I did not want it. I was against it."

"And yet you switched sides the moment you could!" Hex bellowed.

"How could you?" Radnar whispered. The softness of his words was in great conflict with the anger twisting his features. His eyes flashed a dangerous white as he struggled to control the beast he had locked away so long ago. "I never would have suggested it if I had known you'd *asked her*."

"What is done is done," Feliks interrupted.

All eyes turned to him. "What is that supposed to mean?"

Feliks lifted a brow. "Isn't it obvious?" When the only response was an exchange of glances, he sighed. "You cannot change the past. Whether or not the conversation happened, the consequences have not changed. What we need to do now is find a way to remove the Heart, *safely*, before Averie loses whatever is left of herself."

"And how do you suggest we do that?" Radnar asked.

Feliks stiffened. "There is always a way."

CHAPTER TWENTY-SEVEN

Radnar's rough voice filled the air with a grunt as he absentmindedly ran his hand over his unkempt beard. "Of course. But do you know what it is? I'm not sure if you have noticed, but we are running a little thin on time here."

Feliks shook his head. "Not yet. But I believe there is a way. This world was created with the promise of balance. To allow the Heart in, there must be a way out."

"There was," Callen explained. "But when she crossed into the other Realm, something happened, and the Heart was never removed. Because of this, the Heart has grown more ingrained in Averie than ever before."

Feliks frowned, not quite grasping the gravity of Callen's words.

"There was more at play than anyone knew," Hex explained. "The husband and wife that Solara had entrusted Averie and the Heart with had already partnered with Sera. Because of this, the Heart was left inside of her, and the time that would have been safest to remove the Heart has long since passed."

Feliks shook his head. "That is not possible. The Heart cannot reside inside a human body."

Hex lifted a hand. "Hence our current predicament."

As he processed this new information, Feliks viewed the situation from a new perspective. Gradually, the pieces of the puzzle started to fall into place. "That is how Averie was able to come to me," he mumbled aloud. "No one else could have; otherwise, they would have simply died when their essence left their body. But because the Heart was there, her body survived." Feliks met Hex's burning gaze and narrowed his own at the subtle shake of his head.

"But you said that Averie is gone. That she died the moment Thane was taken away. Are you taking that back now?" Radnar asked.

Feliks shook his head. "No, merely amending it. There might still be a way to get Averie back. To get *all* of her back."

Marcus chose this time to slip through the large opening that Averie had made with Callen's body in the Black Mountain, the sounds of rustling leaves and distant birdsong filling the air in contrast to the tense conversation taking place. "I see, once again, I have missed all the fun," he sighed. His eyes swept over Callen's wounded body and noted the stiffness that everyone else held until he settled on the winged man and lifted a brow. "You're new." His black eyes flashed, their dark depths pulsed and swirled until they took over completely, then swiftly returned to normal. "And not quite from this plane."

A smirk played on Feliks's lips as he tilted his head to get a better look at the white-haired intruder. His body thrummed as Hex, Radnar, and Callen's irritation and disgust for the man filled the air. *Only a select few of the fallen can read a person's origins with a mere glance. The Nephilim have long since left this Realm and claimed one for themselves. No, he's not of their kind. A Traveler?* Feliks snorted. *No. Not with those eyes. Then that only leaves...* "Death Walker. I see that your kind has not died out as much as I had hoped. Just how did you come to be with this merry band?"

Marcus shrugged. "Options have been low as of late."

ACCEPTANCE

Radnar growled. "Careful, Marcus, your true colors are showing."

Marcus quirked an amused brow. "Have I ever pretended to be anything other than what I am?"

Radnar clenched his jaw but quickly covered his irritation with a casual stroking of his beard. "Don't worry, Marcus. We all know what cloth you were cut from."

With his hands clasped behind his back, Marcus shifted his weight and rocked back on his heels. Lifting his chin, he smiled a wide, toothy, knowing smile that had Hex narrowing his eyes, Radnar rolling his, and Callen and Feliks slamming down a stony mask. "That is good to hear, Radnar. But the real reason I've interrupted your jolly little chat is because I, and a rather nagging woman, couldn't help but overhear that you were searching for a way to save Averie. And while I think it is a fruitless endeavor, she believes otherwise."

Callen frowned. "I believe you speak of Solara, and yet she is nowhere to be found."

Marcus sighed. "Yes, you are right. She is off taking care of something in exchange for me sharing this message. Meet tomorrow morning in..." He paused and glanced back at the destroyed makeshift war room. "Well, in there. Once it's been fixed, of course."

"Why should we do that?" Feliks questioned.

Marcus shrugged. "Do it or not. I don't care. I have fulfilled my part of the bargain." He hesitated in his retreat. "If I cared, I would tell you that it is in your best interest, and Averie's, to show. I'd bring her along, too. We wouldn't want any more secrets taking root between you all, now would we?"

"Wait!" Radnar snapped, stopping Marcus in his tracks. "What do you have Solara doing for you?"

Marcus winked over his shoulder. "Wouldn't you like to know?"

Radnar grit his teeth, feeling a surge of frustration as he watched Marcus disappear. "He's up to something."

Hex chuckled and crossed his arms. "Isn't he always?"

"We need to be there in the morning. I will retrieve Averie. The rest of you should get some rest before then," Feliks decided.

Hex stepped into Feliks's path. "No."

"No?"

"You need to give her time. We all need to give her time. Let her return when she wishes. Until then, we should do as you suggested. Rest, eat, and in your case," Hex stopped and sent Callen a pointed look, "heal. We will meet back here tomorrow."

A wave of rebellion surged through the crowd as they grappled with Hex's commands. The tension hung in the air for what felt like an eternity until Feliks forced down his own want and led the way, breaking the stalemate. "Fine, I'll leave her. For now. If she is not back by sunup, then I will bring her back."

Dismissing the matter with a shrug, Hex shifted his focus to meticulously mending the Black Mountain. "Whatever. Now, can you all go inside so I can begin?"

Chapter Twenty-Eight

Averie wandered aimlessly through the forest. Her mind was a mixture of disbelief at the path her life had taken and sorrow for the innocent girl she was before. The hollowness that had once thrummed in the background now beat soundly in her chest at the revelation of her situation.

She wasn't sure how much time had passed or which direction she had gone. All she knew was that, when she finally came to a stop, the crashing of water filled the air and all around her was a familiar spring.

"Averie, what are you doing here?" Naiya's twinkling voice rose above the waterfall.

Averie blinked free of her tumultuous thoughts and fell to her knees.

"Averie!" Panic and worry echoed in her name alongside the splash of water as Naiya dove beneath the surface, only to break a foot away. Her incandescent skin was even more vibrant under the Realm's sun as she lifted herself onto the thick grass. "Averie, what's happened? Are you alright?"

Averie shook her head. Her eyes burned from the restraint and the force it took to hold back the torrent of tears. "I can't—I don't—"

Naiya leaned forward and wrapped her in a damp but healing embrace. "Shh, it's alright. Everything is going to be okay."

Averie shook her head and clung to the water sprite. "It won't. Nothing will ever be okay again," she sobbed.

Naiya rubbed a hand over Averie's hair and felt her heart clench at the pain in the young one's heart. "Cry it out, Princess, then tell me what happened."

Averie clenched her eyes shut, and for the first time in weeks, she let the sobs rip through her body. With each tear that fell, Averie felt more and more of her turbulent emotions separate and become clear. She was sad for the loss she didn't remember. Distraught for the boy she once knew, the one that had imprinted so deeply on her

ACCEPTANCE

that she couldn't survive without him. Angry for the girl she once was, the girl she had no hope of ever being again. Betrayed by the ones she called family. But more than anything, she was tired. Tired of being the Queen on the chessboard.

When finally her tears had stopped and their salty treks had dried, she pulled back from Naiya, feeling emptier than she had ever imagined. "They took something from me. Or rather, someone. They took him and called it helping."

Naiya leaned forward, fighting to meet Averie's eye. "Who, Averie? Who did they take? Who are they?"

Averie looked up, and Naiya held back her whimper of sorrow. "They took Thane. Radnar, Hex, Snip, and Callen. They took him away from me and effectively killed the person I once was."

Naiya shook her head. "Hex and Snip? No, they wouldn't. I don't understand."

Averie released a sad chuckle. "Only they would, and they did. To be honest, I don't completely understand their reasons myself, and maybe I never will. That's not even the worst part."

"What do you mean?" Naiya whispered. Fear was clear in the quaking of her voice.

"Nothing can be done now. The Heart is taking control. Whether it has been sped up because of what they did or if it was always going to happen this way, I guess we'll never know."

Naiya leaned back, her eyes wide in disbelief and fear. "The Heart?" She shook her head. "No. You can't... You mean... But Averie, if she gets out..."

Averie pursed her lips and nodded. With her gaze locked on the deep plum waterfall, she said, "I know. It means I'm going to die soon."

"Stop it! Don't talk like that!"

Averie flinched at the heat in the kind water sprite's voice. "Naiya..."

Naiya shook her head and clenched her fists. "They won't let that happen! And if they won't stop it, then I will. I'll... I'll... I'll search through the seas of the other Realms until I find someone to help!"

Averie reached forward and took Naiya's trembling, fisted hands within her own. "Please don't worry about me, Naiya. Everything is going to be as it should be. I do not want you to worry about me. I am going to put an end to this senseless war before anything happens to me."

"But Averie..." Naiya began, her eyes filling with tears.

"And besides, who knows? Maybe what everyone thinks is going to happen won't. After all, me and the Heart have been together for a long time now. Maybe she likes me and doesn't want me to die."

"Please don't joke like that, Princess." Naiya was actively crying now, and Averie couldn't help but smile at the sincerity.

"Thank you, Naiya."

Naiya sniffled and wiped the light lavender tears from her eyes. "Why are you thanking me?"

CHAPTER TWENTY-EIGHT

"For letting me come here and cry on your shoulder. And because you are a pretty great friend." Averie teetered her head from side to side. "Aside from the near drowning when we first met."

"But I—" Naiya grinned at the wide smile Averie had. With a roll of her eyes, she slid herself back into the water. "I see what you did there, Princess. But I'll have you know, if I wanted to harm you, I would have."

Averie's grin broadened. "Yeah, yeah. Sure, you could."

Naiya laid her arms against the shore and rested her head atop them. "So, what do you plan to do now?"

Averie rose to her feet and brushed the debris from her clothes. "Now, I find my way back and figure out a way to end this once and for all."

Naiya frowned. "What about the guys?"

Averie clenched her fists at her sides. "What about them?"

"What are you going to do?"

"What else can I do? I'm going to shove all this way down, bury it as deep as I can, and cover it with the promise that one day, maybe, but probably not, I'll deal with it. Right now, I have bigger issues. The night Sera has waited for is approaching, and I don't have time to sulk over petty squabbles."

Oh, Averie. Slowly, Naiya dipped her head in understanding and traced an unknown design along her arm. "Feliks is gone."

Averie lifted a brow in surprise. "I know."

"He's found you already, hasn't he?"

"Is there something you want to say?"

Naiya looked up with a warning in her purple gaze. "Things are not what they seem, Averie. *People* are not what they seem."

Averie watched Naiya for several moments before tipping her head. "Alright, then. I'll keep that in mind."

"See that you do. I look forward to another visit in the future." With that, Naiya turned and dove deep beneath the water, leaving Averie reeling with a new, more terrifying question. Was anyone as they seemed, or were they all hiding behind their own plans?

CHAPTER TWENTY-NINE

"Averie?"

Averie groaned at the musical voice. She was tired. So very tired. How many restless nights did this one make? If she wasn't fighting, she was preparing to fight. If she wasn't sleeping, she was wishing she was, and now she was being woken up again.

"Averie, what are you doing here?"

Averie frowned. "Doing where?" she asked, peeling her eyes open. It wasn't the shock of seeing a violet sky where the twinkling ceiling of her room should be that frightened her the most. It was the consequences of jerking in shock that did it. The moment her body tensed, she was pulled into the watery depths she hadn't realized she was floating in.

Frantic, she forced herself to the surface, breaking free with a sputtering gasp for air.

"Stars, Averie! Are you alright?"

Averie spun herself in the water and met the worried purple gaze. "Naiya? What are you doing here? What am I doing here?"

Naiya lifted a pale brow. "That's what I want to know."

"Averie!" a male voice beckoned.

Averie's frown deepened as the blood drained from Naiya's already pale face. "Naiya? Are you alright?"

Naiya swallowed through her nerves and plastered on a fake smile. "Of course. I have to go, and so do you."

"What do you mean? Where am I?"

Naiya's lips pressed into a thin line. After a quick squeeze of Averie's hand, she disappeared beneath the water.

"Averie?"

CHAPTER TWENTY-NINE

The deep timbre finally registered in Averie's confused mind. Her heart slammed anxiously against her chest as she shifted in the water. "Feliks," she breathed.

His smile was as blinding as the worry in his eyes was shadowed. "We should talk."

The overwhelming sense of déjà vu pounded against her skull as her body moved forward. The scene continued to unfold, her words tumbling free as though she were trapped in a part she never agreed to play.

Dizziness and warmth washed over her, jerking her back to the present. Feliks's arms tightened around her, and the frantic thump of his heartbeat thrummed against her cheek.

"I need you to focus now, okay? Averie, look at me!" he ordered. Averie opened her eyes and forced herself to meet his gaze. "Things are going to be happening very quickly where you are headed. You need to remember not to forget yourself. Not even for a moment. You have been gone too long. The shift may not be felt right away, but it is there. The Heart has a plan for you, so do not let it deceive you."

"The Heart?" she asked through a heavy tongue.

"Averie!" he snapped. Averie lifted her eyes to his and felt his worry and fear. "Don't forget about this place, okay? Promise me."

Her head dropped in agreement while her eyes stayed fixed on his, both a viewer and participant in one. "Promise."

A pulse shook her body, separating her mind from the scene. Averie watched herself drift in and out as Feliks spoke. His hand rose to cup her cheek, and his thumb ran along her cheekbone as he said the words she never remembered hearing. "I won't let the Heart take you away again. I have fought too hard and searched too long to lose this piece of you. Don't listen to anything it says, do you hear me? No matter what happens. I don't care how bad things get; you can't give up. You can't give in. I am going to save you. Do you understand?"

Averie shot up in bed. Another experience all too real to be a dream. "Damnit," she cursed, her heart thumping erratically in her chest and sweat dripping down the sides of her face.

This time she knew the reason. Feliks had walked back into her life just days ago, and her mind was still putting the pieces together after having so many secrets thrust into the light.

It was late when she had crept back into the Black Mountain. Feliks had been nowhere to be found, and neither had anyone else—something she was sure that the twins had a hand in. Averie pushed the twisted blankets from her body and heaved herself to the bed's edge. "I'm so tired of this," she whispered into the dark. "I just want it all to stop."

ACCEPTANCE

Shaking free of the depressive thoughts, she padded to the nearby sink. A wave of her hand had cool, crisp water pouring from a flower's pistil. After a few seconds, she cupped her hands beneath the spray and splashed it over her face. The chill shook the rest of the sleep from her mind.

Satisfied she had washed the lingering threads of her dream away and had safely stashed the ever-mounting number of questions somewhere deep inside, she reached to the side and plucked the fluffy towel from a waiting vine and dried her face.

It wasn't until she had straightened that she reopened her eyes and hissed when a harsh light burned against her corneas. With a groan, she turned her face to the side and blinked the spots from her vision. Confusion twisted her features as curiosity pulled her eyes back to the mirror.

A world shimmered deep inside. Gone was the reflection of her silken sheets and twisted comforter. A never-ending expanse of cerulean and shamrock replaced the stone walls. A meadow stretched beneath her body, the sea of green rolling over smooth hills. The shadow of a forest darkened into the richest hues as the massive trees stretched high against the pure sky.

"What in Fornax…" Her words trailed, drifting away on a soft breeze as they left her still-parted lips.

Her eyes were wide with wonder and awe as she leaned forward in a daze. She narrowed her eyes slowly, absorbing more of the world that spread before her with every pass. Red, purple, and yellow were dotted elegantly among the sea of green, as if a painter had taken his mighty brush and deemed the addition of color necessary.

The sun was high, bright, and comfortably warm as its rays stretched down and pierced the mirror to warm her skin. The sky above was clear, beautiful, and vividly shaded with every blue Averie had ever encountered. The horizon tempted night in its deep navy before it faded as it stretched, the spots nearest the sun mocking white in their richness.

"Having fun?"

The sudden voice jerked Averie's spine straight as the words and tone settled against her ears. The anger-laced words chilled the air. Slowly, she shifted her attention, committing every blade of grass and rustle of leaves to memory before she turned and found herself staring back.

Averie narrowed her eyes, surprise squeezing her chest when her mirror image did not do the same. "Who are you?"

Mirror crossed her arms over her chest, her brow rising familiarly. "Did you grow dense when I was sent away?"

"What are you talking about?"

"I'm you. The real you. The you that you were before Quen disappeared and the Heart began to take control. The you that always should have been but was sent away the moment you returned to this place, and I think it's time you and I had a talk."

Chapter Thirty

Averie swept her eyes over the mirror image. Her hand lifted and jerked back once she touched the cool, reflective surface. The similarities were much like one would find when glancing directly into their reflection, only the background and sneer of Averie's mirrored self told her something was certainly off. Her hair was the same shade and length, and her body held the same shimmering, golden scars. Her fingernails were clean, if not uneven from lack of attention. She wore a black t-shirt and torn jeans with the recognized, favorite pair of Converse, including the scuffs that never seem to come out, no matter how hard she scrubbed.

Averie completed her inspection and lifted her eyes to meet her mirrored ones. Though both pairs of eyes were vivid emerald, one pair held a thin, golden line that circled the iris, while the other's was circled purple, narrowed, and simmering.

"Are you satisfied with your inspection?" Mirror sneered.

Averie dropped her head to the side with a knowing smile. "You're not me."

Mirror lifted a hand and began to inspect her torn nail bed with a mask of boredom and a shrug. "True. I'm the *real* you. The original." She ended with a smirk.

Averie tossed her head back with a boisterous laugh and shook her head. "No. You are a cheap imitation." Averie rose to her toes and twisted to search her bedroom. "Alright, Sera. Come on out," she called, lifting the edge of her blanket to search underneath the bed. "You almost had me. Haven't you grown tired of the same old tricks?"

Her mirrored self hissed a vicious breath. The sound was harsh as it was forced through her clenched teeth. "Are you done?" demanded her mirror self. Averie shifted from her spot on the ground and let her blanket fall back into place as she made her way back to the fuming version of herself.

The wind whistled as the temperature on both planes plummeted, and gray clouds filled the previously pristine sky. Mirror stalked forward with fists clenched tightly at her sides as she leaned toward the reflective surface. "Don't you *dare* speak that person's name here."

Averie shoved to her feet; the Mirror's anger reflected in every beat that thrummed through her body. "I don't know who you are, but this ends now." She called on the well inside and urged it to send its power prickling along her skin. And found it empty.

Her mirrored self smirked. "Didn't I tell you? The only reason you can see me right now is because you have been caught in my in-between. This isn't your world. This is *mine*."

Averie grit her teeth against a demand for answers and instead asked, "What do you want?"

"Isn't it obvious? I want my body back."

Laughter bubbled from her chest and poured from her lips, the laughter growing until she was forced to grip her sides. "You can't be serious."

Mirror stepped forward until she was nearly nose-to-nose with the barrier. "You're damn right I'm serious. I'm not going to stand by and let you destroy everything."

Averie froze. As if ice had replaced the heated blood in her veins, her body filled with icy dread. "What are you talking about?"

Her mirrored self took a soft step forward, the ground quivering beneath her simmering anger. "They took something from you. Aren't you curious as to what or who it was?"

Averie frowned as she thought back to the fog that blanketed her memories. Pieces of her childhood chopped and haphazardly stitched together with a painful thread that pulled every time she tried to dig deeper. Another wave of pain washed over her as Callen's truth, Emma's story, and her own dreams washed through her mind. Averie forced her eyes back to her mirrored self. "No. I don't care. And I don't know what trick you think you are pulling here, but I'm not going to stick around and find out." With her final thoughts spoken, Averie twisted on her heel and strode away. To where, she wasn't sure. She had nowhere she could go in this room, and she certainly didn't want to venture out into the mountain.

"And if I told you they stole the most important person in your life away? What would you say then?"

Averie hesitated. Her mind slowed until it came to a complete stop. She inhaled a deep, calming breath and twirled back. "I would say that you are full of shit. Sera killed my mother, both of them. *They* are the most important people to me."

Mirror dropped her head to the side in consideration. "And what if there was another? One that shaped you in ways that you hadn't even realized until it was taken away? What if the person you know is the consequence of their selfishness?"

It was Averie's turn to smirk. "If you were me, which you're not, then you would know that I am proud of who I am—mistakes, scars, and all."

CHAPTER THIRTY

Mirror pursed her lips and nodded. "True. But if I was you, which I am, then I would also know that you hate secrets and lies and that you have forgiven only three people in the past when they did either to you."

Averie shook her head and rolled her eyes. "Lots of people know that about me."

Her mirrored self stepped forward with a cruel smile. "Name them."

Averie blinked in rapid succession. "Excuse me?"

"Name the people you forgave."

Averie scoffed at the audacity. "And why would I do that?"

Mirror lifted her shoulders in a drawn-out shrug. "Why wouldn't you?"

"Okay, but why *would* I?"

Her mirrored self pinched the bridge of her nose. "Are we doing this right now?"

Averie arched a mocking brow.

"Will you just answer the question! I'm trying to help you!"

"By doing what exactly? Having me tell you that I forgave people for breaking a child's promise? Fine! My mother, Silas, and…" The heat fled from Averie's words as her brow twisted, and a pain shot through her head. Lifting a hand, she pressed it against her forehead. "And … Thane," she whispered, her foot swinging out to swipe against the stone. "There, are you happy? Does it make you happy to know that, while I know that they took him away, I couldn't care less because I don't remember? Because it's as if he never existed for me? Then fine. It doesn't matter, okay? None of it matters. You are just a figment of my imagination. A dream that will disappear as soon as I wake up. You are nothing more than a game someone is playing with my mind."

"You're wrong," her mirrored self whispered. "It does matter. It matters more than you could ever imagine."

Averie pondered the name, tasting it as it rolled over her tongue and tumbled from her lips. "Thane," she repeated. A moment of silence passed as the two stared at one another. Finally, Averie shook her head. "He may have mattered in the past, but he doesn't now."

Her mirrored self closed the distance between them. "You're right. It didn't matter to *you*. It mattered to *me*. Thane was my brother. And when he died, I went a little off the rails with grief. Callen, Radnar, Hex, and Snip, they couldn't stand it, so they took him away and were left with you."

Averie shook her head at the impossibility. "You're wrong. They weren't *left* with me. I am who I was always meant to be, and whether you want to believe that or not is not my problem."

"Am I wrong? Think about it. You haven't noticed a shift in the way you do things? Do you even question their motives when they aim you? Or do you just start firing?"

"You don't know what you're talking about."

"Do you wonder why they call Callen 'Filling'?" She stopped with a shake of her head. "Or who knows, maybe they don't anymore."

ACCEPTANCE

"Don't be ridiculous. Of course, it slips out now and then, but that's because…" Averie stopped, her words trailing once more as confusion and pain twisted her mind.

Her mirrored self clasped her wrists behind her back and smirked. "Exactly." Her mirrored shelf shook her head and ran a hand through her hair. "We've gotten off topic, and I don't have much time left. I think I have a way for us both to make it through this."

Averie frowned. "What do you mean?"

She smirked. "Just how much do you trust yourself?"

CHAPTER THIRTY-ONE

MEMBRANE – THANE

Thane slammed his fist against the invisible barrier. He watched his friends struggle to plan, strategize, and keep going on. But more than that, something was seriously, deeply wrong with Averie. He wasn't sure what it was or how no one else had noticed when he could nearly see it rising from her in a dark, terrible aura. Bags clung under her vacant eyes, and her hair seemed more unruly than usual. On top of that, a man with wings seemed overly friendly toward her, based on the way he stood a little too close and kept brushing his hand along her shoulders.

Thane glared in Callen's direction. "So much for looking after her. Damnit!" he roared and shoved from the barrier. Frustrated, he resumed his pacing, his hands tugging at his hair as his anxiety skyrocketed. Over the last several hours that he had been going between the Realm and the Membrane, he had only been able to catch bits and pieces of what they were talking about, but between what he had learned from Dar just days ago and what he had been able to do, he had no reason not to believe Dar's words.

"The tears are getting larger, more spread out, and staying open longer."
"What does that mean?" Thane asked.
Dar shrugged, though his eyes held an unusual light that mingled both excitement and worry. "I think something terrible is about to happen."

It had taken him a moment of his five-minute run to understand what he had to do. He needed to do anything and everything he could to help Averie.

ACCEPTANCE

"The Heart is unstable? What does that mean?" Averie asked, pulling Thane from his racing thoughts. Her question halted his steps and pulled him back to watch with a furrowed brow.

Solara's explanation poured from her lips as her hands danced eloquently in the air, accenting her explanation. Thane leaned forward with a pinched expression as he fought against the Membrane's pull. "…the bear. When I sent you away, I had to put it somewhere safe."

Thane's eyes widened in understanding. Piece after piece fell together in his mind with a satisfying click. They were talking about the Heart. About finding a safe way to get it out of Averie so that she could continue to live on.

Averie's head dropped in defeat. "The bear is gone. Has been for years. It got ruined in a rainstorm and I…" Her brow pinched as she struggled her way through the distorted memories. "I threw it away."

A memory, forgotten in the turmoil that had become their lives, fluttered to the surface of his mind and played like a movie before him.

"Oh, no!"

Thane jumped to his feet, frantically searching in the darkened room. "What is it? What's wrong?"

"Bear is outside!" she said.

Thane blinked several times in an attempt to understand Averie's urgency. "Okay?"

"He's all alone in the storm," Averie explained, as though the reason for her upset was obvious.

Thane shifted uncomfortably as he searched for something to soothe the distraught girl, before finally settling on, "He'll be fine."

Averie shook her head as she felt her way to the front door. "I can't leave him outside," she whispered, opening the door.

"Averie!" Thane called. "You can't go out there!"

Averie hesitated on the porch. A flash of lightning revealed her drooped shoulders and bowed head. "I can't leave him."

Keep an eye on Averie for me, Karen's words whispered in his ear. *Mumbling about the stupidity of girls, Thane shoved through the screen door and out into the pouring rain. "Wait for me!" he called and raced to her side.*

Averie's broken sniffle echoed in the sudden stillness as she turned tear-stained cheeks. "He's ruined."

Pain squeezed Thane's chest at her forlorn expression. Before he realized what he had done, Thane wrapped his arms around her trembling shoulders and pulled her into a tight hug. "It's okay, Fox. You can get another one."

"No, I can't!" she cried, the warmth of her tears a stark contrast to the frigid raindrops soaking his shirt.

Thane frowned as he thought of the hundreds of stuffed bears he had seen in the stores throughout his life. "Why not?"

"Because my real mom gave him to me. To protect me," she whispered.

Thane's frown deepened at her revelation. "You're real mom?"

CHAPTER THIRTY-ONE

Averie nodded against his shirt. "Karen's my adopted mom."

"I didn't know," he whispered, more to himself than the little girl trembling in his arms.

"I didn't either. Not until last year. That's why I don't like lies. It's not nice when people lie to you."

Thane cleared his throat. "You know, my mom used to say that sometimes people have to lie until the person can understand the truth."

Averie sniffled. "Did your mom ever lie to you?"

"Loads of times." Thane laughed. "She told me that if I didn't eat broccoli once a week, Santa wouldn't leave me any presents."

Averie stepped back with a laugh. "That's so silly. Santa doesn't care about broccoli."

"I know, right? Wait… What?" Thane asked, his brow furrowing as he struggled to comprehend her words.

Averie shrugged as she leaned down to pick up the destroyed stuffed animal. "Santa doesn't care if you eat your vegetables; you just have to be good."

Thane hesitated, as the right words failed once more to come to him. "Yeah … right. Well, we should get back inside."

A heavy sigh lifted Averie's small shoulders as they made their way to the trash can. Tears filled her eyes once more as she ran her fingers over the matted fur. "Who's going to protect me now?" she asked.

Thane shifted from foot to foot before, finally, he took her smaller hand in his own. "I can if you want."

Averie smiled as she released the sopping, lumpy animal into the trash. "Okay. You can be my new Bear."

As Thane led her back toward the house, he couldn't stop his eyes from wandering once, twice, three times to the trash can. He nibbled the inside of his lip as the little girl at his side continued to ramble and long after they had both changed and made themselves comfortable beneath heavy blankets on the lovingly worn couch.

Averie's soft snore pulled his mind to the present and finally stopped his teeth from gnawing at the raw flesh of his lip. Thane looked down at her cherubic face, and his decision was made. Careful not to disturb the sleeping girl, he slipped free of her and tip-toed from the room and into the dark, stormy night. *This is stupid*, he chided himself. *It's just a stuffed animal.* Even as the thought had passed through his mind, he stepped once more into the chilling rain and plucked the pathetic, sopping animal from the trash and carried it inside.

A quick look at the couch told him she was still sleeping and granted him the time he needed to slip into the bathroom, wring out the worn stuffed creature, and tuck it away until morning. *I'll clean it first, then give it to her.*

Thane broke free of the memory and slammed his fist again and again against the invisible space. "Averie!" Still nothing. "FOX!" he thundered. Desperation dripped from the single word, so potent that Thane nearly collapsed from dispelling the emotion when Solara's head jerked in his direction.

133

ACCEPTANCE

Thane stumbled back in shock before a slow smile crept across his face. He leaned forward. Excitement, pure and raw, coursed through his body for the first time since … well, since before his death.

"SOLARA!" he screamed. His fists pounded against the thin barrier that separated them with more intensity and force than he ever had before. Pain didn't matter in this purgatory he found himself trapped in. He would and had spent hours and days pounding against that thin surface, and never had he felt a twinge of hope that it would work. Not until right now. Not since Solara had turned toward his cry.

Solara frowned and dropped her head to the side as she questioned the strange ring that echoed in her ear. All eyes turned to her as their own curiosity peaked. Marcus shifted at her side. "Solara?"

Averie shook Feliks's hand from her wrist and ignored the worried glint in his eyes as she stepped forward. Her eyes flicked around the room as she scoured the space in search of what had caught Solara's attention. "What is it?" she asked as the silence stretched.

"I think…" Solara started, her feet carrying her closer to the unseen in the corner.

"You think what?" Averie urged as she followed her mother.

Feliks, Radnar, and Callen exchanged confused glances before doing the same.

Excitement burst through Thane's chest as he waved his arms in the air—another attempt to catch attention. Even knowing he was invisible to the eye, Thane didn't stop exaggerating the action. "I'm here!" he called. His hands fell to the top of his head as they grew closer and closer. "Avi! I'm right here!"

Solara stopped only inches away as if she, too, had been taken captive by the barrier that had only served to taunt him with real life. Thane smiled and placed his hand against the space. "Come on," he whispered. "*See me*. Solara, I'm *right here*."

Solara's face pinched as she lifted a trembling hand of her own. Carefully, she tapped her fingers through the air, each tap getting her closer and closer to the barrier. Thane's eyes went wide as the barrier shivered, the moment sending a ripple of déjà vu through his body as he remembered Dar doing the same thing. "That's right," he breathed. "Come down, you son of a—"

"Solara?" Averie called, breaking Solara's concentration and making Thane want to curse his sister for the first time in years.

"Damnit Fox! Seriously?" he groaned.

"What is it? What's going on?" Averie asked.

Solara's eyes refocused on the air as she began to trace a strange symbol. "I think… I think something … or rather some*one,* is here."

Chapter Thirty-Two

Averie's eyes flashed as her magic stirred. *Get ready,* she warned herself. Averie reached down and pulled the dark green blades from her boots.

Callen's eyes flashed like the full moon, and Radnar drew his sword, while Feliks frowned and dropped his head to the side. His eyes flashed with pure light before returning to normal. He sighed, crossed his arms, and leaned back against the wall.

"Who?" Radnar growled.

Solara shook her head as her eyes continued to trace the space. "I'm not sure. But I do not think they mean to harm us."

"He doesn't," Feliks chimed.

Thane shook his head. "Hell no," he promised.

"How do you know?" Averie asked.

Feliks shrugged and leaned his head back against the stone. "I know a thing or two about the prisons within the Realm. Once you have been in one, you get … a sense for these things."

Averie sent a scathing glare that nearly screamed, *You are definitely explaining that later,* before she turned back to Solara. "Can you get them out?" Averie asked, her hands shifting on the hilts.

A slow nod began to tip Solara's head, her brief glance to Marcus going unnoticed by everyone except for Thane. Thane turned to glare at Marcus when he found the man already smirking in his direction. "You son of a… You knew I was here the whole time."

Marcus winked.

"I think so," Solara began. "Though if I am being completely honest, I believe we should do a reveal first."

Averie captured the eye of everyone in the room, and only when she received a nod of agreement in return did she say, "Do it."

ACCEPTANCE

Solara took a visible breath and closed her eyes before she extended her other hand toward the barrier and felt it tremble beneath her touch. "Step back," she whispered.

"Me?" Thane asked, his brow pinching briefly as he pointed to himself before shaking his head. "You can't hear me." He sighed. Shrugging, he took a step back anyway.

"What's going on?" Snip's voice severed the tense silence. Everyone in the room whirled to face the intruders, each with a weapon drawn, and pointed in their direction. "Whoa, whoa, whoa! Calm down. We're all friends here."

"Stars, Snip, can't you see they are clearly trying to focus on something?" Orion groaned as everyone dropped their swords and glared in their direction.

"Well then, shouldn't we be filled in?" Snip asked.

Orion rolled his eyes and pulled a batch of strange orange grapes from the bowl on the table and popped one into his mouth. Shrugging, he stepped forward to join the waiting group. "They didn't know you were here. Why would they—or should they—automatically start to fill you in?"

Snip turned with a disappointed look. "Are you saying I am easy to miss?"

Orion snorted. "No. I am saying you just pop in wherever you want, whether people want you there or not. It's really quite rude. Add that to the constant kidnapping, and you are basically an unstoppable stalker/predator."

Snip's shoulders drooped.

Ryan frowned and popped another grape into his mouth, enjoying the strange citrus flavor as it popped over his tongue. "Why are you so sensitive today?"

"I'll have you know—"

"I am trying to concentrate," Solara snapped through clenched teeth.

Averie glanced over her shoulder and pointed a blade to the space. "Solara said there is some*thing* or some*one* there."

Snip clasped his hands behind his back, his lips pursing as he strode across the room and leaned forward with a squint. A wide, toothy smile split his face a second before he began to frantically wave his hand. "Hey, Thane! How are you, man? How did you get in there?"

The room jolted. Eyes widened as they stared at the manically waving twin. "What did you just say?" Callen whispered.

Snip lifted a brow before rolling his eyes. "'Hey, Thane.' You know, the customary way to greet someone you haven't seen in a while." He shook his head and pointed a thumb over his shoulder. "I swear, since you left, he has just completely lost all understanding of human interactions."

Thane chuckled.

Averie frowned at the reactions around her. "Who's Thane? Your Thane?" she asked.

Sorrowful eyes met hers before quickly fleeing.

Thane gasped. His eyes flew to his sister's pinched and confused face. None of the years spent taking blows in the ring or the pain he felt in his last moments on

CHAPTER THIRTY-TWO

Earth could compare to the crumpling feeling that brought him to his knees as those words tumbled from his sister's lips.

Averie's hands flexed on the hilts of her blades. "He isn't a threat, right?"

Callen flinched. "No, Averie. He is not."

An unsettling feeling crawled across her skin. Even with the truth out on the table and stories from all sides, she was something. Something important. Something that had to do with her but was entirely the fault of those she trusted most. "Where is he?"

"Don't worry buddy, I got this," Snip consoled with a wink and saddled up to her side with his signature smirk and a wag of his brow. "If you ask nicely, I'll tell you."

Ryan smacked the back of Snip's head and consumed the last grape. "Don't be an ass, Snip. Show her."

"I would really appreciate it if everyone would stop doing that! I am a human being, or at least close to it, and I deserve to be treated as such." Snip pouted as he rubbed the back of his head and ignored Ryan's snort as he walked forward until he could touch the thin veil. "Don't say I never did anything for you," he whispered, his eyes searing into Thane's eager ones. A light tap of his finger and, like a bubble, the veil burst.

Thane bounced on the tip of his toes, anxiety rippling his spine, as Snip stepped forward and, with a smirk, tapped his finger against the air between them. A burst of wind rushed over Thane's body as the two worlds collided. Thane blinked several times to clear his vision and swept his eyes from one shocked face to the next. "Hey, guys."

Callen rushed forward, his arms stretched as wide as his smile, ready to embrace his friend, when he slipped through him instead. "What...?"

Snip's chuckle was chased by a yelp of surprise as the echo of another slap sounded. "That wasn't very nice," he whined.

Ryan shook his head and looked at Callen. "He's still dead."

Callen's frown deepened as he looked from Snip to Ryan. "Snip temporarily lowered the veil. He didn't bring Thane back to life," Ryan explained.

Calen's sad realization of the situation showed in the defeated slump of his shoulders. "I see."

Thane smiled reassuringly at his friend. "It's okay, Frosting. I'm just glad you guys can finally hear me."

A frown pinched his brow. "Have you been watching us long?"

Thane shook his head, then shrugged. "I'm not sure. Sometimes I'm able to see you guys for hours, other times only minutes. Speaking of which..." Thane peered over Callen's shoulder and scanned for the familiar redhead, his smile stretching wide as they locked eyes. "Hey, Fox. I told you heroes never die."

"You are dead," Callen emphasized, making Thane roll his eyes.

"I'm sorry. Who are you?" Averie asked.

The room noticeably stiffened, diminishing Thane's smile. "Ha ha, you're hilarious. It was all fun and games when you said it before, and I get that it really sucked,

ACCEPTANCE

and you're probably mad at me for making Callen take you away, but… It hasn't been that long. I was worried when you disappeared. I'm glad you're okay."

Averie took a cautionary step forward, her eyes bouncing from one friend to another before each fell away. Shaking her head, she stopped several feet away. "I'm sorry, but I… I don't remember you. A lot has happened. I'm sure you're a great guy but…" Averie shook her head and stepped toward Feliks.

The lifelike color drained from Thane's face as understanding took hold, igniting a vibrant, angry red. "What. Did. You. Do?" he asked, each word more forced and scathing than the next. "And who the hell is he?!"

Chapter Thirty-Three

Thane whirled on Callen. Red crept up his throat and colored his cheeks as his rage took on a life of its own. "You had one job. ONE! All you had to do was keep her safe! And what did you go and do? You let her get hurt and lose her memory! Then, to top it all off, you're working with Marcus and have a damn birdman flapping around her! Oh, you are so lucky I can't touch you right now. Otherwise…"

The man in question stepped forward with an angry glint in his eye. "My name is Feliks, and I will have you know I have taken care of Averie longer than you have been in existence."

Thane snorted and closed the distance between them. "Highly doubtful, considering I'm older than she is. But nice try, *birdman*."

Feliks leaned forward with a devilish smirk. "It's cute you think you have any idea about *any* of her existences."

Thane jerked back. "What the hell is that supposed to mean?"

"That's enough!" Averie snapped as she stepped to Feliks's side and pulled his arm back. Her intention was obvious, and quickly obeyed, as Feliks shot Thane one last warning look before moving back to his place at the wall. "Can we please get back to the issue at hand?" she asked.

"Which was what?" Snip asked before pulling out a chair and plopping down. Leaning forward, he grabbed a handful of the orange grapes and leaned back into his seat. "After all, you guys still haven't filled us in."

Callen narrowed his eyes. "You were not invited. In fact, we haven't seen you in a while."

Snip rolled his eyes. "It was one day. And if you remember, I left on Hex's orders so…" Snip frowned and searched the room. "Speaking of which… Where is my less attractive other half?"

139

ACCEPTANCE

"He left this morning," Radnar answered curtly, his tone brokered no room for further comment as he retook his own seat. "We were discussing the possibility of extracting the Heart, *safely*, from Averie." Radnar stopped and sent Averie a pointed look before continuing. "The options have been extremely limited and, quite frankly, hopeless, if I am being honest."

Thane shook his head and stepped toward the table. "No, you're wrong. Solara was talking about the bear she gave Averie when I came in last time."

"Yes, but I threw that bear away years ago. The odds of finding it in a trash dump are slim to none. Regardless of having magic or not."

Thane shook his head. His mind and heart still struggled with his sister's vacant look every time she glanced in his direction. "That's only half of what happened."

Averie frowned. "What do you mean?"

Thane smiled a sorrow-filled smile and forced his eyes to meet hers. The vibrant green was just as he remembered, only now a thicker golden circle was encroaching on her iris. "That night Karen had to go to work and left me in charge. There was a storm, and you forgot the bear outside. We had just finished watching a scary movie."

Averie wrinkled her nose. "I hate scary movies."

Thane chuckled and ran a hand through his hair. "Yeah, I know, but you were annoying, and I was hoping it would make you go to bed. Anyways, after the movie finished and the thunder and lightning rolled in, you jumped up, freaking out—scared the crap out of me, by the way—but you kept saying you left the bear outside. I tried to tell you that you could just get it tomorrow, but you weren't listening. You ran outside, and you were crying when you found him all dirty and gross and just soaked." Thane rocked back on his heels and jammed his fisted hands into his pockets as he stared up into the dark ceiling. "You made this big deal about not having him to protect you, so I told you I would be your Bear, hence the nickname, since you always wore those stupid fox ears. Then you threw him away. We went upstairs, and after you fell asleep, I couldn't get it out of my head, so I snuck outside and grabbed the stupid thing."

By the end of Thane's story, the room was deathly still, and eyes were glossy around the table. "Then what happened?" Averie asked in a whisper.

Thane shrugged and met his sister's stare once more, his chest squeezing at the genuine sorrow in her eyes. "I cleaned it and stored it in the bottom of my closet, planning to give it back to you one day. Then time started flying, and I forgot about it."

Feliks broke the spell Thane's story had weaved when he leaned forward and demanded, "Is it still there? In your closet?"

Thane tore his eyes away and nodded. "Should be. I never moved it." He winced. "Although…"

Callen frowned. "What is it?"

"We haven't exactly been there in…" Thane blew out another breath and shrugged. "I don't even know if we technically still own it. Especially after the whole tree thing and then the abandoning-the-entire-Realm-to-come-here thing."

CHAPTER THIRTY-THREE

Averie deflated into a nearby chair. Feliks knelt to her level and placed a reassuring hand on her shoulder. "Don't worry. I'll go and see if it is still there."

"What? No. I can't ask you to do that. Not to mention there isn't any other way back to that Realm."

Feliks smirked, and Thane grit his teeth. "You would be surprised what my kind can do."

"And just what kind was that again?" Thane growled. "And how do you know my sister?"

Averie frowned at Thane. "This is Feliks."

Thane leaned forward, expecting more information but receiving none. A humorless chuckle rumbled. "Oh, Feliks. Right. Because that means something."

Feliks rose to his feet with a smirk on his lips and a warning in his eyes. "To some."

"Mhmm." Thane shifted his glare to Callen. "Really? I'm gone a few months, and this is what happens?"

Callen lifted his arms in surrender. "I was already taught my lesson."

"Not well enough, it seems."

Suddenly Snip's laughter burst through the room, capturing everyone's attention. Too lost in his own laughter to speak, Snip shook his head and waved his hands. Ryan shook his head, rolled his eyes, and sighed. "From what I understand, this dude right here," he motioned to Feliks before sliding his hand to Callen, "attacked this dude … yesterday?" he asked, looking to Snip, who, while still lost in the throes of his own laughter, nodded. "Yesterday. Knocked him around pretty good, from what I heard."

"And why did he do that?" Thane asked, his hands clenching and unclenching as he speared Feliks with another glare.

Ryan shrugged and grabbed another handful of the addictive orange grapes. Popping one into his mouth, he leaned back in the chair and made sure to meet Thane's eyes when he said, "The whole memory wipe thing."

The room went still once more. Even Snip's laughter was immediately cut short.

"The what?" Thane growled.

Radnar groaned and dropped his head to the table as Callen slowly rose to his feet, his hands still lifted in surrender as he revealed, once more, the biggest mistake he had made.

Thane was quivering by the time Callen finished the shortened version of what they had done. He hadn't ever thought of himself as a quiverer up to this point, but it turned out he was wrong. Everything in him wanted to rampage. To fight, destroy, and scream. But he did none of those things. Instead, he bit back his scream and nodded his head.

"So, what is the plan now?"

Frowns of varying depths fell upon the room. "I'm sorry," Snip interrupted with his hand raised. "Did you hear what Callen just said?"

ACCEPTANCE

"Yes," Thane snapped. "And I will deal with that when he can actually feel the force of my frustration. Until then, I know that Sera is planning something pretty big, so who wants to share the plan with me?"

"Sera is going to complete her ritual in the next few days," Averie answered.

Thane's eyes flared. "Few days?"

She nodded. "That's what all signs point to."

Thane blew out a breath and ran his hand through his hair. "And is there a plan?"

Averie straightened. "We're working on it."

Thane opened his mouth to speak when his body jolted. "Stars," he cursed.

Callen frowned. "What is it?"

"I have to go."

"Go? Go where?"

"Back to the Membrane."

Feliks stiffened, and Snip and Ryan exchanged glances. "The Membrane?" Feliks asked.

Thane frowned but nodded. "Yeah. The tears are getting bigger over there. That's why I've been able to get through." He frowned. "Though I gotta say, I think this is the longest I've been able to stay."

"Alright, then. When will you come back?" Callen asked.

Thane forced a smile. "Soon." His eyes met each person before settling on Averie. "You guys work out your issues before this battle happens. We are a family. Regardless of what has happened, that hasn't changed. And you..." he snapped, his hand pointed at Feliks, who lifted a brow in return. "Find that damn bear."

Feliks smirked. "Sure thing. I'll be leaving shortly."

"Good. I'll see you all soon."

Everyone rose from their chair, each reluctant to say goodbye but forced to do so once more. As they left the room, Averie hesitated, her hand hovering above its handle. "I'm sorry I don't remember you. Truly."

Thane smirked. The signature move did not quite reach his eyes. "I know, Fox. Don't worry, though. I'm gonna come back, and when I do, I'll share all the stories of our childhood, and then there's no way you won't remember."

Averie smiled at the door. "I would like that."

"Good. Go get some rest."

Chapter Thirty-Four

The group shifted uncomfortably in the far corner of the gathering hall. The last few days had been filled with nothing but wave after wave of revelations and secrets that were forced to the light, leaving each person in their own mix of uncomfortable awkwardness. Callen, Radnar, Feliks, Averie, Hex, Snip, and a rather disgruntled Orion all stood in a strange face-off with Thane's demand to *work their issues out* ringing in their minds.

"So…" Averie began, drawing the word out and accenting it with a fun snapping of her fingers. "I guess I'll start."

Callen stepped forward with pain etching his flawless features. "Averie—"

"Nope. Stop," Averie affirmed with a lift of her hand. "As I was saying. I'll start. I'm not mad. Well, no, I am, but I am willing to put all of that aside for the sake of what's coming." Sighs of relief whispered around the room. "But—when this is over, we are definitely having a talk."

Callen nodded. "Yes. Once this is over, we will talk."

Averie held his gaze for several moments before the first smile in as long as anyone could remember brightened her face. She clapped her hands and turned to the rest of the group. "Alright! How about a good old-fashioned night of snacks and relaxation before the hell that is going to unfold in a few nights?"

"I'll get the snacks!" Snip declared and grabbed Orion's arm and promptly disappeared into an awaiting portal.

"I will adjust the blankets and pillows," Callen offered and immediately began to shift the assortment of blankets and plump pillows along the long sectional.

"I'll call Seiko and Echo," Radnar said and disappeared down the hall that led to the entrance of the Black Mountain.

Averie frowned and pursed her lips. "Where have those two been?" she asked, struggling to remember the last time she had seen either of them.

ACCEPTANCE

Hex, ignoring Callen's glare, dropped himself down onto the newly straightened couch and shrugged. "Who knows? Those two do whatever pleases them. Sometimes, they are your shadow; other times, they are like ghosts."

Averie nibbled at her bottom lip. "I guess that's true."

"It is. Come on, come sit on the couch. Snip should be back with all kinds of snacks … now."

"I'm back!" Snip announced, bursting into the room with his arms filled with bags, boxes, and bottles.

Averie rushed to his side with an eager smile. "Hey, wait, where's Ryan?"

Snip shrugged and walked over to the center of the couches to release the burdensome load. "He had something to take care of. Now!" He turned back with a beaming smile and a mischievous glint in his eye. "Who wants to play truth or dare?"

"What is that?" Feliks asked.

Averie covered her giggle with her hand and shook her head. "You probably don't want to know."

"Come on, birdman, the only way to find out if Averie is right is to play a round or two."

Feliks shifted on his feet, his eyes bouncing from Snip to Averie. "I'm not sure. There are only a few days before the day of the ritual, and I really should be leaving. I don't have much time to find the bear before…"

Averie leaned in to bump her shoulder against his arm. "Come on. A couple of rounds won't hurt."

Feliks gave a terse nod and let Averie lead him to the plush couch. *Please don't let this be a mistake.*

Averie groaned and threw another cheese puff in Snip's direction and rolled her eyes when the jester of the group leaned back, caught it in his mouth, and winked.

"Alright." Feliks sighed and rose to his feet. "As enlightening as this experience has been, I think it is time that I take my leave."

Averie frowned and popped a cheese puff into her mouth. "Alright, but how exactly do you plan on finding an almost twenty-year-old bear, in a Realm that you have never visited, in a house that has probably been torn down, condemned, or sold?"

Hex and Snip's jaws dropped in synchronicity as two very different phrases left their mouths. "Stars, Averie."

"Little ray of darkness right here."

Radnar chuckled and downed the remaining contents of yet another red bottle and dropped it to the side, where it clinked as it joined the other red and green ones. "You two. Such a strange pair from the very beginning." Radnar shook his head, his eyes clouded with memories of the past. Then, he lifted his head. "I wish you the

CHAPTER THIRTY-FOUR

best of luck, Feliks. I know it will not be a straightforward journey, but I pray to the Stars for your safety and for a swift return."

Feliks forced himself to smile. Even from his prison, he had heard tales of the Memory Stealer and his terrible and heartbreaking past. A past far too reminiscent of his own. "Thank you." He turned to Averie and opened his arms. Averie smiled up at him before climbing from the couch and hugging him closely. "I promise to come back. I won't stop until I find that bear and bring it back to you."

Averie smiled against his chest. "Yeah, sure. Thanks, Feliks. Be safe. It was nice to see you again."

Feliks tightened his grip and ground his teeth against the meaning behind her words. "This is not a goodbye, Averie."

"Of course not."

He wanted to fight with her. Argue and scream and shake some sense into her. He could feel her ready to give up but knew no matter what he said, whether it was the actual truth of her past or the promise that she would have a future, nothing was going to make her believe it. She had to see it for herself. With supreme reluctance, he pulled back, pressed a kiss to her forehead, and looked at the Cursed Pair.

"I'm ready."

Hex lifted a hand and flicked his wrist. A large, deformed, crackling oval opened behind him. Wind whistled from inside as taunting pleas and screams for mercy echoed. Feliks shook his head. "It's there, huh?"

Averie, Callen, and Radnar frowned, their eyes shifting from the soft shimmer of air that rippled behind Feliks to the silent, wordless exchange happening between Hex, Snip, and Feliks.

"Is something wrong?" Averie asked.

Feliks shook his head. "No. I'll be back soon."

Averie wanted to ask more questions, demand answers. Instead, she forced a smile and waved goodbye before turning back to the group.

"So, what are we going to play next?"

Radnar leaned forward and grabbed a longneck green bottle from the center and took a long swig. "Have you ever heard of a game called Reaper?"

Averie twisted her lips to the side in thought and shook her head. "I don't think so."

"Neither have I."

Hex and Snip smiled. "What do you have planned, old man?" Hex asked with a rare smile crossing his face.

"I think it's time this old man teaches you kids a few things."

It was several hours before Averie made her way back to her room, sweaty, dirty, and the happiest she had been in months. Radnar had led them from the Black Mountain and to a nearby forest before he had explained the simple rules. Reaper had been a game that had been extremely popular in Radnar's youth and was actually harder than Averie had expected in the beginning. The rules were simple: the group would choose someone to be the "Reaper." After that, three rounds, each lasting thirty minutes, would begin. At the end of each round, those that had been "reaped"

145

ACCEPTANCE

would become the "Reaper's" minions. The winner would be declared when, after the completion of all three rounds, one or any of the targets remained or when the "Reaper" reaped all of its targets.

 Radnar had easily captured Callen and Averie in the first round as they tried to work out the rules. While Hex and Snip had easily evaded them in the second. By the third round, Hex had sacrificed his brother at the last minute to claim the winner's title. The second and third games had become an all-out war as each person used their skills to the maximum. Whether to hide, sacrifice, or trap the other players, nothing was off the table.

 Averie pulled herself from the happy memories and quickly rinsed herself clean before collapsing onto her bed. *It's almost time. It'll all be over soon.* She sighed. *I'm glad I got to have this night.* Averie rolled to her stomach with a smile on her face and a promise in her heart. *I'm going to protect everyone.*

Chapter Thirty-Five

There was a calm settling over the Realm, as if every living thing that made it knew of the chaos and bloodshed that was to come. Averie sat atop the hill that overlooked the castle and waited for that calm to settle into her. It wasn't as if she were nervous or even fearful of the battle that loomed, but perhaps that was the problem. The war didn't frighten her. Death was a long-awaited and much-evaded companion. Her deal with the Heart was coming to a close, and while she knew she should be afraid or want to live on, there was something peaceful about being free of the world that had claimed so many.

A puff of air left her lips in a white cloud. Straightening her spine, she readjusted the straps around her wrist and slid the bracers up her forearms. Her fingers were tracing the worn leather and embossed scroll work when a throat cleared behind her.

"Am I interrupting?"

Averie turned in surprise. "Radnar, I thought you were..."

"Callen?" He chuckled with a tilt of his head. "Aye, he is coming; do not worry. I stopped him so I could give you these."

Radnar moved from her side until he stood in front of her and crouched down to eye level before he withdrew a cloth-bound bundle from behind his back. "What is it?"

A mischievous light sparkled within the gray depths of his eyes. "A gift from an old friend. I figured you would get more use out of them than I would."

Touched, Averie peeled back the cloth as though the item inside was the most precious thing in the world and gasped. A pair of iridescent sai, blacker than obsidian, gleamed in the darkness of night. The grip was thin and bound in blue straps with an angry, golden-eyed wolf at its head. The guard spread into masterfully molded wings that would both protect her wrists and be deadly to anyone that got too close. "Radnar, they are beautiful." She breathed, running her finger along the sleek blade, and jerked back with a hiss.

ACCEPTANCE

Radnar chuckled. "They are sharp, lass; be careful."

Averie sucked on the bleeding tip of her finger and nodded. "Thanks for the heads up."

Radnar glanced over her shoulder and stood. "I'll give you two some time alone. Oh, and Averie?"

Averie tore her eyes from the enchanting blades. "Yes?"

"They may be a bit … different … from what you are used to. This friend of mine, he isn't from around here." Radnar chuckled to himself and walked away, nodding at Callen as he passed.

Averie frowned at Radnar's back. "What do you think that means?"

Callen glanced at the retreating man and shrugged. "Radnar is a man of many mysteries."

Averie nodded. "I suppose you're right."

"Do you mind if I join you?"

Averie shook her head and patted the ground.

A comfortable silence settled between them as each lost themselves in their own thoughts. Callen tipped his head to her bleeding finger. "Do you want me to bandage that?"

Averie watched the blood drop slide free of her finger and fall to the blades of grass and shook her head. "It'll be fine." She sighed and wiped the tender flesh along her pants before lifting it to him once more. "See?"

Callen clenched his jaw at the thread of the thin golden line that replaced the wound. "She is getting stronger."

Averie pursed her lips and looked off.

Callen adjusted himself against the tree and forced the words from his mouth. "Are you frightened?"

"Of what?"

"Averie."

Averie turned and gave a sad smile. "Yes," she admitted.

"Then don't do it."

"It's the only way."

"No, it is not!"

Averie dropped her head back against the old tree. "Callen."

"We can find another way. We can find a way into the castle and search the old king's library. Or we can send Snip and Hex to find a solution."

Pain fluttered her lashes at the desperation in his voice.

"Feliks said that he would be back. We cannot give up before he does. Thane said—"

When she could take no more, she turned and took his hand in her own. "Callen! Stop! There is no other way."

Callen's cheek jumped at the finality, and then he squeezed her hand in return.

"We've tried everything, looked everywhere. This is the only option, and I don't want to dwell on it."

CHAPTER THIRTY-FIVE

Callen traced the rough pad of his thumb over the thin golden lines that decorated the soft skin on her hand. "You deserve better."

"Don't we all?" she asked, nestling into his side.

"You most of all. This is not a battle we should have dragged you into."

"If you hadn't, Sera would have. She has too much riding on this to have let it go."

"Do you think we would have been enemies had Silas not gotten to you first?"

Averie pondered the question carefully before shaking her head. "No. I don't think it would have mattered. I can never stand on the side of someone who will massacre countless people because of a pipe dream."

Callen frowned. "She dreams of pipes?"

Averie chuckled. "Pipe dream is something unattainable."

"Unattainable," Callen repeated.

Averie inhaled a deep, measured breath before she let the next words tumble free. "Callen, Feliks isn't going to make it back in time, and I need—"

Callen clenched his teeth. "You do not know that."

"Just listen. I need you to make sure that everyone sticks to the plan. No matter what. Can you do that?"

The muscle in his jaw flexed violently. "I will do my best."

Averie nodded her head, knowing that was the closest thing to a promise she was going to get from him, and pointed to the growing light over the horizon. "Today, the sun will cross over the two moons. This is the only time she has to complete the ritual. She's got the blade, the Heart's blood, and a piece of each of the last Seven Kings."

Callen forced his mind to switch from trying to convince Averie to give them more time for the upcoming battle. "She will know we are coming."

Averie chuckled. "When has that ever stopped us?"

"I suppose you are right. Though this one is for all the marbles."

Averie lifted her head from his shoulder and turned the full force of her smile on him. "You got it right! That has to be a good omen!"

Despite himself, Callen smiled. "I have been paying more attention, and getting to speak with Thane has helped things."

Averie's smile dimmed. "How is he?"

"He is well, for someone trapped within the Membrane." For the second time in his long life, Callen felt an uncomfortable nagging that made him clear his throat. "I am sorry, Averie."

Averie lifted a surprised brow. "For what?"

Callen cleared his throat again as the lump grew. "For taking him away. I thought—no—I had hoped it would help. I did not think…" The trailing of his words spoke louder than if he had said them aloud. *I didn't think it would give the Heart a greater hold.*

"You did what you thought was best."

"I took away your choice."

ACCEPTANCE

Averie rested her head against the tree. "Such is the way of war." When her attempt at humor fell flat, she sighed. "I'm not going to pretend I'm not angry, because I am. But nothing we do is going to change the inevitable. This was always going to be the result. The moment Sera left the Heart inside of me, my fate was sealed. This was always going to happen. She needed it to. But you know…" Averie let her words trail and shook her head. "Never mind."

"What is it?"

She looked at the lightened sky and closed her eyes before revealing her darkest secret. "I'm *tired*, Callen," she whispered. "So tired of everything. I'm tired of being a weapon, of being 'the one to save them all.' Just once, I'd like to be the one being saved. The one waiting for the hero to arrive. Those damsels never knew how lucky they were not to have the world on their shoulders. How lucky they were to be so loved that their hero would slay dragons and defy odds just to rescue them. But life isn't a fairytale, and this isn't a story. The hero isn't coming, and the only one that can stop this nightmare is me."

"Averie…"

Averie shook her head with a dark chuckle. "It's fine, Callen. I've accepted this life. The beginning, middle, and end. But it would be nice if things had turned out differently."

At a loss for words, Averie and Callen watched as the sun began to rise and spread its warmth across the slumbering Realm. "You should rest. The sun will rise soon and—" Callen's words froze on his tongue when Averie's head fell to his shoulder, the soft puff of her slow, even breathing tickling the hair on his arm.

A smile crested his lips as he lifted a hand to brush the fallen strands from her face and tucked them behind her ear. "I will not give up," he whispered. The sounds of night continued their soft lullaby around them. After a few silent moments, Callen let his head fall back against the tree and shut his eyes.

One second. One moment. That's all it takes to change everything. To go from a moment of peace to a moment of chaos.

The night's lullaby came to a dramatic close under the blaze of a dark flame. "Callen!" Radnar called, rushing up the hill.

Callen jerked in place, immediately lurching to his feet and withdrawing his blade. Radnar stood a foot away, his body drenched in sweat and soot. "What is it? What has happened?"

"They are attacking."

"Where? How?" Callen demanded, turning to look over the hill at their small, hidden encampment.

"They haven't found us. But they're getting close."

Callen turned back and dropped to his knees at Averie's still slumbering form. "Averie, Averie wake up." At the lack of response, Callen dropped his sword to the ground and lifted Averie from the ground. "Averie!" Nothing. "Come on, Averie. Wake up!" Callen tapped his hand against her cheek.

CHAPTER THIRTY-FIVE

Another blast of heat licked his back. "Crixus!" he cursed. "They are getting closer. Averie, wake up!"

Radnar rushed to his side. "What's going on?"

Callen looked up with desperation in his eyes. "She won't wake up."

Chapter Thirty-Six

"Avi… Averie… AVERIE!"

Averie jerked awake at the shrill scream in her ear. "Crixus!" she snapped and rubbed at the wounded canal. "What?" she asked as her eyes struggled to focus on the new scenery around her.

A radiant, toothy grin came into focus first. "There she is," chimed a familiar voice.

Averie blinked a few more times, dropped back to the stone, and threw an arm over her eyes. "Sera," she sighed. "Where am I? How did you find me?"

Sera shrugged. "Wasn't so hard. Kind of like a game of Battleship. Miss here. Hit there. Line the walls. Follow the screams."

Averie peaked from beneath her arm with a frown. "What kind of Battleship did you play?"

"That's not important right now, is it?"

"Where am I?"

Sera stepped back and swept her arm to the side. "Take a look for yourself."

With eyes locked on Sera, Averie forced herself onto unsteady legs and glanced around. "The throne room," she whispered.

Sera smiled and glanced around the ancient room. "Mhmm. I figured it would be the best way to make a statement. Would you like to see what your new friends are up to?" she asked with a head tilt toward the wall of windows.

Icy foreboding chilled Averie to her marrow as she took slow steps forward. Wrath ignited in her chest at the savagery she witnessed below. Lightning and fire clashed with the clang of metal. Battle cries and curses rivaled the grunts and roars of beasts ripping and tearing their way through the Rebellion forces.

"What have you done?" Averie whispered.

Sera stepped forward and tucked a loose strand behind Averie's ear. "It's war, dear. What did you think it would be? Didn't you know, battles are just foreplay?"

CHAPTER THIRTY-SIX

Averie whirled on her heel and thrust her hand forward, striking Sera in the chest and sending an explosion into the air. The pain was excruciating, the blast of it too much for a normal person to have taken. Her eyes burned as though she had spent the afternoon staring into the sun, and her skin tingled uncomfortably. The sensation was reminiscent of the thousand needle pricks of a sleeping limb. A high-pitched buzz pierced her already sore ears, and air rushed unsteadily from her lungs as her heart beat frantically in her chest.

Sera's haughty laughter filled her head like a hornet's nest as the clicking noise she made with her tongue grew closer. Forcing her eyes open, Averie found herself face-to-face with Sera's crouching form.

Sera dropped her head to the right and gave it a small, disappointed shake. "Oh, how the mighty have fallen. Did you think I wouldn't have a plan for you? That I would fall for that trick again?" Sera tsked, leapt to her feet, spun around, her arms outstretched, and sneered. "Is THIS the great savior? The hope of all? The bringer of everything you thought the future would hold?" Her arms fell to her sides as Averie's grunts met her ear. A mocking, joyful laugh tumbled from her lips as she watched Averie pull herself from the ground. "You know what hurts the most, Avi?" Averie looked up with a glare at the use of her nickname.

Sera didn't wait for an answer as she continued. "I am—" She stopped herself and lifted a hand. "My apologies. I *was* your best friend for *fifteen years*. Did that mean nothing to you?" she finished in a whisper.

Averie sat back on her heels and forced slow, steady breaths as she fought back the surge of rage that plummeted the air temperature and whipped around them. The rustle of rocks scraping the floor filled the silence stretching between them.

Gold clashed with tarnished cerulean. "You were a lie, Sera. Everything about you is, and has always been, a lie. From that fake bottle-blonde hair to the rip-off shoes you wore."

Sera clenched her fists at the biting words. Stepping forward, she kicked her leg out, crossing Averie in the ribs and throwing her back to her side. Sera continued her assault, each blow accenting her declarations.

"We were best friends! We told each other everything! Best Fucking Friends!" Sera cried, the final blow sending Averie skidding across the room and into one of the marble pillars. "Then you find out you are supposed to be some 'hero,' and you drop me faster than last season's scraps. Well, Averie, let me tell you something. I'm not something you can just discard like a broken toy. My strength is palpable, my power unmatched, my cunning and intelligence revered. I have planned every step of this out for the last forty years."

Averie rose to her knees, spat the blood from her mouth, and smiled a red smile. "If that was true, then how do I keep beating you?"

Sera shook her head. "Victory is an illusion. A construct created by man to feel superior in a world where they are the lowest entity on the board."

Averie arched a brow. "And yet you fight so hard for it. You lie and take advantage to get just one step closer to it all."

ACCEPTANCE

Ignoring Averie's comment, she pressed on. "Humans, constantly overwhelmed by their emotions, are the most vulnerable and easily targeted by others. The perfect pieces." Sera looked off, an unknown emotion shining in the depths of her eyes. After a few moments, she shook it off and closed the space between them. "Take Marcus. He was so consumed by his love, no, *obsession* for your mother that he couldn't think of anything beyond having her. So much so that he let his jealousy and envy eat away at him until it festered within the decades-long friendship he had with her and your father until he was begging for a way out. Begging for me to take it all away. So, I did."

"You betrayed him."

Sera shook her head. "No, Averie, I didn't."

Averie frowned at the cryptic words, then opened her mouth with a question when Sera pressed on. "Then there was Silas. The *'Ghost of the Realm.'* The boy that not only haunted an entire Realm, but himself as well." Sera smiled a sad smile to herself. "He was the simplest to understand. An outcast, both feared and hated for being born." She shook her head. "All he really wanted was answers. Well, one answer really. An answer I would have given if only he would do one simple job for me. It wasn't even a hard one. But then he let his silly little feelings for you cloud his judgement, deter his mission…"

"He couldn't do it," Averie whispered. "Whatever you wanted him to do, he couldn't do it."

"NO! And why? Because he *loved* you," she said with a roll of her eyes. "He didn't really, though, did he? I tried to explain that it was just that stupid blood bond but *noooo*. All of my carefully laid plans, and he thought he was going to just throw it all away! Just dismantle it and walk away? Oh, I don't think so! Not with everything at risk!"

Averie rested her head against the wall and watched Sera rise to her feet and pace. The glitter of silver caught her eye. She might be too weak for her magic, but she could still fight. She could still buy time.

Sera continued her nonsensical speech. "It was actually incredibly shocking how quickly he disappeared. How easy he was to get rid of. His bloodline. That's all it took. I never pegged you for being that judgy, but wow, did you prove me wrong. Once you knew who his father was, you threw him away so fast even I was reeling from it. But what I didn't count on was you falling back on Callen." She stopped, looked with a smile, and wagged her finger. "You little minx, you. I knew you must have learned something from me after all those years."

Averie forced a smile. "You got me there. What do you want, Sera? Why are you doing this?"

Sera stopped, her cruel face collapsing into something defeated and innocent that reminded Averie of the lively girl she had once known. "Don't you see? I just want the Realms to be made safely whole again. They are crumbling on their own. Avi, they won't go on like this."

CHAPTER THIRTY-SIX

Averie's eyes widened. "They can never go back to being one. Don't you get that? They have been apart too long. There are entire civilizations spread throughout them all. If you tried to bring them back, their worlds would collide, entire cities would crumble, countless lives would be lost. You have to stop this."

"I can't!" Sera closed her eyes to compose herself before starting again. "You don't—They don't appreciate their world like we do. They are killing it, over and over, throughout each of the Realms. Their greed and selfishness is spreading like a cancer. Tearing down forests, destroying their oceans, killings their *own people*. They will *never* stop. They are getting closer to finding us, Averie. What will you do when their cancer spreads to this Realm, and the next, and the next?"

Averie shook her head in disbelief. "You're insane."

Sera laughed. "I'm insane? Who else appreciates the world aside from us? Only those with magic understand the importance of everything that exists around them. If we're not careful, the Realm will—"

"You are destroying this Realm with your own greed and your own selfishness."

"I am *saving* this Realm. Just like I am going to save the others."

"You are killing your own people! Stripping them of the very thing you are trying to preserve. What makes you any better than them? What makes any of us better than them?"

Sera struggled to explain. *How does she not see?* "Can't you hear it?"

Averie released a heavy sigh. "Hear what?"

Sera lowered herself to the ground and laid her hand against the warm ground, pain crossing her porcelain features. "The Realm is screaming, Averie. It has been screaming for so long, begging for mercy, pleading for help. You have the Heart inside you. Don't you feel the pain?"

Averie nodded her head as the familiar twinge twisted in her chest. "I do, but that doesn't make what you are trying to do right. You have to stop this, Sera. We can work together and get the Realms right, *separately*."

"You still don't get it," she said wondrously.

"Don't get what?"

"I'm not the one pulling the Realms together, Averie. The Realm is pulling itself back together. I've just been trying to prepare this Realm for what's coming."

"You're lying."

Sera shook her head and rose to her feet and looked down at the battle below. "That is what makes us different, Averie. Where you choose to hide from who and what you are to blend in with a world that would lock you away and experiment, I have embraced who I am."

Averie peeled herself from the ground, a dark chuckle cracking her dry lips. "Embraced who you are, huh? Strange, because I don't remember anyone hiding who they were once they accepted themselves."

Sera pulled her attention from the battle below and peered down at her old friend. "I have never run from who I was. From what I was. I am stronger than you because I accept myself and always will. Including the decisions I had to make."

ACCEPTANCE

"So, what was '*The Shadow*,' then?"

Sera crouched down and let the Soul Blade dangle from between her fingers. "A necessary evil." Tense seconds passed before Sera spoke again. "The more you struggle with the decisions that have led you down this beaten and worn path, the longer the pain will last. Take my advice. Forge your own path, as I have."

"You may carve your own path, but at least mine will end with my soul intact."

"And you think mine won't?" Sera wondered, a nagging beginning in the back of her mind. *Something isn't right.*

Averie gave another chuckle, her eyes roaming over the perfect porcelain features. "What makes you think it will?"

A deafening explosion knocked Sera to her knees. Averie tossed her hands over her head, then pushed herself up from the ground the instant it stopped shaking. "This isn't my nightmare, Sera. It's yours," she called, racing for the opened door and jumping through a moment later. Spinning back, Averie turned and gripped the door, a knowing smile creasing her face as she slammed it in Sera's outraged face.

CHAPTER THIRTY-SEVEN

TWENTY MINUTES EARLIER

Another blast of heat licked his back. "Crixus!" Callen cursed. "They are getting closer. Averie, wake up!" he demanded, tapping her cheek with a tad more force than necessary as his panic grew.

Radnar rushed to his side. "What's going on?"

Callen looked up with panic and desperation in his eyes. "She will not wake up."

Radnar nodded his head. "Time to go, then."

"What?" he gasped.

Radnar rotated his hand in a circular motion. "Come on now, we don't have much time. Do you want to carry her, or would you rather I do it?" he asked, moving forward as if to lift Averie's sleeping form.

Callen shook his head and carefully lifted Averie into his arms. "What is going on?"

"All part of the plan." Radnar smiled before he turned and began to jog down the small hill.

"Wait!" Callen called out as he began to carefully race after the excitedly babbling old man.

"I can't believe it worked. Brilliant one, that girl," Radnar complimented over his shoulder.

"What plan?" Callen demanded.

"I'll explain it all soon. Right now, we need to get to the gathering. Everyone should be there by now."

Callen clenched his jaw in a mixture of anger and betrayal. A plan had been made without him. Details listed and fought over … without him. Arrangements and orders given without a single input from him. While it hurt his pride to be a master of war and be left out, it gutted his honor as they approached the soot-and-sweat covered group that he appeared to be the last one to know.

His eyes ran over each grime-covered face within the crowd as he and Radnar made their way to the front. "Where are Hex and Snip?"

Radnar frowned, glanced around, and shook his head. "I don't know," he whispered before he faced the restless group. "Listen up! The plan has been sped up. We move out now! You know your duties and have received your assignments. I wish to the Stars that I could stand here and promise you that we will all meet once more, but I am afraid I do not have that power or knowledge, and you all know what a terrible liar I am." Uneasy laughter rumbled through the group as another explosion ricocheted in the air. "What I do know is that our Queen has given up everything to aid a Realm she did not grow up in. Given up those she loved to save people she had never met before. She is actively fighting a battle none can see to ensure this chance, this slim chance that we make it through that barrier and have a fighting chance. The least that each of us can do is to do the same."

The crowd roared their agreement, swords lifting into the air as another explosion hit where their camp and all of their people had been mere minutes ago. The thirst for vengeance and blood rose and formed a palpable feeling that spread throughout the crowd and washed away the remnants of doubt and fear.

"I was told once by a great man of another Realm that if it meant protecting those they loved, then it would be a great day to die. Now take your places, and may the Stars be there to greet you," Radnar called.

The crowd became a flurry of movement, but Callen acknowledged none of it save the grizzled man standing before him. "What. Plan?" he grit.

Radnar huffed out a breath and clapped a hand to his shoulder. "She didn't want you to worry."

"A bit too late for that."

Radnar's eyes flickered to Averie's sleeping face before rising to Callen's moonlit glare. He shook his head. "I'm too old for this nonsense."

"Just tell me!"

"Averie isn't sleeping." Radnar reached forward and pulled at her sleeve. Callen frowned, then cursed under his breath when the charm shook free.

"The necklace," Callen hissed. His arms trembled with unbridled anger. His stare locked on the chain wrapped around Averie's wrist. "I thought Snip destroyed that! Take it off."

Radnar shook his head and let her sleeve fall back. "Not yet."

"What do you mean? Anything could happen to her in that forsaken place! Where in *Fornax* are those twins?!" he demanded and searched through the bustling crowd once more.

"Callen—"

"This is insanity! How long are we supposed to leave her in there?"

"*Callen.*"

CHAPTER THIRTY-SEVEN

"How are we to keep her safe? I promised I would keep her safe!"

"Shut your mouth, or you won't hear the blasted plan!" Radnar snapped.

Callen narrowed his eyes.

Radnar shook his head. "I'm too bloody old for this nonsense. Averie knows what she is doing. This has always been the plan." Radnar lifted his hand to stop Callen's retort. "She knew you wouldn't approve but was going to do it with or without our help. We chose to help."

"*Our?*"

Radnar met the intensity of Callen's gaze with one of his own. "Marcus is keeping the door open—"

"Marcus?!"

"Enough!" he bellowed. "What is done is done. Averie is buying us time. Time we are wasting here, with your arguments, instead of doing our part right now."

Callen's jaw ticked manically. "Fine. What is the plan?"

Radnar smiled. "It's brilliant, really. Come."

Callen glared at Radnar's back but followed him like the perfect soldier he had always been. "What now?" he asked, adjusting Averie in his arms.

Radar released two high-pitched whistles and smiled as half of their forces poured from the forest. "Now, you dig."

"What?"

"The same way you did when you and Thane saved the Falcon."

Callen's brow wrinkled in confusion before the memories passed like a vison before his eyes.

"Callen! Urgent message has just arrived from the pathway!"

Thane and Callen turned from their impromptu sparring lesson as Trite raced to their side.

"From whom?"

"Falcon. He said that the Savior arrived last night and that the Princess arrived at his house late last night."

Thane's chuckle quickly dissolved into a terribly disguised cough at Callen's glare. "I told you she would not go unnoticed."

Trite cleared his throat. "Yes, well, the King sent out his guard to search the houses for anything suspicious. He also reported a man in a mask appearing to aid in the search. Then Marcus called for a mandatory meeting in the square this morning."

Callen stiffened. "A man in a mask?"

Trite nodded. "Yes, though there was no confirmation if it was, in fact, Ghost."

Thane snorted. "Ghost? Seriously?"

Callen ignored Thane's comment and focused back on Trite. "Alright. Gather a few men quickly and meet me by the ruins. Tell them to prepare for an extraction. We are leaving immediately."

Trite nodded and raced away, his voice carrying Callen's orders. Within minutes, a small battalion stood, ready and waiting, by the ruins.

ACCEPTANCE

Thane frowned. "How exactly are we going to get them out? I don't think just waltzing in and grabbing them is going to work."

Callen turned with a smile. "By going underground, of course."

Thane blanched at the thought of going underground. "Excuse me? You expect us to tunnel there before this meeting is over and they are clearly found out and most likely beheaded or maimed or wait... What kind of punishment do you guys do here?"

"Marcus favors the stripping of power."

Thane nodded. "Oh, yes, of course. The stripping of power."

"Do not worry, Filling. We will not be tunneling; I am."

Thane rolled his eyes as Callen stomped his foot and immediately yelped as the ground beneath his feet gave way, and he landed with a heavy thud. Thane glared up at his chuckling friend. "Not cool, Frosting!"

Smile still firmly in place, Callen dropped to the ground beside Thane and helped him to his feet. "We need to get moving."

Thane watched in stunned silence as Callen moved the earth in front of them with blurring speed and harsh arm movements. "I swear on all that is holy, if you trap me down here, I will make sure you never get a piece of cake again."

A solemn, tinged smile threatened his lips at the memory before Callen forced himself back to the present. "But the barrier..."

Radnar's smile was radiant as he looked down at Averie. "She is keeping Sera busy. It should be adequate to knock her concentration enough to lower the barrier, underground at least. But we don't have much longer."

Chapter Thirty-Eight

Callen grit his teeth in frustration at being left out of the loop and chose to dip his head to show understanding rather than spew the words he so badly wanted at the older man. *There will be time for that later,* he promised himself.

Averie's body tensed in his arms, and his heart stuttered until she fell slack once more. "Hold on," he whispered. "I have quite the bone to pick with you when we get out of this," he mumbled, adjusting her sleeping form in his arms. Once he was satisfied she was secure, he turned to the gathering soldiers and forced a mask of calm before addressing them.

"Being underground isn't for everyone. If you have doubts, back out now. Once you are under, there is no coming back up. Not until we reach our destination." When no rejections met his ear, Callen nodded and turned to face the castle. "Then let us begin."

His foot rose and slammed against the earth, sending each soldier's teeth rattling and feet stumbling as the ground separated a few feet away. Those closest to Callen peered over his shoulder and blanched at the sight. A hole the size of a full-grown man's grave had opened several feet away. Its depths were so deep, there was only darkness when you peered inside.

Callen rolled his eyes when a chorus of audible gulps sounded from behind him. "This is your last chance. If you do not have the strength to leave your fear behind, then turn back now. Those of you with the ability to create light orbs, do so. But we leave now."

With his final warning lingering in the air, Callen began his descent into the earth. The feeling, despite all that was going on around him, felt sweet. Much like the homecoming Thane had always spoken of. Callen shook the painful thoughts away and pressed on. Much to his surprise, all the men that had been left to his care

ACCEPTANCE

had descended into the ground behind him. Pride flared in his chest as he used every step, glance, and flick of his fingers to clear the path before them.

Callen's stomach churned with every step he took. With his arms occupied with Averie's slumbering form, he couldn't easily dispel the earthen adversary with a swipe of his arm. Instead, he was forced to use his eyes within the darkness, limiting his range and forcing him and the army behind him to move at a much slower pace. His eyes shuttered as he reached his mind forward and stretched his consciousness into the Realm. *Just a little farther,* he told himself as he adjusted Averie in his arms. *A little farther.* Averie's body jerked within his grasp.

Callen clenched his teeth against his uselessness, tightened his hold, and pressed on. *Just a little farther.* The Realm stretched out before his molten eyes, revealing the colors of the rainbow with each step. Reminiscent of vines, the colors converged and branched out, expanding their reach but ultimately converging into one before they branched out once more. Callen shook his head against the distortion and shifted the earth from their path. Each step he carved brought them closer to their goal.

Time stretched impossibly slowly before him. Each step it took to forge the path they so desperately needed took more force and energy without the use of his arms. The small space was filled with pants from the men that trailed loyally, albeit fearfully, behind him. Callen grit his teeth.

A tilt of his head widened their path, allowing the convoy behind him to stretch from their tight-knit single file line. The relief of the men behind him was palpable as they were able to fit two men, side by side, on its trail. Callen cursed his weakness in his mind as his eyes drifted to the innocent woman in his arms.

Perhaps Marcus and Feliks are right. Maybe I have strayed too far from my mission and, because of that, have lost my connection. Callen shook the thoughts from his head. There was no time for doubt. Not when Averie and so many others were fighting so hard. Even with that belief burning in his chest, the chilling clutches of regret tightened around his heart.

"I never would have agreed," he whispered. "I did not know the cost." With another flick of his jaw, he took three steps forward. "I would have stopped it," he promised. "I did not know." The words, mere whispers, echoed in his mind. Whether they were truth or fable, his heart clenched with the realization he would never know.

Hang on, Averie. I am almost there. Another flick of his eyes brought a bead of sweat down his brow as the slow trudge of feet echoed in the hollowed cavern. Without the use of his hands, the trip was taking more power and more time than ever before.

Frantic breath and the thudding of panicked hearts raced in his ears and pounded against his own weighted pants. *Just a little farther. Please, Averie, hang on. Do not let me break my promise.*

Callen's thoughts raged against the thump of each weighted step and flick of his eye until, finally, their goal was in sight. His steps rang out in his mind like a countdown until a smile lifted his stonelike features. Callen tightened his hold on Averie and lifted her to meet his cheek. "We are here," he whispered. "Come back to me."

CHAPTER THIRTY-EIGHT

Averie jerked upright with a loud gasp, her eyes wide but vision distorted in the transition and her heart thudding faster and harder than ever before.

Callen jerked in surprise, never thinking that his words would reach her in the dream world. "Averie!" Warm hands cupped her face, immediately clearing her frantic mind.

"Callen," she panted as reality began to sink its vicious claws into her clouded mind. *Now!* it screamed. *You have to act, now!* Averie's words spilled forth, beyond her comprehending mind, and ordered in a voice unlike her own, "Go, go now! Hurry!"

Callen's jaw jumped with the urge to argue when his battle-savvy side forced him to his feet. He looked over the gathering of soldiers and smiled. "You heard her, ATTACK!" he bellowed, his hands slicing through the air.

The earth ripped open and rose beneath thousands of feet, pouring them into the unsuspecting Shadowed like scarabs breaking free and throwing them into the night to claim the existence of countless unexpecting enemies. Inhuman screams tore through the night as the Rebellion army slew beast after unsuspecting beast.

Callen smiled, his eyes glinting silver in the full moonlight. "It worked."

Averie chuckled and rose to her feet, her body alight with golden scars. "They don't know what hit them."

Callen peered down at her, his eyes sweeping her face as though it were the last time. "Are you ready?"

A menacing smile cracked her face as golden light poured from her eyes and lit the darkened tunnel. "Let's finish this."

Chapter Thirty-Nine

"This ends tonight," Averie vowed.

Callen dipped his head in agreement. "Then let us end it."

Averie looked up to the castle and grit her teeth. "I'm going for Sera."

"I will cover you."

Averie nodded, then pulled the new black blades Radnar had gifted her from her boots and began to rise when Callen caught her wrist. She looked back with the question clear in her eyes. "Be safe."

A genuine smile broke free. "Aren't I always?" she asked with a quirked brow.

Callen suppressed a groan and, instead, chose to lift them into the thralls as his answer. As Callen and Averie burst free from the ground, each wearing their own emotionless mask, Callen spurred into action. The castle entrance was directly to their left, along with a line of ferocious, snarling beasts. Averie wrinkled her nose at the sight but was given no chance to release the quip that clung to the tip of her tongue as Callen stepped between her and the beasts, clasped his hands, and drove them into the ground with incredible force. The monsters roared as the ground quaked beneath them before large pikes ripped free and plunged into those too slow to react.

Averie saw her chance and took it without a single glance back. Gold vignetted her vision as she pumped her arms at her sides and raced through the carnage. She moved with practiced ease as she jumped from side to side, effortlessly dodging the protruding and blood-covered pikes.

"DOWN!" commanded a gruff, familiar voice.

Averie instinctively dropped against the ancient stone, feeling its rough texture against her cheek as she anxiously waited. The crunch of bone sounded from above, followed by a steady drip of liquid. "Go now!"

CHAPTER THIRTY-NINE

Averie pushed to her feet, sent Radnar an appreciative nod, and taking the stairs two at a time, cleared the staircase in record time. Fighting against the urge to look back over the battlefield, Averie pushed through the great ornate door and stepped into the castle. A small army of at least twenty Shadowed stood waiting. Their deformed faces and sewn lips distorted the sounds that tried to escape.

"I'll give you one chance," she promised. "Go out there and take your friends out of here and you may live. If not—" Averie wasn't given a chance to finish before the first Shadowed, this one more closely resembling a man, flashed forward so quickly she would have missed it if she hadn't been paying attention.

Averie lifted her sai, deflecting her first blow. "Alright, then. Your funeral."

She fended off those that stepped into her path with the clash of metal and carefully thrown punches. As she took down those who refused to let her pass, her heart pounded. *This is taking too long,* her mind screamed as she felt the warmth of blood splash against her face. *So close, just a little farther.* Averie forced the words to play over and over in her mind as she fought to climb another staircase. Life after life fell to her blade, a haunting reminder of the senselessness of the enemy's mission. Averie bit back her disgust and wiped the sweat and ichor from the side of her face as she kicked the final Shadowed from her blade and watched him tumble back down the stained staircase. *Just a little farther.*

Averie rolled her shoulders and shook out her hands before taking off once more. Her feet slapped against the stone and echoed down the halls as she took turn after turn, letting her instincts guide her to Sera's most likely position. Her heart thumped with unease as she took the final turn and came face-to-face with a hefty gathering of the Elite Shadow Guards, their watchful eyes fixed upon her.

Each man, clad entirely in black, stood tall, their broad shoulders touching as they barred any and all from entering the chamber at their back. Each had a sword in their hands and a mask of shadows covering their face, so Averie was left with only a clear look into their piercing gaze.

"I was wondering what happened to you, boys. I guess now I know," Averie mumbled.

"Turn back," one rasped.

Averie lifted a brow and adjusted her grip on the hilt of her sai. "I didn't know you guys could talk."

"We do not wish to engage in senseless battle."

Averie shrugged. "Then step aside. Because one way or another, I promise I am getting through that door."

The Elite that had spoken tipped his head in acknowledgment and lifted his sword. Averie's eyes widened in shock as she barely had time to lift her blade in defense of the first strike the Elite guard unleashed.

Just as she blocked, another adversary materialized out of nowhere, catching her off balance and demanding more energy than she had initially planned. Twisting and striking her sai, she unleashed a flurry of precise and powerful movements. Even still, Averie struggled to fight her way through the unrelenting guard. Her determination

ACCEPTANCE

to save her power for the impending battle vanished in an instant when a searing, slicing pain stabbed her back and tore through her side.

A cry escaped her lips, echoing through the air beside the clash of steel, as she mustered all her strength to push the Elite Guard in front of her aside, before retaliating against the unsuspecting attacker. The pop of the joint she felt against her told her she had successfully dislocated its knee. As the attacker fell back, a howl breaking free of its chest, the blade inside her slipped free.

"That's it," she growled. "I'm done playing with you."

She couldn't stop; she wouldn't. Today, it was all going to end. *She* would end this. She just needed to get through the door. Turning to the men blocking her path, she dropped to the ground and slammed her fist into the marble floor. The floor tore apart, unleashing a swarm of thorny vines that thrashed and lashed about in a vicious attack against the Elite Guards.

Satisfied with the distraction, Averie rose to her feet and, clutching onto one of the attacking vines, used it to propel her up and over the remaining threat. A smirking, mock salute was all she allowed herself before she slammed her palms against the ancient wood, forcing them open.

With her sai ready and gleaming, an obsidian light in her grasp, she took careful steps forward. Her eyes scanned every nook and cranny, while her body remained on high alert. She was attuned to every sound and movement within the room when a slight tingle began to vibrate out of her hands. Averie frowned to herself but refused to glance down when the realization that the power of every*thing* she slayed was seeping into her. *Just where in the Seven Realms did Radnar find these?*

It didn't matter. She would take whatever edge she could find. Her grip on the blade hilts adjusted as the door slammed behind her. She wouldn't look. She didn't need to. Nothing and no one would be there. Because the one she had come so far for had just materialized in front of the table that Averie and her friends had used not too long ago.

"Welcome, Averie. Shall we begin?"

Chapter Forty

Ten minutes earlier — Sera

A deafening explosion knocked Sera to her knees, the pebbles and rubble digging uncomfortably into her flesh. A flash of movement snapped her head up in time to see Averie leap up from the ground the instant it stopped shaking.

"This isn't my nightmare, Sera. It's yours," she called. Sera frowned as the door materialized.

"No," Sera whispered, her disbelief pounding in her chest as she forced herself to her feet and raced after her. *This can't be. How did she—? When did she—?* There was no more time for thought as Averie stepped through the door and turned back with a gloating smile just in time to slam the door in Sera's face, locking her in this hellish dreamscape.

"Damnit!" Sera roared, running her fingers through her dirty hair as she paced the cracked and uneven stone. "Think, Sera. Think. There is another way out of this. One is to be released; the other is to…" Sera groaned. "To die. Today is not going to be my day. I don't have—"

Sera froze in her tracks as the burn of acidic dread boiled in her stomach. Her head snapped to the side where the large windows showed a frozen landscape locked in battle. But what was strangest of all was that the moons and the sun hung together in the sky in the greatest contrast of all. "I'm running out of time," she whispered to herself.

With no other choice and the threat of the end of everything looming in the background, Sera walked herself to the edge of the Throne Room and looked out over the frozen scene. "One, two, three…" For a brief moment as she fell, doubt crept in and nearly overwhelmed her as the ground rose up to meet her.

167

ACCEPTANCE

In an instant, Sera's eyes snapped open as she was forced back to reality and sat upright, the adrenaline coursing through her veins. Her body was stiff, and her clothes clung to her sweat-drenched skin as her wild eyes scoured her surroundings. She was in the War Room, not the Throne Room, which meant…

"Sera! Thank the Shadows you're awake. What in Fornax happened?!" demanded a familiar voice as pale hands reached up and cupped her cheeks, forcing their eyes to meet.

Startled, Sera instinctively recoiled from the unexpected touch and quickly shook her head. Her forehead furrowed in confusion as she reached and brushed fallen, sweaty strands from her eyes. "Lucas? What happened?"

"That's what I want to know!"

Sera rose, lifted a shaking hand to her neck, and clutched the pendant she hadn't taken off.

Lucas narrowed his eyes and cursed as he launched to his feet. "I told you to take that off! Did you honestly think that they wouldn't use it against you?!"

"I—"

Feral screams pierced through the night air, intermingling with the sudden outbreak of battle roars, the metallic clash, and the mesmerizing sparks of magic. "What's going on?"

With an exasperated sigh, Lucas let out a string of curses and made his way toward the towering windows, which gave him a commanding view of the courtyard. A growl thundered in his throat. "It's Averie. She's breached the castle."

Sera rose unsteadily, her legs shaking, and motioned toward the door with a shaking finger. "Go! You need to stop them before they get inside. We can't let them, or her, get in here before we have a chance to finish what we started."

Lucas's jaw jumped with the need to argue. Even more so when she wavered on her feet. With the sounds of battle reaching a crescendo, he felt a surge of conviction, knowing that his decision was irrevocable. "I'll send the Elite Shadow Guard to watch the door. That should buy you more time. But Sera, you and I both know there is nothing I can do to stop her."

With a determined expression, Sera tipped her head and straightened her spine, ready to face whatever came her way. "I know. Go. We don't have much time. If I made it out, that means Averie did too, probably before I did."

With purposeful strides, Lucas left the sight of battle at the window, grabbed his sword from the table, and headed toward the door, his steps weighted as he crossed the room. As his hand reached out to open the door, a sudden chill of foreboding ran down his spine, causing his muscles to freeze midair. "Be careful, Sera."

Sera smiled at his back. "Aren't I always?"

Lucas snorted. "Not in any Realm I've known you."

CHAPTER FORTY

Lucas strode confidently through the halls of the castle, his footsteps echoing with authority. As he walked, confidence radiated from his every step, mingling with the melodic clash of metal and the enchanting hum of magic that filled the air, resulting in his shoulders straightening and his grip on the sword hilt tightening. As he approached the castle's entrance, he was met with an eerie silence and a formidable sight—a swarm of men dressed in black, with haunting masks and terrifying swords that waited obediently for their commands. They had been careful to keep the Elite Guard hidden, only using them when absolutely necessary to breach the tears and scope out the next spot.

"What are your orders?" rasped the tallest of them all.

Popping his neck from side to side, Lucas brandished his sword and motioned toward the six Elite with a determined expression. "You are to stand guard outside the War Room doors. No one, and I mean no one, makes it through the doors. I don't care what underhanded, backwoods methods you have to use. No one gets through. Am I clear?"

The men in question nodded in agreement and swiftly passed him, their footsteps whispering in the wind as they ascended the stairs to assume their positions. As their haunting presence dissipated, Luca turned to the remaining group and gestured toward the vacant area at the bottom of the staircase. "The rest of you, stay here. Should anyone other than me make it in here, make sure that they meet a swift and decisive end." His eyes roamed over the hodgepodge group with a sigh. Why Sera had insisted on making these mindless things, he would never understand. "Or at least try really hard to delay them for as long as possible. Take a couple limbs off if you have to. Just do whatever it takes. Understand?"

The mishmash of muffled sounds that came after would have to be his confirmation that they grasped the severity of his message. The ground beneath their feet began to tremble, launching another string of frustrated curses from Lucas as he was forced to reach out to steady himself against a nearby wall. "Looks like Callen has finally decided to make his appearance." Without looking back, he warned, "If you do not do your duty and something happens to Sera or… Let's just say that you should end your own vile existence before I do."

With his final vow made, Lucas cracked the castle doors open and slipped away into the throes of battle.

Chapter Forty-One

Twenty minutes earlier – Marcus and Solara

Marcus was giddy with the prospect of completing this particular favor for Callen. The Eternal One knew the risk of asking such a deed from a man such as himself, and yet there was barely a pause or hitch in his voice when he had asked.

Callen lifted his chin, his lips twisting in distaste, and, with clenched fists, said the words that tasted like ash on his tongue. "I need you to do something for me."

Marcus's smile gleamed beneath the moon. "You have captured my attention, Eternal One. Do tell."

"The time is growing closer. When the sun crosses over the two moons, Sera will have all that she needs to complete her plan. If that happens, we are all doomed, and I know that you, even with all of your unruly desires to rule the Realms, do not want that to happen."

Marcus pursed his lips and rocked back on his heels. "What does any of that have to do with me?"

"Everything. Is it not obvious? If the Realms fall, then there will be nothing left to rule."

Marcus smiled. "There is always something to rule, Callen."

Callen clenched his teeth, his jaw jumping so fiercely Marcus lifted a brow. "We are trying to stop it, and when the time comes, I may need your assistance in doing so."

"And how would I do that?"

Callen hesitated. The action was brief but telling. *He doesn't want to ask for help. He* needs *to.* Marcus smiled as the words he had always hoped to hear spilled

CHAPTER FORTY-ONE

free. "When the time comes, I will need you to go into my armory and retrieve a special box and only *this box."*

Marcus bowed, his hand fisted and clasped to his chest. "Your wish is my command."

Finally, the time had come. It was the night before the sun would cross the two moons, and the men were preparing to move out for the battle to come when Callen had sought him out. Though he hadn't been hiding, it had taken Callen longer than necessary to track him down.

Marcus leaned back against the Black Mountain and stared up into the star-filled sky. It was always a wonder to him just how many of the twinkling things there were. How faithful they were to the endless black velvet and the large, purple lit moons. Every night they continued to shine, knowing that nearly no one appreciated their glint and glamour. Knowing that they were nothing but an accessory to the real things people admired, the moons.

Marcus shook his head in disgust at the desperation he had imagined the stars held and smiled to himself at the slowly approaching steps. "Good evening, Callen. Beautiful night, isn't it?"

Callen wasted no time in explanation. "It is time. I need you to go to the armory and retrieve the box that was stolen from you so long ago and bring it to me."

"And just where is this armory of yours?"

Marcus jolted against the tree he rested against, his brow dotted with sweat and eyes clenched tightly closed. "Crixus," he cursed. Solara fluttered uncertainly at his side, wringing her wrists and pacing soundlessly along the grass. "What is taking so long?" he growled.

Solara nibbled her lip. "This was a stupid, stupid plan."

"Hush! I can't concentrate with your incessant babbling and frantic pacing."

"Why did she even ask you? Has she truly lost so much of herself that she would do such a thing? And to not even tell Callen this plan! What is that girl thinking?"

Marcus cracked an eye open enough to glare at Solara. "Have you forgotten that I am the only person who is capable of getting *your* daughter out of this mess *she* has created? That I am here of my own volition?"

Solara stopped pacing and turned a lethal glare in his direction. Her finger lifted and wagging, she stomped through the space that separated them and poked his chest. "Have you forgotten that the only reason she is in this mess is because of you?!"

Marcus smirked and let his eyes close once more. "You flatter me, Solara. Even after all these years, you still know just how to pep me up when I'm feeling low."

Solara fumed in silence, her desire to argue far less than her desire to keep her daughter safe. Time passed with an agonizing slowness that was only accented by her harsh, forced breath. There was nothing like the fear of harm or death as it sought the external embodiment of your soul.

ACCEPTANCE

Marcus jerked once more and pushed from the tree. "She's out. Time to go."

"Go? Go where?"

Marcus shoved his hands into his pockets and smirked. "To the armory of an Eternal One. I'm doing a favor for Callen. Now come along; we don't want to be late."

A sick feeling pooled in the pit of Solara's stomach as Marcus began to slow and finally stop in front of a wall at the end of an empty hall within the Black Mountain. Along their short walk, Marcus had only been too eager to share that Callen had come to *him* and requested the retrieval of the box. He had nearly vibrated with elation as he explained what they were about to see.

It was well known within exclusive circles just how private the tombs, rooms, worlds, and armories that Eternals, Immortals, and Originals claimed as their own. To invite someone in was to allow them into the deepest parts of yourself. These places were used to store memories, objects, and weapons with power far too destructive for man. And most of all, they carried evidence of their weaknesses.

For Callen to allow Marcus into such a sacred place shows his desperation, Solara thought. A soft sigh—whether of regret or exhaustion, she wasn't sure—passed her lips as Marcus completed the opening ritual and let them both into Callen's sanctuary.

Marcus's eyes were wide and manic with possibility as he drank in the glorious wonder around him. Countless weapons of all shapes, sizes, and colors were laid out along the walls. Endless rows of shelves stretched far beyond the eye could see, filled to the brim with objects, boxes, and other unusual things.

"We need to find what you have been sent for and leave before it is too late. There is too much at stake for us to dally."

Marcus waved her off as something shimmered in his peripheral. "We will. Don't worry. I am a man of my word, after all."

Solara suppressed a snort of derision, then feared the action would spur his ire and deter them from their mission. "Where are you going?"

Marcus smiled, the dark curve of his lips a true contrast to any other definition of the action. A terrible glint sparkled in his eyes as he slowly approached a large desk. "The Scales of Life," he whispered with far too much excitement. The ancient-looking apothecary scale trembled beneath his gaze as it shifted from a scale and melted into a pool of the starlit sky.

Marcus continued to watch, his transfixion coming from more than just interest as miniature hands stretched from the puddle. Soon, long, graceful arms could be seen, swaying from side to side as they rose higher, revealing the form of a beautiful woman. Long, flowing hair lifted and swayed in an unnatural air as large, bottomless eyes glared, and a frown attempted, but failed, to mar her angelic face.

The woman crossed her graceful arms over her chest as two thin strands rose from the remaining pool and curled along the length of her body until she was wrapped in a mix of elegant vines that hovered to each side. Each vine ended in a breathtaking flower, one terrifyingly close to the ground while the other threatening to rise above her head. Marcus chuckled as the flowers grew larger, and tree roots

CHAPTER FORTY-ONE

spilled from between the woman's fingers to the table below, locking her into place and cementing her displeasure at Marcus's appearance.

"Death Walker," she sneered, though her lips did not move. Her anger was heavy in the air as her words resounded in the room. "How have you come to be in this place?"

"I was invited, of course. How else does one such as me enter such a *holy* place?"

"Deception, of course," the Scale quipped. "What is it you have come for? I will lead you to it, and you will be gone. I am sure that was the deal you struck, and not one that can be broken when made with an Eternal One."

Marcus rolled his eyes. "I have come for the box."

The Scale tilted her head. "The box? Which one do you seek? As you can see, this place is filled with a great many boxes."

"Dingy, creaky, holding a single stone worth more than any man has ever held."

The Scale of Life hesitated but finally lifted her arm and pointed to the far side of the room. "It is there. Take it and be gone."

Marcus tipped his head in mock thanks before quickly making his way to the shelf in question, plucking the box from its dust-covered space, and slipping it into his pocket.

"Let's be gone now," Solara pleaded. "Something terrible is happening at the castle. We need to get there *now*."

Marcus turned with a smile and tapped his finger on her nose. "Of course, my dear Solara."

Solara's stomach clenched at the action. *What have you done, Callen?*

"Always lovely to see you, Scale, until next time."

"There will not be a next time!" the Scale hissed.

Marcus tsked. "I wouldn't be so sure about that," he said. He looked pointedly at the flower that continued to drift ever so close to the desktop before leaving the room completely.

The Scale of Life looked to her flowers and, for the first time in centuries, was scared for the Realm.

Chapter Forty-Two

CASTLE WAR ROOM – AVERIE AND SERA

"Welcome, Averie. Shall we begin?"

Averie shifted her hold on the hilt of her blades. "I would prefer you just end things here."

"Oh, really?" Sera chuckled. "And just what do you think it is that I need to end?"

Averie circled the blade in her hand. "The nonsense of bringing the Realms together."

Sera released a sound of disgust. "You still haven't been listening. *I'm* not the one forcing the Realms together. The Heart is. Everything I have done has been to prepare us all."

Averie shook her head. "That can't be true. If it was, then why have you hurt so many people? Why did you start this war in the first place? Why did you leave the Heart inside me?!"

"So many questions. I'm afraid I'll have to give you the shortest version of answers. Though I'm not sure you'll like what you hear."

"Try me."

Sera blew out a harsh breath and began to slow her pace as she lifted her hand to tick off each answer on her finger. "I never meant to hurt anyone, well … mostly. The war was actually an accident that spiraled from a young girl given too much power and not enough guidance. The Heart was … an oversight. I thought if I left it inside you, it would make it easier to reason with, but I was mistaken."

Averie's face pinched in disgust. "You're a monster. No wonder you cloak yourself in shadows. You're as dark as they come."

CHAPTER FORTY-TWO

Sera stopped her lazy trek, her blonde locks fluttering in the wind as she turned to look Averie in the eye. "Why do you believe darkness is evil?"

"Because it stains everything it touches."

"But does light not do the same? Spreading its searing light across the shadows? Does evil not stalk the light of day the same way it creeps in the darkness of night? After all, what is darkness but a shade deeper than light?"

"You're twisting words and meanings to make yourself right."

Sera shook her head. "No, not this time. This time, I'm just being honest. Everything in life comes down to perspective. If you were raised to believe that rules are to be followed, no matter who they were made by or when they were thought up, then that is what is right for you. However, if you were raised in a world where the only thing that mattered—your very worth—was based on the amount of power you could wield or the use you were to someone, don't you think you would do anything to raise that worth?"

Averie's jaw ticked as she struggled with the truth in Sera's words. How often had she changed who she was to make herself greater in the eyes of someone else?

"The Realm doesn't need another hero, Averie. It needs a monster. It needs someone that is willing to do whatever it takes, regardless of how corrupt or toxic the task may seem. It needs someone who is willing to be hated in the name of keeping things in order and the Realm safe."

The air filled with magic, popping and hissing, as power raced and cracked along Averie's black-bladed sai. "I hate to admit it, but I understand what you're saying, Sera. But I'm sorry, I can't let you do this. There's too much at risk. Too many *lives* are at risk. I tried to talk some sense into you, but…" Averie shook her head.

Sera smiled and stretched her hands at her sides, calling forth the shadows. Averie watched in awe as they rose and wove into long, thin blades that pulsed with black flame. "I have a feeling it was always going to end this way. But I'm afraid you're too late," she whispered and rested the blade against her forearm and lunged for Averie.

The clash of their swords created a terrifying explosion of fire and lightning that sent shockwaves through the air. Blow after blow reverberated with the same unyielding strength. "You're wrong!" Averie snapped and shoved Sera back. "It's never too late. Tell me how to stop it!"

Sera shook her head and lunged. Her sword came down while her hand rose and fisted. Averie lifted a hand to block Sera's sword, while the other struggled against the razor whip of shadows that snapped and slapped at her.

"You don't understand!" Sera cried and attacked once more.

Averie parried to the side, the heat of the dark blade hissing against the exposed flesh of her shoulder, and shoved her elbow as hard as she could into Sera's side. Air whooshed from Sera's mouth beside a frustrated growl. Anger flared hot and violent as it burned its way through her body. Thick black lines swallowed the bright crystalline color in her eyes and stretched to pulse along the sides of her face. "Damn you," Sera gasped. "That wasn't very nice."

ACCEPTANCE

"I wasn't trying to be. Tell me how to stop it!"

"You can't!" Sera snapped, thrusting her arm out and sending a shadow ball into Averie's chest. "I tried everything! Did everything! And nothing has worked! Nothing can stop it!" Each angered outcry was accented by another blast until Averie was against the wall with her chin to her chest and her eyes closed against the assault.

Averie growled in frustration at her predicament. *It's now or never.* Diving deep inside, Averie imagined herself jumping into the well of molten power that lived deep inside. A moment later, the familiar tingle and heat along her golden scars brought a smile to her lips. Opening her eyes was like seeing for the first time. Everything was sharp, bright, and in complete focus. A slow smile split her face. *I love this part.* She sighed in satisfaction as raw power thrummed through her veins and slowed the beat of her heart. Sounds were clearer and more crisp than ever before. Somewhere in the back of her mind, she knew it was just one more sign, one more way that the Heart was consuming another piece of her soul, but she didn't care. All that mattered was stopping Sera before she could force the Realms together, effectively destroying them all.

She lifted her hands and, with a swift flick, twirled the blades until they ran the length of her forearms, and smirked as she walked toward the oncoming attack. Her eyes flashed a deep fluorescent amber. As Sera lifted her sword high above her head, Averie slammed her hands to the ground. The stone shook and stuttered before it ripped free and rippled like a tsunami. Sera's alarmed cry echoed as she was thrown from her feet and sent head over foot through the air like a child tossing its old rag doll.

At the last moment, Sera called to her shadows and used them like a rope to catch herself before she was thrown from the castle entirely. As her feet touched down, the air shifted, and Sera prepared to counter. Averie shoved from the ground and used her own wave to carry her after Sera. Bringing her blades up, she leapt from the stone wave and brought both arms down unilaterally.

Dodging Averie's blow, Sera leaned to the side and slammed her elbow into the center of Averie's spine, which dropped her to the ground immediately with a thunderous *thud* and sickening crack of bone. Her vision swam as blood immediately began to seep from her forehead and burn her eye. Averie cursed as a prickle of awareness had her rolling to the side a moment too late. Pain tore into her as Sera's black flame pierced her shoulder with a cauterizing burn that clashed against her flesh in a pain so vicious it stole her voice as her mouth opened in a cry. Sera lifted a foot and pressed into Averie's chest, eliciting another painful cry as she ripped her blade free.

Sera's eyes widened in a mixture of shock and awe as the wound she had inflicted on Averie's arm failed to heal. "It appears that the Heart has forsaken you, Chosen One."

Averie stared down at her arm in disbelief. Sera was right; she wasn't healing. The blood wasn't slowing, and the pain was agony. With a sharp cry and a furious wave of her arm, the stone was jettisoned from the ground and into the far wall.

CHAPTER FORTY-TWO

Sera slammed against the window wall with enough force to crack the glass. "Ugh," she moaned and let herself slide to the floor. The flicker of magic and glint of metal from far below caught her eye. Her breath came in short, ragged pants as she stared down.

A terrifying mix of Shadowed, beast, and Rebellion soldiers filled the courtyard below. Some engaged in a fight to the death, while others were being trampled upon as the fight for life grew more perilous than ever.

"Averie—" Sera stopped, her eyes growing impossibly wide as her heart stuttered a painful and uneven rhythm in her chest. A scream pierced her consciousness, crippling her mind and temporarily paralyzing her body before consuming her in agony. Sera fell to the ground while clutching her head and crying out in fear, pain, and sorrow as the Realm jerked. The movement was so quick only those most in tuned could feel it.

"What the hell is happening?!" Averie screamed.

Slowly, Sera dropped her hands to the ground and forced open her tear-filled eyes. "It's started."

Chapter Forty-Three

Averie shook her head. "No, no it couldn't have. Feliks is… Tell me how to stop it!"

Sera rose to her hands and knees, one eye forced shut to keep the blood from seeping in. "You think you can stop this? You can't! You're too late! It's already started. Nothing can stop it now."

Averie's chest heaved as she forced her body to keep on living. Her limbs shook from exhaustion, and blood seeped from the wound in her shoulder. Like a river, it trailed down her useless arm. Sera was right. The Heart had forsaken her. Now it only waited for the moment it could take control and claim her body as its own. A growl rumbled in her chest as she forced the thoughts away and stumbled to the cracked window that overlooked the Realm and gasped.

A scene straight from one of the old science fiction movies that her mother had enjoyed so much played out in the sky of the Realm she had come to love. Large black dots marred the sky as far as the eye could see. For a moment, Averie wondered if they were a blemish on the battle-dirtied glass. At least until they began to stretch like a rubber band before elongating.

They were falling. The Realms were falling. Each colliding into the other, leaving nothing but destruction and death in their wake. Stars, moons, and suns encroached closer and closer until, suddenly, everything stopped. Screams echoed around them, the smell of blood and war spreading faster than anyone could stop. Races tumbled into each other as fear spurred a new kind of battle. One driven by fear. The Realms would be destroyed if things were left like this. But what hope did she possibly stand? She had already lost so many… Was it possible? Could it even be stopped?

CHAPTER FORTY-THREE

I've lost. Averie felt the desire to cave within her chest. There was nothing left to give. She had nothing left. *Maybe it's time for me to rest...* Averie felt the weight of her eyes as they began to slip closed.

Don't give up.

Quen? Is that you? Quen's smiling face flashed before her eyes. *I thought you were gone.*

Quen shook her head. *Not gone, just preparing.*

Preparing? For what?

Do you trust me?

Yes, Averie swore without delay.

Explosions sounded in the distance, quickly joined with loud pops and the whistle of electricity. It was happening. The Realms were at war.

Averie forced her eyes open, her decision made. Using the wall for support, Averie pushed against the smooth surface and forced herself to her feet.

"It's not over," she breathed.

Sera sat back on her haunches as a sad smile marred her once-clear features. "Aren't you listening? The Realms have fallen once more. The war has started, and soon, there will be nothing left. There's nothing you can do. It won't be long now, and the Realms will be forced back into one. I have failed, and there is nothing I can do about it."

Averie smiled as her eyes traced the expanding cracks running along the castle floor. "You said so yourself. There's still time."

Sera's eyes narrowed as she rose on shaking legs. "What are you saying?"

Anguish claimed Averie's body as she drew from the nearly empty pool of magic within. Her eyes flashed, and relief thrummed in her blood as the familiar burning flowed down, igniting her scars. A nervous chuckle rattled her chest as she tightened her grip on the hilt of her sai. Her decision was made, and for a moment, she let her eyes close. Flashes of broken memories played behind her dark lids, giving her the strength to do what she prayed to the Stars would end this. She couldn't stop the Fall, but she could save what was left. "There is always another way, Sera."

Sera's head jerked to Averie. The resignation in Averie's voice ignited a fear Sera hadn't experienced in far too long. "Averie, no!"

The world slowed as everything happened at once. Sera twisted on her heel, her arm stretching toward Averie as she sprinted across the short space separating them. Her shadows, desperate to follow their mistress's order, raced from every crevice and corner. Averie lifted her own arm, twirled the sai Radnar had gifted her in her palm until the blade faced her, and plunged it into her heart.

A gasp puffed across Averie's lips as the pain she expected to consume her body was nowhere to be found. Confusion knit her brow as she dropped her eyes to her chest. She hadn't missed. Her armor had been pierced with barely any effort, leaving the black blade buried to the hilt deep inside her. Then suddenly, everything was different. Her vision swam, and a chill spread from the blade's intrusion, weakening her knees, and yet, somehow, she remained standing.

ACCEPTANCE

"Averie!" Sera's fear-filled voice steadied her eyes as her former friend cupped her cheeks. "What have you done?"

A broken smile twitched across Averie's lips. "Isn't … this … what you … wanted?"

I'm sorry, she thought as Callen, Radnar, Hex, and Snip's faces passed through her mind.

Callen slashed his sword through the distracted Shadowed's throat, severing its head from its body, and launched himself into the growing mayhem. Sweat, blood, and grime streaked down the sides of Callen's face, neck, and back as he continued to fight his way through the endless waves of beast and Shadowed. Radnar bellowed an angry war cry from somewhere to his right, followed by a gargled cry and a spray of liquid against his side. Callen grit his teeth against the sickening smell and turned to glare at Radnar. The older man cackled, then widened his eyes, his lips forming a word Callen didn't need to hear to understand.

A chill racked his spine, a tell of someone corrupted creeping up from behind. Callen twisted, his foot digging into the soiled earth as his sword lifted and clashed against a familiar, misted blade. "I was wondering if you would show your grotesque face."

Lucas chuckled. "If I didn't know any better, I would say you missed me, Callen."

Callen growled and shoved the pale man backward. "In your nightmares."

Lucas frowned. "I want to say you got that one wrong, but you actually nailed it."

Callen smirked. "A man much better than you made sure to teach me several important distinctions between our worlds. Including—"

Lucas and Callen broke apart, stumbling as the world shook beneath their feet.

Snip appeared at his back. "It's started," the man hissed.

"Where in Fornax have you been?!" Callen demanded, though his eyes followed the previously missing twin's eyeline and did nothing to stop his jaw from dropping. His eyes locked on the sky as long tears began to spot the clear, cloudless blood. Lucas frowned. It was the perfect time to take out the one that Sera had called Eternal One, and yet, for some reason, he couldn't do it. Instead, he, too, looked to the sky and felt the return of his dread.

The tears were stretching and elongating until the familiar flint of skyscrapers from the world Lucas, Thane, and Averie had come from began to drift into a world of magic. On the other side, flying cars and ships poured from buildings, decimating them entirely.

"What in Fornax…"

"The Realms are colliding." Callen gasped.

Lucas's head snapped to the side as if the very words Callen had spoken had inflicted a physical blow. "No," he whispered. "Sera!"

CHAPTER FORTY-THREE

Snip reached out and grasped Lucas's shoulder, stopping him in place, as a swarm of trolls erupted from the ground like ants and sent the men scattering in all directions.

"It is not over yet!" Callen called.

I'm sorry.

Callen froze as the familiar voice echoed in his mind. His hands squeezed against the man's throat as raw, unfiltered emotion swarmed him. "RADNAR! HEX! SNIP!" Callen bellowed as blood seeped between his fingers. Dropping the lifeless corpse, he threw his body over the next wave of enemies and slammed his fist against the dampened and cracked surface. Radnar, Hex, and Snip raced to his side with questions clear even through their war-painted faces.

He lifted a hand. "Averie..."

Blinding light exploded from where he pointed before any explanation could be shared. Arms, shields, and hands were brought up to cover faces as each man, being, and creature struggled to protect themselves against the searing blaze. Slowly, the light faded away into nothing, and with great caution, hands, arms, and other protective gear were lowered as all eyes lifted to the sky. A single, petite figure hovered above them all. Her hair was long, and as dark and shimmering as the star-filled sky, as it lifted and swayed around her as if it had a mind of its own. But it was her eyes that held all captive, for they shined brighter and fiercer than the sun itself.

"Who in Fornax...?"

"Atria." Callen gasped.

This is only the beginning...
To be continued in The Empty

Epilogue

A hooded figure appeared on a moonless night in the small, sleepy town. Its citizens slumbered peacefully, oblivious to the heavy, foreboding air that billowed in like fog. The soft wind dragged the autumn leaves rustling across the stranger's path as it ambled down the streets in a heavy silence. Step after silent step, the figure wandered the town, stopping on occasion to peer into a darkened shop window before pressing on.

The streets were lined with carefully painted and restored buildings, remnants of a town gasping its last breath but fighting for survival. An old ice cream shop, adorned with pink-and-white striped awnings, was placed purposefully after a quaint cafe. A hint of fresh rose permeated from the blooming flower shop nestled next to it. Logos were elegantly scrawled against the wide storefront windows with splashes of vibrant colors in hopes of bringing wanderers close. The figure, seemingly indifferent to these attempted drawls, passed by unabated.

A small light at the edge of town drew the figure closer. Something about the warm glow always intrigued the figure enough to cause pause in its mission. The old redbrick building's small, circular window flickered by candlelight, illuminating a bartender, dutifully wiping down the worn and chipped counters, while a waitress flitted around the room to collect the empty bottles and glasses. Nursing the darkened liquid sitting before him, a lone patron sat at the end of the bar. The dark figure watched in thoughtful silence for a few moments before continuing its worn path.

As is the standard in most small towns, the end of the main road signaled the end of the town itself. The hooded one gently stepped off the edge of the sidewalk and onto a small gravel path that wound into a dimly lit park. Though its steps made no sound that humans could hear, the energy pouring off the figure was not so kind to the animals of the park. A rabbit family, once happily asleep, crept from its burrow for a closer look. Birds peeked from their nests, the ruffling of their feathers echoing

ACCEPTANCE

into the night. Predator and prey alike momentarily set aside their differences in the neighborhood in the spirit of protection. An owl hooted into the night, eyeing the gracefully silent being with skepticism.

It was a strange figure, neither resembling man nor woman, human nor animal. There were no limbs or unusual movements revealed, no flash of hair or hint of face to give the possible distinction between one or the other. If someone had seen it pass, which no one had, they would only be able to remember the distinct bloodred cloak that seemed to be abnormally immune to the darkness of night.

Reaching the end of the manicured cul-de-sac, the figure slowed, tilted its hooded head, and admired the two-story colonial home. The pristine white coloring seemed to shine even on this moonless night, leading one to believe it had been painted recently. Its windows were framed with hunter green shutters, while a generously sized covered porch held three differently colored chairs and a dainty, square, glass-and-wicker table. Flowers, pushing their fresh fragrance into the cool night, hung between the wooden beams, while vibrant, green ivy grew lazily over the railings.

The being righted itself before drifting forward, following the siding around the silent house before coming to a stop once more and peering up to the far curved window. The figure looked around, once, then twice, somewhat cautiously, before leaping into the nearby tree and evaporating into a fine red mist and gliding forward. The mist filtered through the cracked window and pooled onto the floor. As the last particles filtered to the ground, the mist began to slink across the thick, soft carpeting, before finally rematerializing into the cloaked figure once more.

The room was painted a simple white and held a long-distressed white dresser, mirror, and matching nightstands on each side of the queen bed. One of which held a small clock with glowing red numbers and a book, while the other held a collection of picture frames. A combination of photos and posters spread across the walls in a chaotic collage. From the side, a soft light spilled from the bathroom, casting a warm glow and drew attention to the partially opened closet door. In the middle of the room sat the bed, holding a multitude of pillows, the center of which held a disheveled, sleeping figure.

The hood drifted to the edge of the bed and, for a long time, peered down at the sleeping woman. It watched her lips part on soft puffs of air and her chest rise and fall with deep, even breaths. One of her smooth hands lay carelessly against her chest, while the other was tucked deep into the pillows behind her head. It continued to watch until lightning flashed from beyond the wind, igniting her red hair, giving birth to fire within the darkness of the night. She was close enough to reach out and touch and yet still so far.

She knew nothing of the true world around her, of the things that were creeping at her door once more. Of the part she had to play in the upcoming scenes or of the events destined to befall upon her.

It was time to begin things once more.

EPILOGUE

Filled with a new resolve, the hooded one leaned down. Its hand, appearing from beneath the cloak's wispy material, delicately clasping a silver-like powder. The hand moved closer and closer to the sleeping woman until it was just inches away. After a slight inhale of breath, the figure's lips parted, ready to blow the powder from its hand when another's clamped over the figure's mouth, sealing the breath within before it was jerked back. Shock trembled the strange figure as it watched the slumbering woman rise to a sitting position on the bed. Her lips curved in a vicious, knowing smile. "Not this time, big boy."

"It's time this game came to an end," whispered another.

The Realm Series

Denial
Anger
Bargaining
Depression
Acceptance

Broken Beginnings: Story of Thane
Sins of the Father: Story of Silas
Shattered Start: Story of Sera
Honorable Darkness: Story of Hex and Snip
A Love Lost: Story of Radnar

C.R. Rice

I am a fantasy/sci-fi writer, currently immersing you in the Realm Series. As someone who grew up in a small town, I have always loved escaping into the world of fantasy, paranormal and legend. I have dedicated myself to create that same escape for anyone who wants to escape the boring reality of real life. Through the years, I have traveled to dozens of different states and countries. Plus, I have lived in North Carolina, Pennsylvania and now Florida! While they all have their own unique treasures, I must admit to favoring the sunny southern states over the chilly northern ones, though there is nothing like curling up with a good book by the fire as the snow falls outside the window. Some of my favorite reads are Terry Pratchett's Disc World series, The Uglies Series by Scott Westerfeld, and The Hallow Kingdom by Clare B Dunkle. When I am not reading or writing I enjoy teaching and learning from my mini-superhero three-year-old and spending time with my husband by the pool.

authorcrrice.com
facebook.com/authorcrrice
x.com/authorcrrice
instagram.com/authorcrrice

Book Club Question

1. Before starting *Acceptance*, whose side were you on, Averie's or Sera's?

2. Would you still go to the Heart Realm?

3. Have any of your views on the characters changed? If so, how and why?

4. If given the opportunity, would you erase your most painful moment?

5. Do you think people really impact you in a way that would change who you are?

6. Did you have a favorite scene? If so, which one?

7. Who do you want to learn more about? Why?

8. If you could ask the author anything, what would it be?

9. Were there any twists that you loved? Hated?

10. What are your lingering questions?

11. Are you excited about the Empty?

12. Are you satisfied with the ending of the Heart Realm?

Discover more at
4HorsemenPublications.com

10% off using HORSEMEN10

www.ingramcontent.com/pod-product-compliance
Lightning Source LLC
Chambersburg PA
CBHW021457171224
19163CB00025B/167/J